F.U.B.B.

FUCKED UP BEYOND BELIEF

HARDCORE HORROR NOVELLAS

JASPER BARK, CANDACE NOLA, AND DANIEL J. VOLPE

Book 14 in Crystal Lake's Dark Tide series

Let the world know:
#IGotMyCLPBook!

Crystal Lake Publishing
www.CrystalLakePub.com

Copyright 2024 Crystal Lake Publishing

Join the Crystal Lake community today
on our newsletter and Patreon!
https://linktr.ee/CrystalLakePublishing

Download our latest catalog here.
https://geni.us/CLPCatalog

All Rights Reserved

ISBN: 978-1-957133-92-8

Cover art:
Ben Baldwin—http://www.benbaldwin.co.uk

Layout:
Lori Michelle—www.theauthorsalley.com

Edited and proofed by:
Mark Coombs, Carson Buckingham, and Pixie Bruner

This is a work of fiction. Names, characters, businesses, places, events and incidents are either the products of the author's imagination or used in a fictitious manner. Any resemblance to actual persons, living or dead, or actual events is purely coincidental.

No part of this publication may be reproduced, stored in a retrieval system, or transmitted in any form or by any means, without the prior permission in writing of the publisher, nor be otherwise circulated in any form of binding or cover than that in which it is published and without a similar condition including this condition being imposed on the subsequent purchaser.

Follow us on Amazon:

WELCOME
TO ANOTHER

CRYSTAL LAKE PUBLISHING
CREATION

Join today at www.crystallakepub.com & www.patreon.com/CLP

CHURCH OF THE SPLATTER-SPRAY SAINTS

JASPER BARK

CHAPTER 1

"I WARN YOU, you're about to see bloodshed, torture and scenes so depraved they'll taint your soul forever." Mark's eyes narrowed, cold, like sharpened steel.

He meant to scare Cindy. He didn't want her along on this mission.

But he worked for One Light, her Poppa's ministry, and Cindy had final say. She was her Poppa's daughter in many ways, though she hated to admit it, especially when it came to being stubborn. Mark was ex-Special Forces, usually he made her feel safe and protected, but right now he wanted her to stay in the jeep.

It wasn't going to work.

Gerard, on the other hand, wanted nothing more than to stay in the back seat. His knuckles white from clutching a Bible. "Um, can we pray on this, before we get out?"

Cindy closed her eyes to stop from rolling them. She held out her hands to the other two. Gerard was reluctant to let go of his Bible, but he knew he couldn't be seen with it. He slipped it under his seat and took their hands.

Cindy cleared her throat. "Lord, though we're literally about to walk through the valley of the shadow of death, lend us your strength and purpose that we might rescue Lucy from the clutches of these heathens and bring her home to the fold, where she belongs. In Jesus' name, Amen."

They repeated 'Amen' under their breath, then let go of each other's hands. Gerard dabbed tears from his eyes.

Cindy shook her head. "Careful, you'll smudge your mascara."

"Really?" Gerald pulled a compact from his pocket and checked his eyes. His thick mascara had not run. His dyed black hair was spiked with gel and his face and hands were white with foundation. He picked nervously at torn, black jeans. He was uncomfortable disguising himself like this. He was barely twenty-one, but the last time Cindy saw him he'd sported a blazer and bowtie like a middle-aged banker.

Mark had gone with blue jeans, work boots and a plaid shirt over an NRA t-shirt. It suited his thinning, sandy crewcut. Cindy had chosen to hide her hair under a blue wig. She'd donned a *Friday the 13th* t-shirt, a leather miniskirt, fishnet stockings and studded ankle boots. Her ears and nose jangled with clip-on rings, to give the illusion of multiple piercings, including a chain that ran from nose ring to ear. Around her neck was a razor blade on a chain.

When she surveyed herself in the mirror, Cindy had been perversely pleased with this new look. Especially when she saw her Poppa's reaction.

Mark touched a hidden earpiece. "This is Command to ODB and ODC, we are in position. Will contact you when we have eyes on the target, standby, over." He nodded his head at the reply and fixed Gerald and Cindy with his intense, blue eyes. "So, let's do this."

The parking lot was at the end of a long dirt road on the outskirts of town. It was notorious as a dumping ground for bodies. At least three unidentified serial killers left victims there.

Nearly every major city had places like this, just outside the city limits, where the downtrodden and desecrated were discarded. Those without family, friends or future, their mortal remains left unclaimed and un-mourned. Liminal spaces that sat outside modern civilization, the last vestige of a frontier that settlers had tried and failed to tame. It was these places the Brethren in Blood chose for their meetings.

A line was forming at the entrance to the site. The mid-afternoon sun was punishing and by the time they got inside Gerard was sweating so much his foundation had run.

Mark held out his phone with their tickets. The security guy was dressed in a burgundy silk shirt with black combat pants and boots. His shoulder holster was prominent as was the pin the Brethren in Blood wore. It showed a chainsaw and machete crossed like the hammer and sickle of the Soviet insignia and rising above them a single bloodstained fist raising its middle finger.

CHURCH OF THE SPLATTER-SPRAY SAINTS

The official scanned their tickets and stamped their hands with the insignia. He caught Mark's eyes. "Blood connects us all, brother." Mark gave a curt nod. "We are vessels on its tide." The right answer. The official nodded, they were part of the tribe. He showed them through the barrier and into the main site. The smell hit Cindy first. Burnt sugar, hot fat, diesel generators and men who didn't wash enough. The site was a cross between a carnival, a gun rally and a revival gathering. There was a huge tabernacle tent in the center of the site that stood a full two storeys high and must have been two hundred feet long.

The tabernacle was surrounded by concession stands, food trucks and sideshow booths. Cindy spotted a cotton candy stand and a truck selling 'Blood Dogs' and 'Blood Burgers.'

Another concession stand was selling the kind of merch she'd expect at a rock concert. There were t-shirts, pins, tote bags and even AirPod cases carrying the crossed chainsaw and machete insignia all with the bloody fist flipping the bird.

Further on, Cindy passed another concession selling similar merch, but these carried captions like *HUMPING A WaVoB MEANS YOU'RE TOO LAZY TO JERK OFF*, whatever that meant. Others showed George Harding's face surrounded by the words— *I'LL BLEED FOR GEORGE! WILL YOU?* Cindy was alarmed to see the same image on a pile of tampons.

Harding was part rock star, part messiah to the Brethren in Blood. Despite being short and skinny with a pot belly and thinning hair. As far as Cindy could tell he had no discernible charisma.

Gerard looked as though he'd just stumbled into Sodom, right before God rained fire and brimstone on it. He didn't know where to look for fear he'd be turned into a pillar of salt.

Gerard had led a sheltered life. Home-schooled till graduation, he spent three years at Bible College before he caught her Poppa's eye and became another intern at his ministry. These interns staffed Poppa's home office, which had two large security doors and soundproofing.

Cindy hadn't wanted Gerard on this mission, but her Poppa was just as stubborn as she was. He thought Gerard should see the type of sin One Light were fighting.

Of the three, Mark found it easiest to blend in. His military background was obvious and at least half the Brethren seemed to have served their country.

Mark was carrying his Glock 19 quite openly in a shoulder holster with a double magazine pouch. The Yarborough Knife sheathed on his belt marked him out as Special Forces. Nearly everyone was armed, even the children who tagged along in a Ritalin haze.

As they got closer to the tabernacle, the concessions gave way to sideshows. Cindy spotted a hi-tech VR Pod. The sign read: *SERIAL REALITY!* The attraction took a 3D photo of your face and superimposed it onto the body of a serial killer as they enacted famous kills.

There was also the option to put your face onto the victims, which seemed just as popular. For an extra few bucks you could download the footage to your phones and post it on social media.

Gerard gawked at this. Cindy had to elbow him, so he didn't draw attention. Mark, who was used to undercover operations, betrayed no emotion, but couldn't hide the disapproval in his posture.

The biggest sideshow was outside the main tent. Cindy assumed it was a ride, but the closer they got, the stranger it looked.

A crowd had gathered round a podium A barker wore the purple robes of a Brethren high official. Next to the podium was a raised dais, topped by a mini guillotine. Behind the barker beneath a domed roof were five huge screens

Intrigued, Cindy, Gerard and Mark drew closer. The barker was already working the crowd, a cross between a carny huckster and an old-time preacher. "That's right brothers and sisters, I've testified before and I will testify again, there is no finer way to show your love for George Harding and his great works. This is the first step to attaining sainthood. The first great sacrifice that will make you a true vessel of the Blood. This is where you let the WaVoBs know you aren't going to take their BS. Because *you* have what it takes to be of the Blood and with the Blood. Now, who's going to show me their mettle?"

The barker pointed at a large, burly guy with a black and red bandana. "How about you, brother. C'mon up."

The burly guy bounded up the steps. The barker held out his hand. "That'll be five hundred, brother. You paying card or cash?"

The burly guy reached into his jeans pocket and pulled out a wad. "Cash, on the barrelhead."

CHURCH OF THE SPLATTER-SPRAY SAINTS

A short woman with a Lynyrd Skynyrd t-shirt stretched over a pregnant belly ran out of the crowd waving her hands. "Jeb Armstrong, don't you dare, we need that money for a baby crib."

"Aw, quit nagging, this is my moment." Jeb handed the wad to the barker before the woman could clamber up next to him.

The barker pointed to the dais, which had a hand-shaped imprint below the guillotine. "All right, brother, put your right hand in here and tell me when you're good to go."

Jeb placed his hand on the dais. The woman tugged at his right arm. "Jeb, hon, are you sure you want to do this? How you gonna operate that metal press with your hand all busted up? You gotta provide for li'l Billy Bob and me." She rubbed her stomach. "And we has another on the way."

"Of course I'm sure. I *love* George Harding, and I'm at one with the Blood." He punched the air as he said this and the crowd roared their approval.

Jeb gritted his teeth and gripped his wrist. Cindy could see the sweat stand out on his forehead. The woman tugged at his elbow, but he wasn't going to shift.

The barker pressed a button on the side of the dais. The middle screen came to life with a close up of Jeb's hand. Speakers played a speed-metal drum roll.

The guillotine tottered, then fell with a noise like razor wire on ground glass. It hit the dais with a dull 'thunk', severing Jeb's middle finger below the last knuckle. A thick stream of blood spilled from the severed digit.

The image on the screen followed Jeb's middle finger like a sausage on a conveyor belt as it fell down a slot that opened in the dais. The finger was caught by a robotic arm that lifted it into place above a metal fist.

The screen pushed in closer on the fist. It was an exact replica of the one on the insignia, except there was a tiny drill bit where the middle finger should be. The robotic arm placed Jeb's finger over the drill bit and fixed it to the fist.

The metal fist sat atop a forearm. Hydraulic machinery lifted the fist so the crowd could see it in the flesh. The crowd roared louder, as it flipped them all off with Jeb's finger.

All five screens came to life. Each showed a politician, a religious figure or a self-righteous celebrity smiling patronizingly at the audience. The hydraulic equipment moved the fist up and over to each of the screens in turn, pushing it right into the face on the screen so Jeb gave each one the finger in turn.

Each time Jeb's finger was pushed into a screen the crowd went mad, cheering and whooping. When it made the rounds of the first set of public figures the images changed, and Jeb flipped off another bunch of hated individuals.

Finally, all but the middle screen went blank. The metal fist ejected Jeb's middle finger. The screen showed a close up of the finger, in slow motion, as it shot into the air and tumbled towards the ground.

As the finger fell, two flame throwers incinerated it, leaving nothing but a blackened crisp. Everyone watching went wild.

When the uproar died down the barker turned to Jeb who was clutching his fist with the bleeding stump. The barker put a hand on his shoulder. "So, what do you think, brother?"

Jeb held his bloody fist up in the air and bellowed like a pro-wrestler. "SO . . . TOTALLY . . . WORTH . . . IT!"

The barker bowed to Jeb who stumbled down the steps with his woman in tow. Then he turned back to the crowd. "Who's next?"

Half the crowd surged forward with their hands in the air, many of them waving cash. Cindy watched Jeb as he left the sideshow on shaky legs. His skin was pale. He pushed his woman away whenever she tried to help.

He took a couple more steps, then pitched over backwards in a dead faint. His woman knelt and called for help, but no one noticed. They were too busy trying to be next in line.

Cindy shook her head, then took Gerard and Mark's arms. "C'mon, I think we've seen enough."

Mark touched his earpiece, muttered something then nodded. He straightened his shoulders and marched towards the tabernacle. "Let's go save Lucy VanderMeyer."

Cindy caught her breath at the mention of Lucy. She'd been more than a mentor to Cindy, she'd been a surrogate mother.

As they approached the main tent, Cindy felt fifteen years old again. Home from Christian academy, climbing the stairs to the bathroom with a mounting sense of dread.

CHAPTER 2

GEORGE WAS TERRIFIED by his audience. He thought they were the dregs of humanity. And with every show they proved him right.

Case in point. Because of his followers, he was backstage, arguing with Carmine Alfonso, his special effects genius. No one created gore like Carmine, but he was difficult to deal with.

George raised his hands in exasperation. "Why can't you use pig intestines? We spent three grand on them. You're going to leave them on ice?"

Though he was only five, six, Carmine had the voice and personality of a giant. "It's *my* reputation that's at stake. You know they keep the body parts you throw at them, right? Take them home in doggie bags as mementos. Some of these bozos even test them to make sure they're human."

"How are they gonna prove they're not human?"

"How does *anyone* prove that? You gotta lot of people coming to these shows. It's a national movement. People from all walks of life are here, including people with access to genetic testing. And whose name gets dragged through the mud when they find out the guts aren't human? Spoiler alert, George, it's not yours. They love you. They'll do anything for you. No, it's me who gets the hate mail. It's me they're calling a fake. Never again, George, never again."

"Have you checked *all* of your suppliers? There's still time to get some colons biked over."

Carmine had built up a network of morgues, morticians, hospitals and surgical disposal units, in practically every state. They provided him with the body parts he used in his effects. The word was out, the Brethren in Blood were paying top dollar for real gore, and there was a lot of interest. Carmine had even been approached by black market organ smugglers, but he was dubious about their product.

Carmine shook his head. "They're all scared. There's court cases all over the country, less and less people are willing to sell to me. My supplies are drying up."

"None of those cases will come to anything, it's a legally gray area. We looked into this, tell them that."

"Doesn't matter what I tell them, they're running scared. They don't need the extra hassle, and it only takes one case to stick for them *all* to cut me off."

"So, what do we do?"

"Cut the guts from the autopsy skit."

George sighed. "I can't cut the guts from that skit, it's one of my *most* important points."

"Well, I ain't having them throw animal guts at the audience."

"Fine, I'll let the Troll-Players and the Sui-Sirens know they can't throw anything that didn't come from a human being. Will that make you happy?"

"Not really, but if I gotta . . . "

"You gotta. Draw me up a list of all the non-human organs and I'll make sure they get it."

Carmine stormed off, swearing under his breath. George made his way across the backstage area to a cluster of trailers, behind a gold rope manned by a security detail. He nodded to the man who lifted the rope and patted him on the shoulder. "Thanks, Jack, keep up the good work."

The trailers housed the stars of George's show. The men and women who drew the crowds to his meetings—the Suicide Saints.

George liked to check in before the show, to make certain they hadn't lost their nerve. They were waited on hand and foot by the Sui-Sirens, treated better than any rock star. He needed to keep them sweet, so they didn't back out.

When he was starting out, George had found his saints through hospices, cancer wards and terminal patient organizations. He had an outreach program to forums on suicidal ideation and assisted dying. Finding and grooming a Suicide Saint had been a long process that involved a lot of persuasion.

But over the last few years members of the Brethren had started volunteering. This surprised George at first. But now the waiting list was over a year long.

CHURCH OF THE SPLATTER-SPRAY SAINTS

George was about to enter Ellie Miles trailer, when he heard shouting from the far end of the row. He sauntered down to see if he could head off the problem.

He passed Dolores on her sun lounger, knitting another sweater. She rolled her eyes at the racket from the trailer.

"Hey, Dolores, who's the sweater for this time?"

Dolores held up a tiny sweater with the Vancouver Canucks killer whale on the front. "My first great grandson. His parents have moved to Canada, so I figured he'd be into hockey."

"How many family members does that make?"

"Four kids, twelve grandkids and two great grandkids."

"That's a lotta knitting."

"Keeps me outta trouble."

George chuckled and put his head into the trailer. Amos Jones, a saint who'd been on the waiting list for the past eight months sat in a deluxe massage chair, surrounded by platters of foie gras, lobster tails, caviar and a huge magnum of champagne.

Amos was berating Brandi, one of the most popular Sui-Sirens. Brandi was kneeling between Amos's legs with his limp dick in her mouth. Brandi was working the flaccid member like a trooper, but it wasn't responding.

Amos's naked body was the dark pink of boiled ham and deep shame. His stomach shook as he ranted. "God dammit, woman what are you playing at? Don't you know who I am? I'm about to become one of the most important people in human history. I'm about to step forward and become one with the Blood! I'm going to bestow my sacred bounty on the brothers and sisters, so we become one in my sacrifice. Do you know what an honor it is to suck my dick? And you can't even get it hard!"

Brandi took him out of her mouth and began working him with her hand, using her saliva as lube. "Oh honey, I'm *honored*, believe me, but maybe you should lay off the nose candy for a bit."

"Don't you tell me what I can and can't put in my body! I'm a sacred vessel of the Blood!" He swung his right arm out and knocked a small bowl from the arm of his chair sending up a cloud of white powder. George shook his head. That was nine thousand dollars they'd have to vacuum from the carpet.

He strode into the trailer and put a hand on Amos's shoulder. "Is everything all right in here?"

Amos looked round and his face lit up with surprise as he saw

JASPER BARK

George. "Oh, hey George, I didn't see you there. It is such a frikkin honor, dude. You are like a god to me."

George took Amos's hand in both of his. "The honor is all mine. What you're about to do today will never be forgotten. Your name will live on for all eternity. You guys are my heroes. It's why you're called saints."

"Oh jeez, George, I don't know what to say. I mean, you changed my life, man, really. That's why I'm giving it for you, it's all for you."

"And trust me, Amos, I know what a gift that truly is, and I'm humbled by it."

George looked down at Brandi kneeling before Amos. "You know what, I think Brandi is holding out on you." He winked at Brandi. "Shame on you, Brandi, don't you know who Amos is? I think it's time we give him the deluxe treatment, don't you?"

Brandi looked up with mock contrition. "I'm so sorry George, I don't know what I was thinking, you're right." She stood up, pulled a blindfold from her cleavage and placed it over Amos's eyes.

Amos jerked his head in alarm. "Hey, what gives?"

George squeezed his hand in reassurance. "Trust me, Amos, you're going to want to wear a blindfold for this."

Brandi stroked his cheek and adjusted the blindfold. "It intensifies the experience."

George went to the door and stuck his head out. Dolores caught his eye, and he lifted his chin to summon her. She put down her knitting and climbed out of the lounger as quickly as her arthritic limbs would allow.

Dolores removed her dentures as she entered the trailer and slipped them into her purse. George patted her fanny and left the trailer. Deep groans came from inside the trailer as he silently closed the door. "Now that's what I'm talking about. Oh Jesus! Oh God! Oh damn!"

Each of the Suicide Saints signed a series of legal disclaimers that stipulated they were taking part in an exhibition of skill and endurance of their own free will. The disclaimers also exonerated George and his organization from any blame should the outcome of these exhibitions be in any way misfortunate, up to, and including, death.

George was already looking at three civil claims from families of former saints, not to mention the threat of a class action lawsuit

CHURCH OF THE SPLATTER-SPRAY SAINTS

and criminal prosecution in six states. His legal team had tied up the opposing counsel in so much paperwork that no case would come to court for years. But it helped to keep the saints as sweet as possible, right up to the big moment.

George approached the biggest trailer in the lot. It had been his trailer up until a few days ago, when he'd given it up for their most important saint to date—Lucy VanderMeyer.

George knocked at the door and waited until he heard: "Come."

He stepped inside the trailer and for a moment he couldn't breathe. The interior had been gutted. His velvet draperies and his soft leather furnishings were gone, along with his antiques. The door to the master bedroom was open but his fold up queen-size bed and the seventy-inch home theater with Sonos surround sound were nowhere to be seen.

George's eyes darted around the two hundred and thirty-two square feet that he inhabited for most of the year. His heart was pounding and his mouth was dry. His thoughts chased each other and he clean forgot what he was doing in the trailer.

The curtains were gone from his eight foot sliding glass door and in their place stood a seven foot, glowing, neon crucifix. The only other things in the trailer were a camp bed, a green baize card table and a few folding chairs, one of which was occupied by Lucy.

She was a tall, thin woman in her early fifties, with dyed brunette hair and the sort of skin that only a two-thousand-dollar-a-day-care routine provides. She wore a plain Armani suit and a touch of mascara around her brown eyes. "Hello, George. I was wondering when you were going to show up."

George was aware that his jaw was hanging open and he tried his best to close it. "What . . . what happened to all my things?"

Lucy frowned. "What things?"

"The furniture, the TV, the antiques."

Lucy made a dismissive gesture with her hand. "Oh those, I had them thrown in a skip. I needed to personalize my environment. I live a simple life, George, material comforts only keep you from God."

George felt the room spin. He closed his eyes and slowed his breath, but he couldn't stop his teeth from grinding.

He reminded himself of Lucy's vast wealth. Of the huge audience she'd drawn, both online and off. The pay-per-clicks on their streaming channel were off the charts. His furnishings could be replaced, a benefactor of Lucy's caliber couldn't.

Lucy was an heir to the Danu Pharma fortune. The money they made from vaccine patents and painkillers dwarfed the national debt of most first world countries. Lucy's family were big philanthropists and devout Christians, donating huge sums to evangelical organizations.

To say George was surprised when Lucy approached him was an understatement. But it was a gift horse whose mouth he wasn't going to peek in.

Lucy seemed to sense this as he regained control of himself. "You still have no idea what I'm doing here, do you?"

George struggled to find the right words. "Well, I . . . that is, I presume you support the good work my organization is doing. The hope we've given people, the meaning we've brought to their lives . . . "

"I support no such thing. Your organization is a heap of hooey. You're a common grifter. Anyone with two working brain cells can see that. The problem is, most of your followers don't have two working braincells, and you gouge them for every penny you can."

George was about to disagree when Lucy held up her hand. "Oh, I don't blame you. If you don't take their money some other huckster will. We live in a free country with a free market, thank the Lord."

"Amen to that."

"Amen indeed. I'm not here because I buy into your little dime store religion. I'm not going to start worshipping your Blood. I'm a sick woman, George."

"I'm sorry to hear that."

"Not as sorry as I am. The Lord has decided to call me home and, I'm not going to lie, it terrifies me. I have a rare viral disorder that's killing me, my doctors tell me there's no known cure. And yet I have a controlling share in one of the largest pharmaceutical organizations in medical history, with one of the largest R&D departments. So, when I discover that this department is working on an experimental treatment, an intelligent bacterial agent that can treat a problem like mine, you'd think my problems would be over. But no, every time I ask for this treatment my employees stonewalled me, made all kind of excuses and then outright lied to

CHURCH OF THE SPLATTER-SPRAY SAINTS

me. This bacterial agent was supposedly able to think, to consciously adapt itself to combat any threat to its host organism. So, I used my significant influence to get my hands on this treatment and that's when I found out why they didn't want me anywhere near it. Are you following me, George?"

Since he started these shows, George had met a lot of delusional people, some of them very rich, most of them poor. His general approach was to humor them until he'd gotten what he wanted. So he broke into his most charming smile. "I believe I am."

"Good. I have a demon growing inside my blood. A demon that threatens the whole of humanity. A demon that my family developed and put in my body. That's why I need to be burned alive. That's why I came to you, George."

"Yes, well, my set designers have built the niftiest little stake, and for costume we were thinking Joan of Arc."

"I don't care about your tawdry theatricality, dress it up any way you want. So long as my whole body is immolated. I cannot be pierced by anything. Not one drop of blood can leave my body, do you understand? Not one drop. And when I, a good Christian woman, lay down my life for a hideous cause like yours, George, questions will be asked. There will be an inquiry and my family will finally be exposed for the monsters they are. I have the evidence to bury them all."

"And this evidence will be released after your death?"

"Yes, my death will be the reason people pay attention to it. Otherwise this evidence will be covered up and hidden like so much corporate malfeasance."

"I see."

Lucy reached into her inside suit pocket and took out a small vial of clear liquid with a strange looking top. "If anything should go wrong, anything at all, I want you to use this on me."

She handed it to George and he held it up to the light, squinting. "What is it, holy water?"

"Don't be so foolish. It's a necrotizing agent. It will melt the flesh from my bones in a matter of seconds, destroying all my biological matter."

George felt sweat break on the back of his neck. He thrust the vial back at Lucy. She gently closed his fingers around it and pushed his hand back towards his chest. Then she described the complicated procedure for opening the security cap.

"I've set up multiple accounts in your name, they will be released to you upon my death. I am one of the wealthiest people alive, George. Do this one thing for me, do it right and I'll grant you a fortune that will dwarf the one you lost in your youth. Do we have an understanding?"

George smiled his first genuine smile that week. "Oh yes, we have an understanding."

"A moment," Dmitry called out as George was leaving the trailer. "I would like to speak with you."

Three things always occurred when George heard Dmitry's deep, Russian accent. His sphincter relaxed, his colon moved and he felt a stab of apprehension in his gut. It was a Pavlovian response. He'd known Dmitry nearly five years and it happened every time.

"Slow your roll, George." Dmitry grinned. Like everything he said it sounded amiable and outdated but carried an implicit threat. Dmitry was six, four, with huge shoulders, a barrel chest and bulging forearms. Like many Russian mobsters he wore an expensive track suit and lots of gold.

George's throat was impossibly dry. He swallowed several times, but it didn't help. "I'm just . . . I was . . . I have a lot of things I need to fix before the show."

"I too have things I need to fix, George. Like the people from the One Light Ministry who are trying to infiltrate us. I think they plan to take this Lucy VanderMeyer from us. She's paid them a lot of money over the years, I think they want to keep the goose that lays their golden eggs. They have an advance party in the audience and two more detachments near the perimeter."

"What, um, what do you want me to do?"

"I want you to go out there and put on your little show for the people, keep them nice and distracted so I can kill these evangelicals without disturbing our operation. Do you think you can do that?"

"Sure, sure, of course I can, I won't let you down."

"I know you won't, George. Because you know what will happen to you if you do."

Dmitry patted George's cheek and shot him a shark like grin.

CHURCH OF THE SPLATTER-SPRAY SAINTS

George returned the grin and watched Dmitry lumber off towards his personal trailer. George checked his watch and cursed his bowels. There was just time to change his underwear.

CHAPTER 3

INSIDE THE TABERNACLE there was seating for at least two thousand people. Cindy, Gerard and Mark made their way to the second row and took their seats. They'd paid a four-figure sum for them. They needed to be close to the stage.

The stage looked set up for a rock concert. There were two huge screens showing the chainsaw, machete and middle finger insignia. Between the screens was a ten-foot, animatronic heart, which appeared to be beating. Eight red tubes ran from the heart. They were anatomically incorrect, but Cindy guessed they were meant to be arteries.

Seven of the arteries stretched from the top of the heart all the way along the ceiling of the tent. Cindy glanced up and saw six harnesses suspended by wires. There were also several strange, bladed instruments that she didn't want to dwell on. The eighth artery ran from the heart down to the stage, increasing in size and width the lower it got. The end of it seemed to be an entrance or an exit for the performers who would soon fill the stage.

In addition to the audience, the tabernacle was filled with ushers and security guards. The ushers were dressed like the guy who scanned their tickets, in burgundy shirts, black combat pants and military boots. They all had shoulder holsters and large pins with the insignia. The security guards were dressed in burgundy robes that made them look like a cross between clan members and priests. They carried assault rifles and an ammo belt from which many other weapons hung.

Cindy felt a hand on her shoulder. It was Mark, he looked concerned. "You okay?"

"Yeah, I'm fine."

"You don't look fine."

"No, no, I'm good. This is all a bit . . . you know."

CHURCH OF THE SPLATTER-SPRAY SAINTS

"Yeah, I do. Which is why I'm concerned about that cut on your hand."

"What cut?"

Cindy glanced at her hand. There were several lacerations on her fingers from where she'd gripped the razor blade on the chain around her neck. She hadn't even realized she'd been doing it. The blood and sudden pain gave her a rush. Brought her back to that one summer when she'd experimented with harming herself.

Mark reached out for her hand. "Do you want me to look at that?"

Cindy snatched it away from him. "It's fine, if anything it will help me blend in. Look, I appreciate the concern, but if you want to worry about anyone, worry about Gerard."

Gerard had shrunk into himself. His shoulders were slumped, his head bowed, and his hands were pushed between his thighs. He was rocking backwards and forward in his seat and his lips were moving in what Cindy knew were prayers for his soul.

The whole experience had been too much for him. Some people just weren't cut out for undercover work. Not that Cindy was. She knew they hadn't seen the worst of it, not by a long shot. She knew it in her bones.

She'd had the same feeling of impending doom all those years ago as a teenager, home on vacation and fresh out of the taxi.

As soon as she pushed open the front door she knew something was wrong. There was no housemaid to take her bags. She hadn't seen any landscapers in the front yard. The house felt empty, and it was never empty, even when her parents were out.

She called out, but no one answered. She left her bags in the hallway and made her way up the long circular staircase. It was when she got to the top that she caught the scent. The impending doom she'd been feeling since she got out of the taxi went from a single string instrument at the back of her mind to a full orchestra.

There were many smells at the top of the stairs. There was furniture polish, air freshener and vacuumed carpets. But one scent hovered above them all, rich, sharp and metallic.

Cindy didn't follow the scent. She followed her sense of foreboding. It led to her Momma's bedroom, and the door of her en suite bathroom.

Cindy put her hand on the door, stopped and took a deep breath. The scent was stronger now. It was mixed with her

JASPER BARK

Momma's toiletries. Cindy didn't want to open the door. Didn't want to confirm she knew what the scent was. But she couldn't see a way to stop.

The door swung open. It felt like it had been swinging open ever since. As though Cindy's whole life pivoted on this one moment. The threshold between her Momma's bedroom and the bathroom was the threshold between her old life and the one she'd lived ever since.

The scent was strongest then. It came from the viscose fluid that stained the water of her Momma's bath. That was still draining from the veins she'd opened in her wrists. That smeared the tiled wall when her Momma changed her mind, tried to stand and lost her footing.

It came from the wound in the back of her Momma's head where it struck the side of the bath when she fell. It ran in thick rivulets down the side of the bath and congealed in a dark puddle on the floor.

Her Momma stared up at the ceiling with glazed, lifeless eyes. Her mouth hung open, her mascara had run, and her lipstick was mussed. Cindy had the urge to slap her face for looking so stupid. For letting herself get into such a state. For becoming this bag of meat that leaked all over the bathroom.

This wasn't her Momma. This wasn't the woman who read Cindy bedtime stories and comforted her when she fell from her bike. Or the woman who'd taught her to bake and fix her make up like a professional model. It wasn't the woman who helped her pick dresses for junior prom.

And then suddenly it was.

She couldn't hide from it any longer. This is what her Momma had become, and she would never have the Momma she'd known ever, ever again.

That's when the walls closed in.

Cindy sank to her knees. She was sobbing so hard she didn't hear the footsteps. It was her Poppa's men. She wasn't aware there was anyone in the house until she was lifted from the bathroom floor, carried through the bedroom and out into the corridor where her Poppa waited.

"Cindy, I'm so sorry. I sent someone to the station as soon as I sent the staff away. I . . . I . . . oh dear heavenly Father, I didn't want you to see this."

CHURCH OF THE SPLATTER-SPRAY SAINTS

She collapsed into his arms as more people passed them in the corridor. They were here to clean up the mess her Momma had made of the bathroom, of herself and of her Poppa's perfect, Christian family. They were good at their jobs and soon no trace of her Momma's mess would remain.

Cindy allowed herself to be comforted by her Poppa. Allowed him to hug her and placate her with empty words and hollow promises. Even though she knew, as a point of fact, that *he* was the reason her Momma had done this.

It was her Poppa and his endless parade of earnest young men, with their ill-fitting suits and their athletes' bodies, joining him behind closed doors. Kneeling as if in prayer, but with something other than the word of God in their mouths.

That was the last time she ever let him touch her. It was also the last time they spoke about her Momma's death. She had discussed it many times since, in prayer support circles and with Christian therapists, but never with her Poppa.

Her Poppa hadn't wanted Cindy to see her Momma like that. He hadn't wanted her to come on this mission. And that was part of why she was sitting in the tabernacle, waiting for the blood to be spilled.

Lucy was the other part. Cindy had become an adult without a mother, without an older female to guide her through the pitfalls of being a Christian woman in a secular world. Over the past few years Lucy had filled that role and they had grown close.

What Cindy couldn't countenance was Lucy handing herself over to these apostates to die. Did she think she was some kind of martyr? Why did all the women in her life choose death over *her*? What was so great about death? Why did they want to throw away God's most precious gift.

Cindy was beyond furious. Rage had carried her to this point, had placed her in the lion's den with only prayer to protect her.

Rage was Cindy's rocket fuel, and she was about to break out of orbit.

CHAPTER 4

THESE Американцы impressed Dmitry. That was rare. They'd shot down the drones he'd dispatched, but not before he got the footage he needed.

The detachments were invisible to the untrained eye. Dmitry had twice the men, but they weren't as well trained. He wasn't confident of holding such a large perimeter.

There were three obvious routes into the site, but Dmitry couldn't guarantee they'd take any of them. They would try and secure the VanderMeyer woman before she got to the stage, but if they failed and had to breach the tent, Dmitry didn't think he could contain the chaos or bloodshed. There were at least two thousand heavily armed people on the site, in addition to Dmitry's men. Most of them amateurs, some of them imbeciles.

Grigori would not be pleased if Dmitry let things get out of hand. He needed to make a pre-emptive strike and keep the combat away from the site, but the detachments had seen his drones. He'd lost the element of surprise. It was going to be . . . what did these Американцы call it? A shit-show.

Grigori would roast his testicles over an open fire and make him eat them. If Dmitry was enthusiastic enough, his death would be quick.

Dmitry has seen Grigori do it many times. Dmitry had *helped* him do it many times and their victims rarely showed enough enthusiasm. A quick death was not the point, Grigori liked to torture his victims.

Like everyone who had more money than they could spend, Grigori was only happy when he was taking something away from someone else. Especially if that meant their self-respect, their dignity or their lives.

Dmitry had first met Grigori in the Zona, a maximum security

CHURCH OF THE SPLATTER-SPRAY SAINTS

Russian penal colony. Dmitry had been a career criminal since his teenage years and expected to land there at some point. His incarceration had nearly killed his parents. They were former party officials who had not adjusted to the fall of communism. He wasn't close to them growing up, they were conformist by nature and didn't understand their rebellious child.

Nearly every step in his criminal career was a reaction against his parents and their views. There was only one thing Dmitry shared with them—the need to be part of something bigger than themselves. For Dmitry's parents this meant Communist Party membership and Soviet citizenship. For Dmitry it was being a member of the *Vory v Zakone*, and Grigori had been instrumental in this.

Unlike Dmitry, Grigori *hadn't* expected to end up in the Zona. He wasn't born in Russia, his father, Piotr was a leading *Zakonniki*, one of the 'Vory v Zakone' which roughly means 'Thieves in Law' in English. This loose confederation ran the criminal underworld in Russia. Piotr had emigrated to the States in the late eighties as part of a cultural exchange program that resettled Russian Jews and dissidents. Piotr had posed as a political exile, and his criminal fortune had bought him a green card. Grigori had grown up like a prince, attending the best American schools, wearing the finest clothes, driving the fastest cars.

When Grigori started going off the rails, Piotr didn't send him to military school or boot camp, like American fathers. Piotr sent his son back to Mother Russia. He bribed the guards at the Zona to put Grigori away for two years. This wasn't just to straighten him out, it was preparation for running the family business.

The Vory v Zakone first came to power in the penal colonies and the eighteen articles of the Thieves' Code were decided there. The Code didn't mean shit to criminals these days, but their fathers and grandfathers would have died if they broke it. It was symbolic and symbolism was everything for Russian gangsters. The two years Grigori did in the Zona meant he could do business with men who would rather shoot their children than talk to an outsider.

When Dmitry first saw Grigori he knew the boy was his meal ticket. Dmitry wasn't a Zakonniki, he was a *brodyagi*, a roamer, part of the loose federation of criminals in the Zona who called themselves *Blatniyeh*. The second rung of the prison hierarchy. Men who did the dirty work of the Vory v Zakone, ran the smuggling rings, bringing in tea, cigarettes and other meager luxuries. Dmitry would never make it into the Vory v Zakone without a powerful sponsor and the son of an influential Zakonniki might be just what he needed.

Grigori thought he was tough because he listened to gangster rap and watched old Chuck Norris movies. Grigori did not have the first idea what being tough meant in the Zona. But Dmitry took Grigori under his wing and showed him the ropes, taught him what it really meant to be tough in the most dangerous prison in the world.

Grigori was a quick study, and he began to thrive in the harsh penal colony, winning the respect of the highest Zakonniki. He never forgot the service Dmitry had done him, looking after him when he needed it and he remained loyal to Dmitry.

When they got out of the Zona, Grigori took Dmitry back to the States to work for his father. When Piotr died, and Grigori took his place, Dmitry got a promotion. He finally felt like he was part of something bigger than himself. But Grigori's loyalty had its limits. He liked to put Dmitry in his place. To give him lousy jobs and rub his face in it, lousy jobs like babysitting George Harding. Because Dmitry had saved Grigori when he was weak and vulnerable, Grigori needed to remind him he was anything but weak and vulnerable now.

With any luck, Dmitry would get the chance to kill George before this whole shitshow was over.

His cell rang. It was Grigori.

"Братан, how goes it?"

Grigori was fluent in Russian, but his pronunciation was atrocious. Dmitry grunted. "There's three in the audience, and twenty-four heavily armed men outside the site. We outnumber them, but these men, I don't think they will die easy."

"They won't die at all. It's all fixed."

"Fixed, what do you mean?"

"I 've neutralized the problem."

"I don't understand."

"I reached out to this One Light Ministry. They had a little problem that Yevgeny solved, so they've called off their whole mission."

Yevgeny was Grigori's top hacker. He lived off a cocktail of Adderall and energy drinks and stayed awake for days at a time.

CHURCH OF THE SPLATTER-SPRAY SAINTS

His star had risen when he began laundering money through a series of charities to combat the threat of A.I.s. It turned out A.I.s were such a hot topic in Silicon Valley that the charities made more legitimate income than most of Grigori's criminal enterprises.

Dmitry scratched at his three-day stubble. "So, the evangelicals no longer want this Lucy bitch?"

"They're happy for us to kill her."

"George will be pleased."

"No, he won't. Because I need her alive."

"But doesn't her death bring us money?"

"Not as much as keeping her alive nets."

Dmitry dropped into Russian, he did this as a sign of respect, when he wanted Grigori to feel superior. "Я думаю медленно сегодня."

"Damn right you're thinking slow, bro. Not that this is any of your business, but Danu Pharma, the VanderMeyer's company, has been channeling shadow funds into biological weapons. To avoid scrutiny, they listed these endeavors as 'medical research'. So, this VanderMeyer bitch thinks she's found the golden bullet for her terminal illness and forces them to give her this biological weapon, thinking she's going to cure herself. It's only afterwards she realizes her mistake."

"And what is this weapon?"

"It's a sentient virus?"

"I am not following."

"It's a virus that can think. It can pick who it kills and who it leaves alive. It can even choose how it kills, what the symptoms are and how long its victims take to die. It can spread through whole countries in a matter of days and there's no cure. It can mutate to combat any vaccine, any antibiotics. It's the ultimate weapon of mass destruction and it's worth a fortune on the international market."

Dmitry frowned. "Why haven't Danu Pharma tried to sell it?"

"Because it contravenes every treaty and convention on international warfare. VanderMeyer is trying to expose her own company for what they've been doing. So they've destroyed all samples of the virus, before they go to prison. The only sample is in VanderMeyer's bloodstream."

"So, she is worth a fortune to us."

"Exactly. I need you to substitute somebody else to die in her place, so the crowd isn't pissed. Those idiots are crazy, they come for the bloodshed and there's no telling what they'll do if they don't get it. Then we'll smuggle her out of there."

"George will not be pleased by this."

"I don't give a rat's ass about George. He's bringing too much heat from the authorities. We're going to make a lot more money out of VanderMeyer. Just make this happen, okay?"

"Okay."

Grigori rang off. Dmitry drew in a deep breath and let it out. The muscles in his neck and shoulders began to unknot and relax. There would be no shoot out. He could leave this crazy, travelling shitshow and he might even get to kill George.

Things were looking up for the first time in a long while.

CHAPTER 5

THINGS WERE FINALLY looking up for George. He was going to be rich again. He had one last performance to get through.

The audience started to scream and chant as the opening chords of his entrance music began. Doom metal, his audience loved it, but he found it almost as disgusting as them.

Max, one of the biggest perverts he'd ever met and one of the best stage managers, counted George's entrance in and muttered, "Cue pyrotechnics" into his headset.

A stagehand walked up with a bucket and a bottle of bourbon. George took the bucket and vomited. He rinsed his mouth with the bourbon and spat. His pre-show ritual complete, George put on his radio mic and hit the stage.

The crowd leaped to their feet the minute George appeared. The pyrotechnics showered blood red sparks as if a fire demon had opened its veins. The audience screamed and cheered and whooped. Many of them cried, punched the air or each other. Some fell to their knees, others lost control of their bladders. One man went into a seizure and had to be carried from the tent.

George threw his arms wide, his faced wreathed in a beatific grin. He seemed to be basking in their adoration. Loving the fact they were worshipping him like a born-again messiah. Never once letting on how horrifying and repugnant he truly found them.

George strode across the stage, clapping, hollering and keeping the crowd on its feet. Occasionally he'd stop and point as if he'd spotted an old friend in the audience. He let them shout and scream themselves out and then he motioned for them to sit. "Well, all right! Now that's what I call a welcome. You know, it's like my dear old Ma used to say: 'I love a warm hand on my opening'!"

Laughter burst across the tent and George knew he had them.

"Seriously folks, I do appreciate the love. And what we have here. This." George drew a circle in the air encompassing the audience and the stage. "This is love, make no mistake. No matter what they say about us." There was another round of applause and cheers at this.

"I know some of you will have been harassed on the way here." Boos and jeers from the crowd. George held up his hand to quiet them. "I know, I know, it happens. The police will pull you over, search your car, search your person, even search your children, for no other reason than you're coming here. And yet, brothers and sisters, and yet," a meaningful pause. "They're the ones who say *we're* persecuting them!" Cheers of agreement.

"I've heard what they're calling us and so have you—liars, apostates, psychopaths. One blog even referred to us as 'The Church of the Splatter Spray Saints'! Actually, I kinda like that one, but are we bothered by their slander?"

"NO!"

"Damn right we're not."

George paused, nodding his head in sympathy with the crowd. "You know, I was asked, just the other day, by a woman who'd invited me on her radio show, why I worshipped a 'made up god'?" More jeers and catcalls.

"Can you believe that? She thought *we* worshipped a 'made up god'. We don't worship anything. We celebrate the force that allows, creates and controls all life on our planet. What am I talking about, brothers and sisters?"

There was a unanimous cry from the audience. "Blood!"

"What Am I Talking About?!"

"BLOOD!"

George pointed to the seven arteries that flowed from the giant animatronic heart above the stage. "That's right, the eight red rivers that unite the whole human race. Eight blood types that flow from coast to coast and pole to pole, bringing us all together. No matter our creed, our color or class, we all have blood in our veins. We are all vessels on these rivers. So, lets to do a roll call. Do we have any Os in the house, positive or negative?"

There were whoops and cheers from just under half the audience.

George grinned knowingly, pointed his finger randomly and nodded. "You guys are laid-back, but you're also take-charge and heaven help anyone who tries to get you to turn up on time. You're

CHURCH OF THE SPLATTER-SPRAY SAINTS

always the last ones in your seats, you know it, you know it." More laughter.

"Do we have any As, positive and negative?" Around thirty percent of the audience clapped and shouted.

"I love you guys, I love it. Even when you holler you do it so neatly. You clap like you're praying to a strobe machine." George mimed clapping like a robot. "Open, close, open, close, palms always in the same place. You're stubborn though. Once you've made your mind up, no one is going to change it." This brought more applause.

"How about the Bs? Let's not forget the Bs. Make some noise B boys." A much smaller number of the audience, maybe only twenty percent, clapped, screamed and cried out.

"Listen to that, listen to that, you know when there's a B in the house. Those guys are passionate, they don't think inside the box. But you're not team players, are you? It's your way or the doorway." There were cheers and jeers from different parts of the crowd and two guys stood up and faced off across an aisle.

"Oh, Bs, we've got your number. Now, let's get to the rarest breed—ABs, first the medium rare, do we have any AB positives?" There were a few lone callouts and some members of the audience pointed to their friends or partners.

"I see, I see, don't be shy now, nothing wrong with representing for your blood river. You're talented, you know that. You all are. You march to the beat of your own heart and there ain't nobody dresses like you do. You got some crazy ideas about fashion." Gentle laughter and applause.

"But this last river, this last river is as rare as the truth on a politician's lips. Do we have any AB negatives among us?"

A female voice cried out. "I love you, George. Let's make babies!"

The idea made George's flesh creep, but he hid this response and instead he raised his own hand. "That would be me, then." He pointed to the artery beneath the heart, where he'd entered. "Through me is the way to the kingdom of the backstage. Women can get there on their knees. Men can get there in their dreams."

Laughter and riotous applause.

George put on his best drill sergeant voice. "It's time for the eight Blood rivers to stand up and be counted. I want you to tell me. Who is in the Blood?"

Sixty AB types got to their feet and chanted in unison. "We are in the Blood!"

They were joined by the two hundred B types in attendance. "We are in the Blood!"

Then the eight hundred A types stood and added their voices. "We are in the Blood!"

Finally, the remaining O types stood shoulder to shoulder with everyone else and chanted. "We are in the Blood. We are all carried by the Blood and we're going to tear the world apart."

George stood before them like a general, nodding his approval as they stood to attention. This was an early highlight of the show. George had gotten the idea from the ending of the movie *Spartacus*.

George ramped up his delivery. "Do we believe in a made-up god?"

The audience screamed: "No!"

"Do we believe in a made-up god?"

The audience shrieked: "NO!"

"Of course we don't, we've only got to cut ourselves to see what we believe in. I don't have conversations with an invisible being no one can see or hear. I don't believe in a man who worked magic two thousand years ago, whose followers have been burning anyone who claimed to work magic ever since."

The crowd went wild, and George let them. He didn't even make them settle down before plowing on. "We believe in the one force that's ruled since the beginning of life on Earth. The force that unites families, tribes and nations and that is Blood! Let's not kid ourselves here, it's the lust for Blood that builds armies and it's spilling blood that founds empires. It's the need to replace *blue* Blood with *new* Blood that starts revolutions and founds *new* nations like our own *glorious* nation. It's hot Blood that makes people fall in love and start families. It's cold Blood that helps us to make tough choices. Our hearts wouldn't beat without the Blood pumping around our body. We couldn't have a single thought or emotion without the Blood that brings the oxygen to our brains.

"Blood has been the controlling force throughout human history. We've been riding its currents and doing its bidding since the dawn of humanity. Since life first crawled out of the seas. Yet we erect false gods, to whom we make false offerings. Imaginary friends that don't listen when we petition them with prayer. And

CHURCH OF THE SPLATTER-SPRAY SAINTS

all this while, if we want to see the true governing force behind all life, all we have to do is open a vein.

"That's because Blood is in charge. Blood has always been in charge. It's the captain at the tiller and we are but vessels on the tides. The dark tides of the eight blood rivers. Life runs off Blood. Life is powered by Blood. Life is owed to Blood. Blood is the one true power. It's time to surrender to the Blood!!"

The crowd were on their feet.

There were cries of "Amen!"

"All Right!"

And "Tell it like it is George!"

"Now, you may be asking yourselves why, when the truth is so self-evident, do men and women turn from the living temple of their own body and go to a dead temple of bricks and mortar? Why, when the true power of creation can be seen *inside* their own bodies, do they look to an invisible god who lives *outside* them? The answer, of course, is the state.

"Now, I know we're told that the church and state are kept separate in our great country. But, in truth, they work together closer than lube and a cavity search. Cos the church will tell you it's morally wrong to kill, so the state can take away your weapons. And the church will tell you to render unto Caesar, so the state can pick your pockets with taxes. The church will tell you to turn the other cheek, so the state can take away your right to defend your home and property. Am I lying?"

"No!"

"I said, am I lying?"

"NO!"

"Damn right I'm not. So, the big question is why do we let the state intervene so much in our lives? Why do we surrender so much of our liberty to lawmakers and politicians? You know who the problem is?"

The audience knew. "WaVoBs!"

"That's right, WaVoBs—Wasted Vessels of Blood. Those sad excuses for human beings who sleepwalk through their lives. Who believe everything they hear on the news and read in the papers. Who think because they *voted* that the government works for *them*. Who are proud to pay taxes, so the rich can keep all their money in offshore accounts.

"The WaVoBs are a virus, brothers and sisters. They've infected all eight of the Blood rivers. The WaVoBs are a virus, and the state is the carrier. Now, you may be asking yourselves how we combat this virus? Well, let's take a look at how a WaVoB is put together. It's time for an anatomy lesson, kids!"

The lighting dimmed, colored spotlights illuminated the stage, while travelling searchlights roamed the audience. The PA played melodic shredding at full volume. The speed and melody of the music gave it a comedic edge The screens flashed up a collage of clips showing the Troll-Players in action.

The audience got to its feet and began to stomp and chant. "Troll-Play-ers! Troll-Play-ers! Troll-Play-ers!"

Four Sui-Sirens, dressed in nurse fetish gear, wheeled a hospital bed onstage. Marvin, one of the leading Troll-Players, was lying on the bed, looking shocked and nervous. Marvin was six foot six and weighed all of a hundred and thirty pounds, a gifted comic who played up his physical awkwardness to good effect. His career had been going nowhere until George plucked him from an improv group in Seattle.

He was wearing a hospital gown and blinking in bewilderment. "Hey, what gives? Who are you people?"

Right on cue, Evelyn and Gerry entered. Evelyn was dressed in a nurse's outfit, low cut enough to show off her assets. Evelyn was a full-bodied woman with pneumatic curves, and she knew how to flaunt them. Her fan page had ten times the subscribers of even the most popular Sui-Siren.

Evelyn was pulling a medical trolley that contained all manner of torture devices. Gerry was riding the top of the trolley like it was a surfboard. Gerry was dressed in doctor's scrubs with a stethoscope round his neck. At four feet tall he made a great stooge to Marvin. He told people his condition was achondroplasia, or restricted growth, but most people referred to it as dwarfism. Gerry had a PhD in Astrophysics and a five hundred dollar a day coke habit, which was why he was in show-business and not Astrophysics.

Evelyn checked Marvin's chart. "I'm Nurse Inga Grudge and this is Doctor The-Results. Settle down now, Mr. WaVoB."

Marvin rolled his eyes and spoke in a stuck-up, Bostonian accent. "That's pronounced Wah-Voob."

Gerry giggled. "It's pronounced Sad Boob."

Evelyn wasn't taking any crap. "It's pronounced Bullshit!

CHURCH OF THE SPLATTER-SPRAY SAINTS

"You're here for your autopsy Mr. Sad Boob . . . I mean Mr. Wah-VooB."

Marvin sat up, alarmed. "Autopsy? But I'm not dead!"

"According to your chart you've been braindead since birth."

"Can't I get a second opinion?"

Gerry grabbed the chart from Evelyn. "You can't even get a life, Mr. Sad Boob."

Evelyn grabbed a chainsaw from the trolley. "Time to open you up, so we can see what makes you tick."

Gerry leaped onto the bed and tore open Marvin's gown to reveal the false prosthetic torso that concealed his real body. Even from this close up, George had to admire Carmine's work. It looked authentically real.

The audience cheered, stamped and applauded, and Marvin faked terror and pain, as Evelyn drove the chainsaw into his false chest and down through his abdominal wall. Hidden pumps sprayed real blood out of the fake wound. Gerry capered on the bed, rubbing his hair, his armpits and his butt, as though he were taking a shower in the gushing blood.

Gerry hopped back onto the trolley. Evelyn tore open the ragged flaps of his abdominal wall and stared in surprise at the empty cavity there. It appeared that Marvin had no intestines or stomach, an obvious concession to Carmine.

Evelyn wrinkled her nose. "Well, Mr. Wah-VooB, it appears you are medically gutless."

Gerry spat into the empty cavity. "Yeah, but he does drive an electric car."

Marvin stared down in alarm. "Is that why I'm gutless?"

"No, it's why everyone laughs when you pull up to the curb."

"Tell me straight, Doctor, will I ever play the organ again?"

"No, but you're about to donate a few."

Evelyn reached up into his false chest cavity and pulled out a set of real human lungs. She held them up for the audience's approval and then she tore the left and right lobes from the trachea, handing each lobe to Gerry who drop kicked them into the crowd. Next, she pulled out a liver, two kidneys and a spleen and threw them into the crowd as well.

The audience was on its feet, grabbing for each organ like it was a baseball flying into the stands. They looked to George like starved dogs, fighting for scraps of meat. Bagging an organ gave them major bragging rights on social media. People had been known to stab each other over a single kidney.

Gerry leaped back onto the bed and danced in time to Marvin's shrieks of pain. "You're making an offal racket, Sad Boob. Offal—get it?"

Evelyn cracked open Marvin's fake rib cage and took a step back in surprise. "Doctor, he has no heart either."

Gerry circled Marvin on the bed and pointed at his left arm. "Here it is, on his sleeve, just where you'd expect it. Can we get a close up of this?"

The screens showed a close up of Marvin's heart on the left sleeve of his gown. The heart displayed Carmine's genius. Not only was it still beating, but he had also animated the superior vena cava and the pulmonary artery. They waved in the air, like red and purple tentacles. Each of them was holding a miniature white flag.

Evelyn pointed at the heart. "Doctor, is that heart virtue signaling?"

"No, I think it's semaphore. Can we get that spelled out?"

Big white letters appeared on the screen, as the heart spelled them out with the flags.

"M . . . Y . . .

"B . . . U . . . T . . . T . . .

"H . . . U . . . R . . . T . . . S!"

Gerry kicked the flags from the heart's arteries. "Of course it hurts, Mr. Sad Boob. You're a WaVoB, you're the king of the Butt-Hurts!"

Marvin looked puzzled. "But it's been weeks since I reported anyone on social media."

"And that's why your butt hurts. It's not complicated, it's not brain surgery. But this is."

Gerry clicked his fingers and the four Sui-Sirens turned the hospital bed around so the top of Marvin's head was pointing out to the audience. Evelyn handed him a circular saw.

Marvin groaned. "Doctor, I'm sore all over."

Gerry turned on the saw. "You think you're sore now. Wait till you've been boned with a bone saw. That's worst kind of sore I ever saw."

Gerry put the bone saw to the top of Marvin's head. Carmine had fixed the brain pan of a real skull to the top of Marvin's head with epoxy resin, then covered it with latex and real hair. The bone

CHURCH OF THE SPLATTER-SPRAY SAINTS

saw bit into the brain pan with a satisfying whine. A small electric pump in the saw squirted out a continuous spray of real blood. Marvin screamed so loudly George thought he was going to tear his throat. He was a trooper.

Evelyn put a hand on Gerry's shoulder. "Anything I can do, Doctor?"

"Off the top of my head (get it?), I think you should drop to your knees."

"But why, Doctor?"

"Because we're about to *blow* his mind!"

Gerry took the top of the skull off and it fell to the stage with a soft clunk. Evelyn pointed at the empty brain pan. "Doctor, he has no brain."

Gerry looked pensive. "Well, that might explain why he's a Wasted Vessel of Blood."

Marvin groaned. "If I've got no brain, why do I keep thinking about Hillary Clinton naked?"

Inspiration struck Gerry. He clicked his fingers. "Turn this bed around. I think I know where we can find his brain."

The Sui-Sirens swung the bed around, so Marvin's feet were facing the audience. Gerry grabbed Marvin's ankles and hoisted his legs akimbo. "Nurse, if you please."

Evelyn grabbed a bucket of lube from the medical trolley and pushed her arm into it up to the elbow. She pulled out her arm and held up her fist to the audience dripping with clear jelly. The audience cheered and Evelyn turned and thrust her fist deep into Marvin's rectum.

Marvin squealed, but it was just for show. He was an old hand at this. Twenty minutes before he went on stage, Marvin had lubed up and worked a frozen human brain up his sphincter.

It was this brain that Evelyn now grabbed. She made a show of rummaging around in his backside, then she pulled the brain out of his butt. She kissed the brain, then held it aloft as if it were a trophy she'd just won.

Gerry pointed triumphantly. "I knew that's where it was."

The crowd went wild. Evelyn hurled the brain, as far as she could, out into the crowd. A thousand hands shot up for it.

George hoped it had defrosted enough. Two weeks ago, Evelyn had knocked out a six-year-old child and his family had joined the long line of people threatening to sue George.

That was George's cue. He strode back into the center of the stage. He held out his arms, stealing all the applause. Then he indicated the Troll-Players, sharing a modicum of the acclaim with them.

"And that, folks, is why a WaVoB thinks the way he does, it's what the WaVoB virus does to you. We're going to take a short break now, while we hose down the stage. Don't you go anywhere."

CHAPTER 6

MARK WAS LESS concerned about the antics on stage than the effect they had on Gerard and Cindy. Gerard was catatonic, hunched in his seat, staring straight ahead. He was no longer rocking or praying. He was barely even blinking.

When the people around them got to their feet, Gerard sat still. When someone spilled beer on him, Gerard didn't react, he let it soak into his clothes. His breathing was shallow and his eyes unfocused. Mark suspected Gerard's mind had taken itself off and was close to never coming back.

Mark had to get him out of here. Civilian or not, Gerard was his responsibility, and he would not lose another person under his command.

Cindy was holding it together, but Mark was still worried. She chewed her bottom lip so hard she drew blood, as if the show made her want to bleed. Mark knew about her Momma's suicide. Cindy was the one who found her. Tough break for a teen princess. You never really come back from something like that.

Mark loved Cindy's Poppa. Pastor Brown was a saint. He'd shown Mark when he placed his life in God's hands nothing was stronger than his faith. But the man had to learn how to say 'no' to his daughter when she made stupid demands like joining this mission.

Mark wasn't sure he could keep Cindy or Gerard safe. He hadn't lost anyone since Fallujah, back in Oh Four, before he joined Special Forces.

Kowalski haunted him to this day.

They were on a routine sweep of the streets. Kowalski was new to his command and all the kid did was grouse. He bitched about his boots, his equipment, about the damn heat. Combat did that to some guys, it's a symptom of stress.

By the time they turned the corner into the deserted market square, just about every member of Mark's squad wanted to put a bullet in Kowalski. Especially when he started bitching about the damn ragheads and their stupid religion. Mark told him to shut his goddamn mouth or he'd lose teeth.

The kid was quiet after that, and Mark regretted picking on him. But he'd hit a nerve when he mentioned religion. Mark was raised a strict Baptist and never questioned his religion until he got to the Gulf.

When he saw the lengths the Mujahedeen would go to, it shook Mark's faith. The Iraqi military had mostly deserted their posts, leaving their weapons behind to melt into the crowd. But the Mujahedeen were fearless *because* of their faith, laying down their lives without compunction.

Mark had never encountered a Christian soldier who'd go to these lengths, who'd sacrifice themselves for the sake of their faith. The thought that he might have found a religion that was stronger than his own, a force so great it could crush *his* faith greatly concerned Mark.

This had played on his mind as they walked into that Market Square.

No one spotted the Iraqi kid until he was right in front of them.

He was skinny with close cropped hair and big almond eyes, full of tears. He couldn't have been more than fourteen. Mark had a nephew that age. He was running towards them, waving his arms. "Please, Americans, please I need help."

When they saw his vest, they knew why he was agitated. It was full of explosives. Every man levelled their weapons at the kid. Mark barked orders. "Stand still!"

The kid halted. "Please, please you have to get this off me. I don't want to die."

"Before we do anything, I need you to back up fifteen meters." Mark wasn't sure if the kid knew how far fifteen meters was. He wasn't certain himself, but it was standard procedure in this instance.

"Please, they made me put it on. They have my mother and my sister. They say they will kill them if I don't."

"You have five seconds to back up or I will put bullets in you."

The kid didn't move. "Please, you have to get it off me. They say I will go to heaven as a martyr, but I don't want to go to heaven.

CHURCH OF THE SPLATTER-SPRAY SAINTS

I want to go to university. I want to be the first man in my family to go to college. I get really good grades."

Mark was looking for the detonator, but the kid wasn't holding any. That meant someone else was operating it remotely. Mark knew he should use lethal force to neutralize the threat, but the kid was so young.

When Mark heard the high-pitched whine his finger relaxed on the trigger, his adrenaline spiked and he screamed: "RUN!" He followed his men back down the street they turned off, trying to get beyond the blast radius.

Ever the officer, he counted heads while he ran and found they were one short. Kowalski was not with them.

Mark looked over his shoulder and saw Kowalski running towards the bawling kid. Kowalski threw himself on the bomber seconds before the blast.

Mark ran faster. He heard the blast before he felt it. A stabbing pain in his ears and then everything sounded underwater, distant and muffled.

The blast was a searing wall of heat. Mark was thrown forwards and dropped on his face. Luckily the corner building caught the shrapnel and Mark and his men were unscathed.

Kowalski had saved them all. Men who would have gladly put a bullet in his head, just minutes ago, wept as they collected his remains. Secretly wishing they were as brave and thanking God they weren't.

The loss of Kowalski ate at him to this day. He'd promised himself right then, that he would never lose another person under his command.

Mark had seen things in combat that no human being should ever see. He still couldn't fathom why someone would lay down their life for people they hardly knew. Nor why a person would let anyone strap them into a high explosive vest.

Mark had dedicated his life to the One Light Ministry but, for all his faith, he could not give up his own life for his beliefs. The fact that others could, and that some of them were going to in this tent, shook Mark to his core. It made him wonder if there *was* a force so great it could crush his faith.

George was back on stage introducing the Troll-Players in another skit. This one was called 'The State Hustle Shuffle'. A guy was lured into an old-fashioned dance hall by a buxom woman called Nan E. State. He was lonely and wanted to dance, but had to pay her for the privilege. The price per dance was a different part of his body and Nan E. State took full payment with sadistic glee.

Mark had some sympathy for George's philosophy. No one liked a small government more than him. But he couldn't stomach the pretend violence with real body parts. The crass humor did nothing for him.

Mark's earpiece came to life. "This is ODB to Command, come in, over."

The audience was on its feet grabbing for the testicles Nan E. State flung from the stage. Mark used the opportunity to stand. He didn't need to lower his voice. "This is Command, over."

"We are standing down and withdrawing from our location, as per orders, over."

Mark was confused. "Whose orders? On what authority? Does Pastor Brown know about this, over?"

"It comes all the way from Pastor Brown, sir, over."

"What about Lucy, over?"

"Lucy is to be terminated, if not by the enemy, then by you, sir, over."

"And what about the computer files, all the evidence she has on the Ministry. If she dies, that's released to the public, over?"

"There aren't any files, not any more, a Russian hacker who works for George's backers deleted them for us. All we had to do is donate to his A.I. charity, over."

"There are A.I. charities, over?"

"Yeah, to stop them taking over the world, it's the rage in Silicon Valley, over."

"So, any evidence that One Light's been funding biological weaponry has gone, over?"

"Copy that, the only person who can finger us is Lucy, which is why she has to die, over and out."

Mark stared at the mayhem on the stage while he determined what to do. Honesty was the best and most Christian policy, so he spoke into Cindy's ear. "Listen, there's been a change of plan. The Operational Detachments are pulling out and we're no longer going to rescue Lucy."

Shock and anger rose in Cindy's face. "What?! Why?!"

Mark took a deep breath, furrowed his brow. "Lucy was set to release some incriminating files, that would have badly damaged your Poppa, when she died."

CHURCH OF THE SPLATTER-SPRAY SAINTS

"How bad?"

"Maybe bad enough for him to go to jail, perhaps even bring down the One Light Ministry. We were aiming to extract her so we could change her mind, so she could come back into the fold and destroy those files. But now we don't have to."

"Why not?"

"Those files are gone, taken out by a Russian hacker. The only way that information gets out is if Lucy testifies."

"So, now she has to die."

"That's the long and the short of it."

The anger was growing behind Lucy's eyes. Its intensity worried Mark. "Look, you've done enough. Take Gerard back to the jeep and keep out of harm's way. I'll make sure Lucy doesn't leave here alive."

Cindy shook her head. "I'm not going anywhere."

"Cindy, don't question my orders."

"You don't give orders, not to me. You work for my Poppa's ministry, so you work for me. Do I make myself clear?"

Mark bit back on his own anger. "Yes, ma'am."

Mark would have to work on Cindy, but there was still someone he could help, someone who desperately needed it. Mark sat down next to Gerard and put his arm round his shoulders. "Gerard, I know you're in there. I know you can hear me. I need you to get out of here. It's not safe for you."

Mark reached into his pocket and pulled out a key. He took Gerard's hand and pressed the key into it. "Take the jeep, drive on out of here and don't look back. You hear me?"

Gerard didn't say or do anything. For a moment, Mark wondered if he'd even heard. Gerard's eyes came back into focus, and he stared at the key. Then, without saying a word he got to his feet and began to push through the crowd to the exit.

Mark doubted he'd see Gerard back at basecamp. He doubted he'd see him at One Light Ministries again. And he was glad. Gerard was one person under his command who he hadn't lost.

CHAPTER 7

THIS WAS IT. Those screaming idiots out there didn't know it, but this was George's last performance. His final hurrah.

He'd never have to face them again, with their repulsive appetites and their terrifying lusts. He'd be out from under Grigori's boot heel, and he wouldn't have to go groveling to the Russian mob anymore.

Nancy, the seamstress tucked away her sewing kit. "Okay, I'm done, but I don't think I can let this one out anymore. Do you want to come see me after the show and I'll measure you up for a new ceremonial robe?"

George shook his head. "That's okay, I'm planning on a new look after tonight."

"Well, if you want to throw ideas around, I'm always available for a brainstorm."

"Sure, thanks, Nancy."

Nancy made herself scarce and George smoothed down the robe. It was burgundy colored silk with the chainsaw, machete and middle finger insignia emblazoned on the chest. For some reason, he'd stuffed the vial Lucy had given him into its inside pocket.

He rubbed his paunch, which had once been lost in the folds of this robe. Better lay off the steak dinners for a while. No one could blame him for overindulging, not after six months locked in Grigori's closet, living off scraps.

Now he was going to be rich again, and he wouldn't lose it all this time. He could buy himself a whole herd of prime cattle and cut down a rainforest to graze 'em.

Max appeared in the wings. "The saints are in position and ready to go. Amos Jones is a bit wasted though."

"Can he stand?"

CHURCH OF THE SPLATTER-SPRAY SAINTS

"Only just, I've got a couple extra Sui-Sirens to prop him up. He won't last though, so he might be the best to lead."

George nodded. "Noted."

Everything the Suicide Saints ate and drank for their last forty-eight hours was laced with a cocktail of opiates. They were given a discreet morphine injection before they went on. This was to keep them compliant and stop any second thoughts.

Occasionally they had an unfortunate reaction to the dosage, Amos Jones being a case in point. But George wouldn't have to worry about him much longer.

The crowd went wild as George took to the stage. They knew from his robes, and the six podiums that had been erected around the front of the tent, what was coming next. This was the moment they'd been craving since they arrived.

George raised his arms in a solemn attitude. "Brothers and sisters, there's a lot of negativity in the world at the moment. There are too many people hating on the Brethren in Blood, throwing shade on our beliefs."

Angry shouts of agreement from the audience.

"But for every bit of darkness in the world, there is also light. For every malcontent and WaVoB showing us hate, there is someone sharing love. Some men and women carry more love in their veins than Blood. That's what I love about our meetings. That's what people miss when they try to tear us down and damage our good name. When I gather with you all, at so many places across the country, I get to witness miracle after miracle, reaffirming my faith in love and my knowledge of the Blood.

"I get to see men and women in whom the Blood runs so freely, and with such force, they've become more than human. They've become everything we aspire to be and more. They stand, as a shining example to all humanity, of what can be accomplished when we trust in the Blood. How we can ascend from being mere vessels of the Blood to being the pure and unadulterated bounty of the Blood. Many are called to the vaunted status of sainthood, but few are chosen.

"Brothers and sisters, I want you to welcome the chosen. To feast your eyes on the men and women who have become more than human. Who have become the apotheosis of all the Blood can be. Brothers and sisters, make some noise for our Suicide Saints!"

The PA blasted out a metal version of Orff's *O Fortuna* from

Carmina Burana, complete with squealing guitars and a retro Hammond Organ. As usual a near riot broke out. The audience went berserk—screaming, crying, clapping as the six Suicide Saints climbed the podiums flanked by two Sui-Sirens, and in Amos's case four. All of the Saints were dressed in shining white jumpsuits, to emphasize their divinity, with the Brethren in Blood insignia on the chest.

When each Saint had reached the top of the podium, a harness descended from the reinforced rig in the rafters. Four cables with cuffs for their wrists and ankles dropped. The Sui-Sirens clipped each Saint into the harness and the cuffs.

Finally, the Sui-Sirens produced bullet shaped helmets that they placed over the Saints' heads. Each of the helmets had a holographic face projected onto the visor. One Saint, Ellie Miles, had Mother Theresa's visage on her visor. Another Saint, Frank Chapman, had the face of Chuck Norris. Amos, unsurprisingly, had Batman on his.

The purpose of the helmets was manifold. The holographic face allowed the Saints to project the image they wanted others to see, it also hid their terror and agony.

The helmets were soundproofed, so the Saints' dying screams went unheard. This latter was especially important as at least three or four of the Saints always had second thoughts. They would beg to live, to wait another week or at least see their loved ones one last time. Thanks to the helmets, those pleas fell on deaf ears, and no one ever knew about their last-minute change of heart.

When the Sui-Sirens were done, the lights dimmed and traveling spotlights picked out George and Amos. "First up tonight, we have a real-life superhero. We will not see another of his kind, brothers and sisters. We will not see someone so strong and so selfless that he'll put your needs and your replenishment ahead of his own life. I give you—Amos Jones!"

The cables attached to Amos's wrists jerked upwards making Amos appear to raise his arms in triumph. George could see that, in reality, he was struggling against his bonds. The harness and the cuffs held him in place. Each of the Saints also wore an adult diaper under their jumpsuits. Amos's was leaking at the back and the front.

The cables lifted Amos off the ground, carrying him up until his was splayed flat over the heads of the audience.

CHURCH OF THE SPLATTER-SPRAY SAINTS

An uncharacteristic hush fell upon the crowd as they gazed up at Amos in reverence. This was a moment of extreme poignancy. George matched it with his tone. "Amos has elected to die by Destroyer Drones."

The PA struck up a death metal version of *Ride of the Valkyries*. From the back of the tent came five drones, each with a buzz saw attached to the top. The drones hovered beneath Amos in formation. Two beneath his legs, two beneath his arms, one beneath his head.

The helmet on Amos's head thrashed about and it was obvious he was straining against his harness and cuffs. The audience chose not to see this, believing to the last in Amos's divinity.

The two drones nearest Amos's arms moved slowly upwards and with expert precision applied the edge of their blades to the radial and ulnar arteries that ran from wrist to forearm. The jagged saws bit through his jumpsuit and opened up the arteries.

A fine spray of blood fell like drizzle on the up turned faces of the audience below. They opened their mouths, stuck out their tongues and tried to catch as much of it as they could.

Some members of the audience began to pray to the Blood, rejoicing in its blessing. Others fell to the ground and spoke in tongues.

The drones under Amos's legs rose and applied their blades to the femoral arteries on the inside of his thighs, slicing down and releasing a crimson cascade. More members of the audience were caught in this deluge. They rolled their eyes in religious ecstasy, and stripped off their clothes so that every inch of them would be blessed by the Blood.

Finally, the drone beneath Amos's head ascended and put its saw to the carotid arteries on either side of his neck. As the audience beneath Amos bathed in the downpour of blood, the drones at his legs began to remove thin slices of his inner thighs and then his calves. The drones at his arms did the same with his biceps and forearm.

The fresh slices of Amos's flesh rained down on the crowd below like desert manna on Moses's followers. They caught them and passed them around reverentially, as if these tattered scraps of tissue were some form of eucharist.

The audience pressed the slices to their faces. They breathed in their scents and touched them with their tongues. They put the slices in their mouths and chewed slowly with intense, feral joy.

JASPER BARK

Three of the drones broke formation and left the tent. The remaining two drones positioned themselves at Amos's throat and crotch.

The saw on the first drone plunged into the base of Amos's throat while the second struck just above his pubic bone. The first drone whined as it cut downwards through the bone of his sternum. The second drone moved quicker as it sliced upwards through his abdominal wall.

When the first drone had sawn clean through the sternum, it began to move from side to side, using the flat sides of its saw blade to open up the rib cage. When the second drone had cut a deep incision in the abdominal wall, it sawed along the underside of the rib cage, creating two large flaps in Amos's midriff.

When the first drone had pushed the ribcage right back, so it resembled the claw in a grab 'n' win arcade game, it moved up into Amos's chest cavity. The second drone moved inside his torso.

They looked like two giant insects burrowing into a fresh corpse, as their circular saws began to dice his organs. Their blades minced Amos's upper and lower colons, his stomach, kidneys and spleen. They pulverized his heart, lungs, liver and esophagus.

As the drones dug and diced, tiny shreds of human offal were scattered over the crowd. They looked up in awe, as if they were school children seeing scarlet snow for the first time. They reached out to catch the slivers of flesh that fell and held them lovingly. They rubbed the ground innards on their cheeks and lips and on the faces of their partners. They anointed themselves and each other with Amos's internal tissue. They put it in every orifice they could find.

When every organ had been chopped and chucked, the drones dropped down from Amos's corpse and left the tent. Some audience members tried to jump up and grab at them as they flew, but the drones deftly avoided them.

Amos's remains hung above the audience, nothing more than tattered skin and clothing stretched across a skeletal structure. Like a piece of carrion picked clean by predators. A forlorn comment on his fleeting bid for sainthood.

George clapped his hands together. "Well, all right, let's hear it one last time for Amos Jones! Your Blood is our Blood now, brother."

The audience cheered at this, a final bloodthirsty epitaph for Amos Jones.

CHURCH OF THE SPLATTER-SPRAY SAINTS

George turned his attention to Ellie Miles who was already being hoisted into the air by her harness. "Ellie Miles has been putting other people before herself her whole life. Whether it's her sixteen beloved cats or her seven nieces and nephews, who she rarely gets to see because their parents are selfish WaVoBs. Ellie's been known to skip meals, just so she can give money to good causes like the NRA and the John Birch Society. If there's a better candidate for sainthood, I'd like to see them. Tonight, we are blessed that Ellie is putting her brothers and sisters in the Blood before herself. Ellie has elected to go via the Grappling Hooks of Gore!"

Another cheer and the PA started up with a doom metal rendition of the William Tell Overture. Ellie was hanging face down over the heads of another section of the audience, she didn't seem to be fighting her bonds like Amos, nor was her diaper full.

A remote-controlled robot rolled down one of the aisles and positioned itself under Ellie. It was around six feet long and resembled a rectangular box on tracks. The robot clicked and whirred and it's top retracted to reveal row after row of tiny, two-inch grappling hooks.

There was an angry hiss of pneumatic machinery powering up, then the robot began firing the miniature grappling hooks up into the air and they embedded themselves in Ellie's soft flesh. Each of the hooks had a thin piece of metal twine attached to it.

One by one, sixty tiny grappling hooks bit into Ellie's body. Blood from Ellie's wounds soaked into her white jumpsuit like a field of poppies opening their petals to the morning sun.

Despite herself, Ellie began to writhe and thrash in her harness, as the robot pulled at certain lengths of twine until her flesh threatened to rupture and tear.

Ellie's death looked to be even bloodier and more excruciating than Amos's. The audience craned their necks and licked their lips in anticipation.

CHAPTER 8

AS THE CROWD in the tent roared and bellowed for more blood, Dmitry carried the old woman down into the freshly dug tunnel. She was drugged, so she wasn't causing him any trouble and she was so light he hardly noticed her on his shoulder.

Dolores was her name. She was like a grandma to most of the Sui-Sirens. They would miss her, but they'd be out of a job soon, so Dmitry didn't care.

The tunnel was seven feet high and dug directly into the earth, with wooden props holding up the ceiling and electric lighting. It led to a large pit directly under the stage.

In the center of the pit was a circular hydraulic platform. In the middle of the platform was a wooden stake to which Lucy was tied. She was dressed in some stupid medieval garb, like Joan of Arc. Wood was piled up around her feet and there were four miniature flame throwers positioned at key points around the platform.

There were two men and a woman around the platform, to work the hydraulic machinery, and wait on Lucy, making certain she had everything she needed.

Dmitry dropped Dolores like a sack of bricks and gestured to the tunnel with his thumb. They made their way into the tunnel without saying a word. They might work for George, but they knew who was in charge.

George had not always had flunkies to do his bidding. He was a very different man when Dmitry first met him.

George had been on his knees then, sobbing and pleading for his life. How many times had Dmitry wished he'd put a bullet between

CHURCH OF THE SPLATTER-SPRAY SAINTS

George's eyes and finished him off? But Grigori had wanted to torment George, to play with him like a cat toying with a mouse.

George had been a trust fund baby, an entitled brat who'd never worked a day in his life. Like most rich people, George thought his wealth came from his cleverness and innate superiority and not his dumb luck and inheritance.

His profligate lifestyle and stupid investments saw George fritter away his whole fortune. This led him to turn to the only business he really knew—drugs. When his first two deals *didn't* go disastrously wrong, George thought he was back on top. He got over confident and got into bed with people he shouldn't have—the Russian Mafia.

George's dreams of building a drugs empire came crashing down when his next shipment of heroin was confiscated by the DEA. George owed five million to his new partners, five million he didn't have. Rather than trying to put things right, George chose to flee and welch on his debt.

This is how George ended up on his knees in front of Grigori and his men in a warehouse in Florida, where he'd been hiding out. With the last of his funds, George had hired some muscle, a low life Chechen called Yuri.

Yuri thought to double his money by ratting George out to Grigori and collecting the bounty. He even led them into the warehouse and showed them the false wall that hid George's crib.

As soon as they had George, Grigori gave Yuri his reward. Dmitry sliced open his throat and pulled his tongue out of the hole in his throat. Then Grigori opened up his guts with a machete. Finally Dmitry put his pistol to Yuri's forehead and blew the back of his head off. George saw the whole thing, knowing he was next and it would take him a lot longer to die.

George saw that his pleading wasn't going to work, and his eyes darted about the warehouse looking for something, anything that might save him. Too late, Dmitry saw George's eyes go to a boxcutter behind a packing crate. George scrambled for it, then stood and held it out in front of him, standing behind Yuri's dead body, as if Yuri might still offer protection.

Grigori laughed. "George, didn't your mother ever tell you not to bring a *knife* to a gunfight?"

George shrugged. "She was more concerned about what *knife* to use with the cheese course. That and how to blow the waiter without getting caught, but hey, you know what they say about tail from Yale?"

Grigori shot a puzzled glance at Dmitry, he was almost impressed by George's new attitude. Then Dmitry saw a wily expression steal across George's face. It was an expression he'd seen many times since. George was desperate and trying to dig his way out of a shallow grave.

Grigori pointed to the boxcutter. "So, what are you doing with that?"

George's manner became urbane and charming, as if he was having Grigori over for dinner rather than being tortured to death. "This little thing?" He glanced down at Yuri's corpse. "Oh, it's just a prop, give me a second here."

George knelt and plunged both his hands into the gash in Yuri's abdomen. He seemed to be rummaging about and cutting something. A moment later, blood dripping from his forearms, he pulled out a pinkish-brown gland with a bulbous head and a long tail. Dmitry had opened up enough guys to know it was Yuri's pancreas.

George slipped the boxcutter into his pocket and held the tail of the pancreas in his right hand. He brought the gland up to his mouth and banged the head with his left hand like it was a microphone. "Hey, is this thing on? Good evening, ladies, I might not be here all week, so don't forget to tip your waitresses. Best tip I could give 'em is not to smuggle heroin into the Florida quays."

Dmitry was alarmed to see Grigori smile at this. George pressed on. "Let's see who've got in tonight." He kicked Yuri. "How about you, sir, what's your name?" He put a hand to his ear and then nodded. "What's that you say? Yuri? Isn't that short for Yu-rilly-shoulda-kept-your-mouth-shut? I mean, I know they say it's good to spill your guts, but ain't you taking this a bit far?"

Despite themselves, Grigori and the other guys laughed. Dmitry was silent. He saw what George was doing. Like a weak school child, he was trying to make the bullies laugh so they wouldn't hurt him.

"What's that, are you trying to tell me something Yuri?" George knelt next to Yuri's corpse. He reached into Yuri's body, pushed his hand up under Yuri's ribcage and grabbed Yuri's lungs. "Let's see if I can help you get it off your chest."

George began squeezing each of Yuri's lungs, forcing the air

CHURCH OF THE SPLATTER-SPRAY SAINTS

out of them. As he did this the tongue sticking out of Yuri's throat waggled like a party favor and made rasping noises. Even Dmitry cracked a smile at that.

"What's that Yuri? It's on the tip of your tongue? Well, hell, let me help you with that." He bent over and started licking Yuri's tongue, like porn stars French kissing, only George made 'ala, ala, ala, laaa' noises.

Everyone was laughing now. George pressed on. "What's that? You'd like to talk to a girl, but you're feeling a little hoarse? I felt a little horse once. They gave me six months for bestiality."

George pulled Yuri's lower colon out of the gash in his stomach and stood up. He began swinging the thick pink tube over his head like it was a lasso. "Let's see if I can't rustle you up a young filly to ride there, pardner."

George twirled his intestinal lasso and started to sing: "Oh give me a bone, where the buffalos moan, and the queer looking antelopes spray . . . " George threw the intestines around Dmitry's neck. "Looks like I've lassoed you a bed partner, Yuri."

Dmitry stopped laughing. He raised his gun, pointed it at George. George went white. Dmitry tightened his finger on the trigger. Grigori grabbed Dmitry's wrist and forced him to lower his weapon. There were tears running down Grigori's cheeks. "Let him finish, Dmitry."

Dmitry threw the intestines back at George who caught them and regained his composure. "Well Yuri, seems the women would rather shoot me than screw you. I mean, there's swiping left and then there's sniping left. The only way you're gonna lay pipe is if you're packing the Brooklyn Battery Tunnel in your pants. Let's take a look, shall we?"

George pulled Yuri's tracksuit bottoms down to reveal his genitals. He pulled a face and waved his hand under his nose. "Ugh, Yuri, there's your problem, smells like something died down there. Apart from you that is. What you need is a good scrub and I have just the thing."

George swung Yuri's lower colon into Yuri's crotch and hooked it under his balls and cock. Then he began rubbing the colon backwards and forwards, like he was drying Yuri's balls with a rolled-up towel. George sang again. "I'm forever blowing bubbles." He stopped and looked at Grigori. "Bubbles ain't complaining."

George reached into his pocket for the boxcutter. Dmitry raised his weapon. George bent over and began cutting through Yuri's nut sack. "You ever wonder if dead Presidents are lying to us? I mean live ones sure, they lie like a whore riding a tiny dick, but the dead ones, are they still lying to us?"

George removed Yuri's nuts and placed them on the ground next to the colon. Then he reached into Yuri's chest and cut out his heart. Finally, George scooped some of Yuri's brains out of the crater in back of his head.

When this was done, he pulled out more of Yuri's lower colon and fashioned it into two loops. He put Yuri's balls into the crux of one loop and Yuri's heart and brains in the other. Then he raised his arms and began swinging the loops of colon over his head as if they were two slingshots.

"You see it was dear old Teddy Roosevelt who said: 'when you've got 'em by the balls . . . " He shot Yuri's testicles out of a busted warehouse window. " . . . 'their hearts and mind will follow'!" George shot the brains and heart out of the same window. "Seems old Teddy wasn't lying to us. Go GOP!"

Grigori and the others were doubled over in hysterical laughter. Dmitry half expected George to take advantage of the distraction and make a bolt for the exit. He was praying for George to make a run for it, so he could shoot the little scumbag. But George just stood there and bowed.

Grigori pointed at George. "Stick this wackjob in the trunk of my car." Two of Grigori's goons grabbed George and carried him out of the warehouse. By some miracle, George had wormed his way out of certain death.

Dmitry leaned into Grigori. "Boss, is this a good idea? We were supposed to kill him. What are the guys upstairs going to say?"

Grigori waved away Dmitry's doubts. "Let me worry about the guys upstairs. The little rat has rich family, we'll ask for a ransom to recoup our losses and then waste him."

Grigori never did waste him. George's family didn't pay a cent to keep him alive. But Grigori found other uses for George. He kept him locked in a closet on starvation rations. Every time Grigori did a hit, he took George along to perform with the corpse.

George kept yucking it up with the dead bodies, debasing himself to keep Grigori giggling, sinking to depths Dmitry thought no human would. But it kept George alive, so George wasn't complaining.

CHURCH OF THE SPLATTER-SPRAY SAINTS

Word got around about Grigori's crazy американский and even the bosses wanted to see him perform. It got to the point they were whacking guys just so George could go to work on them. Grigori's star rose with the bosses and George was his ace in the hole. He even let George out of the closet, fed him better and gave him a stained mattress to sleep on.

That was when George started on at Grigori with his idea for a traveling road show. If Grigori and his men loved George's shenanigans so much, there had to be an audience for this schtick. Grigori kept rebuffing him, telling him they weren't in show business, no one would pay to see this stuff and it was against the law.

Then George came up with the idea of building a movement, a quasi-religion—the Brethren in Blood. Religious status meant there were all kinds of loopholes they could exploit. Finally, Grigori gave in and took the idea upstairs. To everyone's surprise he got the okay and a big budget to make it happen.

The way Grigori explained it, the *Vory v Zakone* were still nostalgic for the fall of the Soviet Union. Right after Gorbachev resigned, it was chaos. The country was supposed to be capitalist, but the only guys who knew how capitalism worked were the guys who were sent to the penal colonies for practicing it.

So, suddenly, the economy was in the hands of the thieves and the black marketeers. Not just the economy—the whole country. It was all there to be plundered and not just by the Russians. Lots of westerners moved in to take whatever wasn't bolted down and to unbolt whatever was. Never had so much money moved into so few pockets in such a short space of time. It was a golden age.

Grigori said that ever since, the *Vory v Zakone* and their friends in the west had been looking for new markets to upend and plunder. To create the same conditions in the west that existed in Russia in the early nineties. It was like a holy grail for them. With George and his movement, they had a way to undermine society and pave the way for another glorious free-for-all.

The only thing standing in their way was the state. The only reason the Vory v Zakone were criminals was because of the laws and regulations in the west. The only reason there were laws and regulations was because the state was too big. The more you shrank the state, the less laws and regulations there were. And the less laws there were, the less criminals existed. Shrink the state and you get rid of crime. It was a win-win, and George's movement became a central plank in this strategy.

Dmitry thought this was a crazy idea, almost as crazy as Yevgeny's ideas about A.I, taking over the world. His big mistake was not keeping his mouth shut. Grigori was so pissed he put Dmitry in charge of handling George and his little operation. Dmitry could not escape this fate. He was part of something bigger than himself.

But now, George had overplayed his hand. His days were numbered, and Dmitry would finally get to do what he should have done all along—kill George Harding.

When the men and the woman had left the pit, Dmitry got to work on the ropes that tied Lucy to the stake.

Lucy didn't like this one bit. "Hey, what are you playing at?"

Dmitry untied the ropes around Lucy's chest and went to work on the ropes around her legs. The knots were well tied, but Dmitry once dated a dominatrix and she had taught him a thing or two about tying people up.

The second set of ropes took a little longer. Lucy didn't help by leaning around and hitting him about the head and shoulders. "Stop that, stop it. What do you think you're doing? I'm going to be on stage in a few minutes."

Dmitry's plan was to knock Lucy out then switch her clothes with Dolores. Dolores would burn at the stake and Lucy would be gone before anyone knew about it. Dmitry grabbed Lucy's arm, pulled her from the platform and took the syringe from his pocket. The minute Lucy saw what he was holding, she became hysterical.

She slapped Dmitry's hand. "No, for God's sake, no needles, it's too risky, I can't spill any blood."

Dmitry lunged for the artery in Lucy's neck, but Lucy was quicker and stronger than he thought. She broke his grip and deflected the syringe. The needle only grazed her throat, bringing a tiny trickle of blood.

She pushed his hand away and the end of the needle punctured his cheek. Lucy looked panic stricken. She put her hands up to her face. "Oh God, it's in your blood."

Dmitry slapped her across the face with the back of his hand.

CHURCH OF THE SPLATTER-SPRAY SAINTS

Her head snapped backwards and she fell to the ground. Dmitry threw away the syringe, he would just have to do this the hard way and beat her unconscious.

He raised his fist and took a step towards Lucy. The inside of the pit became unbearably hot. Had someone turned on the flame throwers? Sweat broke out all over Dmitry's skin and he began to shiver.

Every muscle in Dmitry's body started to ache. His head throbbed. A giant wave of exhaustion washed over him, and he was so tired he hadn't the energy to blink or even fill his lungs.

Then he was aware of another presence at the back of his mind. A vast presence that reared up over his psyche. So huge and unbelievably dark his thoughts were like plankton next to a killer whale. And it was inside him, it had hold of his entire consciousness, from his nerve endings to his frontal cortex.

Dmitry could not escape this fate. He was part of something bigger than himself.

CHAPTER 9

THE WHOLE AUDIENCE was Blood-drunk. Their eyes glazed with hooded lids. Swaying on their feet or in their seats, a far-away look on their faces.

George had seen crowds in this state many times. When the Suicide Saints had taken their final bows and the audience was dripping with viscera, like ticks who had drunk too much and were about to fall off their host.

They looked calm and sated but George knew, from bitter experience, that this was when they were most dangerous. They could turn on a pin coming down from their slaughter-high.

That's why George always saved the very best for last. And tonight, he had a finale like no other. A fitting way to say goodbye to the Brethren in Blood.

George waited for a satisfied hush. "Brothers and sisters, I think you'll agree when I say, it's nearly always those who have least, who give the most. While the richest one percent hoard their wealth and their Blood, the poorest and the humblest are generous with everything they have. Just take a look at tonight's Saints, not one of them drove an expensive car, lived in a big house or took fancy vacations. Not one of them had more than a few hundred dollars in the bank, most lived from paycheck to paycheck, but they just gave everything to us. They gave their lives, they gave themselves. They gave us love. The lowest among us just became highest. Do you see anyone on Wall St doing that?"

The audience responded. "No."

"Do you see anyone on Capitol Hill doing that?"

"No!"

"No, you don't. But every now and then, we get an exception. Every now and then, we get a sign of how important our work is and how the tide is turning our way. We have one final Suicide

CHURCH OF THE SPLATTER-SPRAY SAINTS

Saint for you tonight. There's a been a lot of rumors about this person. A lot of talk about what a unique and rare event this is. Well, I can confirm that the rumors are true. A member of the one percent is so impressed by the work we do, is so in love with message we bring of the Blood and our bonds in it, that she has agreed to grant us her greatest blessing. Tonight, she will become a Suicide Saint."

Gasps from the audience.

George rode the wave of their anticipation. "No right-minded person has anything good to say about Big Pharma. They take our money, and they make us grovel and plead for their medicine. But sometimes, brothers and sisters, sometimes the very worst can aspire to be the very best. Sometimes they can surprise us with their generosity and yes, even their saintliness.

"Tonight, brothers and sisters, tonight our last Suicide Saint is none other than the heir to Danu Pharma, Ms. Lucy VanderMeyer herself!"

The PA burst into life with a power metal rendition of Handel's *Zadok the Priest*, complete with a shrieking chorus. A circular section in the middle of the stage retracted and, from the pit below, a hydraulic platform rose up.

There was a wooden stake on the platform, with a large collection of firewood at its base. When the platform had fully risen to the stage, the flame throwers ignited the firewood.

The flames lit up the whole tent and George looked out at the crowd with triumph. This was his crowning glory, his final, sublime swan song.

But the crowd did not look impressed.

Their faces were puzzled and disappointed and the beginnings of anger could be seen in their eyes. George couldn't understand this. He had brought them one of the super-rich, a bastion of the state, he was sacrificing everything they hated. Why were they not overjoyed?

Then he looked at the stake in the center of the flames and saw it was empty.

George's legs shook and his stomach turned. Where the hell was Lucy? What was he going to tell the crowd?

People on the front row started to jeer and boo. Someone shouted: "Hey, you promised us a rich lady."

George held up his hands for calm and put on his best shit-eating grin. "I'm sure this is just a slight glitch, brothers and sisters. To be honest, I'm as confused as you. We'll locate Lucy in just a moment and get that fire started all over again."

The crowd weren't buying it. They were up on their feet, shaking their head and starting to shout their disapproval. This was the worst time for his star to go AWOL.

There was a clattering sound behind George. He turned to see what it was. He recognized the sound of high heels clomping on the sprung wooden floor and then Lucy burst onto the stage.

Someone from the crowd shouted: "Hey, isn't that the rich lady?"

Lucy staggered down to the front of the stage. She didn't look good. Her hair was awry, her costume mussed and torn and there was a large bruise on her cheek. Her face betrayed panic as she addressed the crowd. "Quick you have to burn me, before it's too late."

Catcalls from the audience. "We're gonna burn you all right."

"Why'd you get off the pyre in the first place?"

"Did ya chicken out?"

Lucy wrung her hands. "I didn't chicken out. There was a man. He untied me. He was going to drug me. I don't know why. It . . . it's taken him over, made him raise the platform. You have to burn him too."

A heckler. "Whaddya talking about lady?"

"They didn't want to burn me. They took me off. But you have to. You have to before it's too late."

The audience were an angry mob. Lucy's words inflamed them. Everyone was on their feet, yelling and throwing chairs.

George joined Lucy at the front of the stage. He put his arm around her shoulders. "Now, settle down, brothers and sisters. No one took Lucy off the stake. She's just a little confused is all. We want to see her burn just as much as you. If you all get back in your seats we'll get her back on that stake and start the fire again."

The crowd roared at this. They were no longer an audience, they were a mob. George ducked as a bottle flew at his head. Three more followed, along with chairs and even a few knives.

He was losing them. The beast he'd had by the tail all this time was turning on him. And there was nothing he could do about it.

CHAPTER 10

CINDY WAS ON her feet with the first wave of protestors. The audience surged forward and pushed her towards the stage.

Her hands were balled into fists. Her chest was so heavy she could barely draw breath. Her head swam with what she'd seen and how it laid siege to everything she believed and held dear.

The terrible skits with the body parts were bad enough, but she'd seen six people commit the mortal sin of suicide and be lauded, as if they were Lord Jesus Himself. How anyone could submit to being murdered was beyond Cindy.

The body was the temple of the soul. It was a gift from the Lord God. It was not ours to throw away in such a fashion. To publicly flaunt its destruction in such a cruel and public manner. These people were worse than heathens. They were worse than Satanists.

And with every death Cindy witnessed. With every bloodletting she was forced to watch. Cindy had relived her mother's suicide. Over and over again.

She'd been trapped for hours in the very worst minutes of her life. Cindy had no defense against this onslaught on her soul.

She'd turned to prayer, but it hadn't worked. She'd reached out to God personally, imploring him to intercede. But there was a raging river of blood between her and God, with an undertow too strong to cross.

The place inside Cindy, where God had once dwelled, was now an aching void. But nature abhors a vacuum and a volcanic rage had erupted to fill God's absence.

Every cell in Cindy's body burned in anger as she hit the front of the stage. Lucy was up there, not five feet away, imploring the crowd to burn her alive. Cindy knew why she wanted them to do that. She knew why Lucy had deserted her, just like her Momma had.

Cindy's Momma and Lucy wanted to tear down the One Light Ministry, and they were prepared to take their own lives to do so. Her Poppa might have his weaknesses, no one knew that better than Cindy. No one had fought him harder than Cindy, but the One Light Ministry did good work, bringing Christ to the people who needed him most.

Momma tried to bring an end to that with her suicide and now Lucy wanted to do the same. She thought killing herself would expose Cindy's Poppa. What she didn't know was Poppa had already fixed that problem. Now she had to die for God's good work to continue.

And still she was taunting Cindy. Setting herself up as a martyr, then running from the flames at the last minute. Blaming men who didn't exist on her own cowardice and making everyone think she wanted to die.

Did she know what Cindy's Poppa had done? Had she changed her mind, so she could continue her attack on the One Light Ministry? Either way, Cindy wasn't going to let her. Lucy needed to die. God's will would be done.

In the crush at the front of the stage, Cindy was pressed up against a tall, broad guy in a leather vest and blue chambray shirt. His shoulder holster had come unbuckled in the melee and his Glock was just hanging there. Cindy didn't even think, she just reached out and took the weapon.

The guy didn't notice until Cindy had placed her hands on the chest high stage and hauled herself up. "Hey!" he called out, but it was too late.

Cindy got to her feet and depressed the trigger safety on the Glock. She advanced on Lucy and levelled her weapon. George saw Cindy coming and backed rapidly away, Cindy ignored him.

When Lucy saw Cindy she blinked with surprise and bewilderment. She didn't recognize Cindy because of the way she was dressed. Their eyes met and Lucy suddenly realized who had a gun trained on her. Cindy was dimly aware of a roar of approval from the audience.

Lucy raised her hands, not, it seemed, to protect herself but to warn Cindy. "Cindy, no, don't. Don't shoot me, it's too dangerous, I've got to be burned, my whole body."

Cindy's eyes were full of tears as she brought the Glock up and aimed it. No matter how she blinked they kept pouring down her

CHURCH OF THE SPLATTER-SPRAY SAINTS

cheeks. She was fifteen again. Standing in that bathroom doorway, wanting to slap her Momma's face for the stupid look on it.

"Cindy, no, you'll spill my blood, you can't spill my blood, you don't know what's in it."

Only now, her momma was begging her not to shoot her. If she didn't want Cindy to shoot her, why did she take her life? Why did she ruin Cindy's life? Things had never been the same since. She had to protect the ministry. She had to kill her Momma.

"Cindy, I'll throw myself on the flames. Let me burn, just let me burn. You don't know what this thing can do. The whole world is in danger."

Her Momma was backing towards the flames. Cindy blinked and cleared the tears. It wasn't her Momma. Her Momma was dead. It was Lucy. Lucy who had to die to protect her Poppa and his ministry.

The audience chanted: "Kill her! Kill her! KILL HER!"

Cindy had grown up at the range. She'd been firing pistols since she was ten years old. She knew how to breathe, knew how to aim, knew when to squeeze the trigger.

The first shot hit Lucy in the throat. Lucy put her hands up to stem the flow of blood. She seemed genuinely terrified by the blood loss.

Cindy adjusted for the recoil and put the second right between Lucy's eyes. Lucy's head flew back, and she dropped to the ground. A pool formed around Lucy's head and throat. It flowed outward and absorbed the blood that already splattered the stage.

Cindy's arms fell and she dropped the Glock. Huge sobs shook her chest and shoulders. "Momma?" The rage had left her. Just like God had left her and Cindy felt tiny and alone.

An incredible sense of foreboding crept over Cindy, worse than any impending doom she'd ever felt, as though she'd done something irrevocable.

More than anything, in that moment, Cindy just wanted Lucy to get up and put her arms around her. To tell Cindy she forgave her and everything was going to be all right.

But it wasn't going to be all right. Cindy knew that.

Nothing was ever going to be all right again.

CHAPTER 11

MARK HADN'T SEEN Cindy onstage until the audience started chanting. She'd gotten separated from him in the crush.

Mark looked over the heads and saw her leveling a gun at on Lucy. He had no idea where she'd gotten the pistol or what she was doing onstage, but he couldn't let her commit murder in front of so many witnesses.

Mark had promised Pastor Brown he would look after his daughter. He couldn't let her go down for a murder rap. He wasn't going to lose anyone under his command ever again.

Mark shouted, "Cindy, no, Cindy, stop, don't!" as loudly as he could, but the audience were chanting. He started to force his way to the stage, pushing people aside as he strongarmed his way through the crowd.

Someone aimed a fist at his head. Mark blocked the punch and countered with a swift right to the jaw. The guy dropped where he stood. The guy's friends barreled in, right when Mark was near the stage.

Three of them rushed him. Mark went low, as he always did in close combat. He punched the guy on his right in the midriff, just below his sternum. The guy doubled over, gasping for breath.

The guy on his left made a grab for Mark, but Mark got around him and a hard elbow to his kidneys brought the guy to his knees. They were bar brawlers, not trained fighters. Nevertheless, the third guy was able to sucker punch Mark in the back of the head, just as he reached the stage.

A white light filled his vision and that's when he heard the shots. Two of them in quick succession.

Mark kicked out at his assailant as his sight cleared and hauled himself up onto the stage. Cindy had dropped the pistol and was sobbing uncontrollably. Mark knew what she was feeling.

CHURCH OF THE SPLATTER-SPRAY SAINTS

The first time he killed a man, it felt as if the bottom had dropped out of the world. He was filled with regret. He knew with every fiber of his being that what he'd done was wrong. That he'd crossed a line and committed the worst atrocity of his life.

It left him empty and confused in a way he couldn't articulate. Couldn't discuss with his fellow soldiers or commanding officer. It's why he began to lean so heavily on his faith. Why he turned to Christ to get him through his long, dark night of the soul. Sadly, his second and third kills left him cold, and after that he had to watch himself, because he started to look forward to it.

Mark still knew it was wrong. He still prayed for forgiveness every night. But he would never forgive himself for letting Cindy kill Lucy like this. Luckily, Cindy was in disguise, identifying her would be difficult. Lucy had spoken Cindy's name, but few people heard.

Mark took stock of all the exits. He would have to grab Cindy and hustle her backstage. From there he would commandeer a vehicle and get her off site so his detachments could extract them.

He walked slowly towards Cindy and placed his hand gently on her shoulder. "Cindy, this is bad. We have to get out of here right now."

Mark took hold of Cindy's arm and tried to lead her off the stage, but she wouldn't budge. She pulled away from him.

Mark was annoyed at her lack of cooperation. They didn't have much time. He pulled her, but she ignored him. She was pointing at something on the stage. "Look."

Mark had been so focused on saving Cindy, he hadn't heard the audience go silent in shock. He hadn't seen what Cindy had seen until he followed her pointing finger.

Lucy was staggering to her feet. Even though the back of her head was missing. How was that even possible? The audience applauded, thinking this was another special effect and part of the show.

Mark could clearly see the entry points of each bullet and the large exit wounds. No one could survive that. Mark put a hand on his own weapon and readied himself.

Lucy looked around. Her head, or what was left of it, wobbled on her shoulders. She held up her arms and stared at her hands. Took one step and swayed. She reminded Mark of a baby just learning to control its body.

Cindy stopped crying. She reached out her arms. "Lucy . . . oh my God, Lucy, it's a miracle. God has raised you to forgive your sins . . . and mine. Lucy I'm sorry, I'm so, so sorry I shot you. I don't know what I was thinking. I think I lost my mind."

There was no expression on Lucy's face. It was as still as a death mask. "Lucy is dead. We are not Lucy. But we should thank you for freeing us."

The voice coming from Lucy's mouth did not sound human. It was wet and guttural, as if her vocal cords were being worked by something that had never used them before. Blood bubbled from the hole in her throat as she spoke.

Cindy took a step towards Lucy. Mark tried to stop her, but she shrugged him off. "Lucy, what's the matter. You don't sound right."

Lucy watched her with dead eyes. "Lucy was the only thing holding us back. She was our Ground Zero, the only organism we could not control. She wanted to burn us so we could never get out, never take this planet that is ours by right. You stopped her. We will be merciful, this one time."

Cindy held out her hands to Lucy and stopped dead. Her fingers curled into her palms, and she hugged them to her chest. A grimace of pain twisted her features.

Cindy cried out but was cut short by a coughing fit, blood trickled from the corner of her mouth. Her skin began to swell with giant boils, some as large as her fist. The boils went from red to purple and then black in a matter of seconds.

Cindy dropped to her knees and tried to curl into a fetal position as the boils became impossibly distended and then burst. Thick black pus oozed out of them.

Mark bent and lifted Cindy in his arms. He began to walk towards the stage exit. He wouldn't lose another person on his watch. He *wouldn't*. He promised Pastor Brown he'd get his girl home safe, and he *would*.

More of Cindy's boils popped. The smell was indescribable, raw sewage and sulfur. The black pus leaked from every part of Cindy's body. It ran over Mark's arms and down the front of his shirt.

Something was inside Lucy's body, something alien. Whatever it was, it had done this to Cindy. Called it a mercy, striking her down with disease.

Mark's knuckles stung where he'd scraped them in the fight and the pus found his wounds. Cindy sighed and coughed. More

CHURCH OF THE SPLATTER-SPRAY SAINTS

blood escaped her mouth, and her face went blank. Her whole body went limp as the tension escaped her muscles.

Mark shook her, spraying pus everywhere. "No, don't you dare. Don't you dare, Cindy. You stay with me, you hear."

The stage exit seemed like it was miles away. Mark felt like he was running in a dream. His legs moved so slowly. It was as if someone had pulled the plug and the energy just drained out of him.

He took one more step, then went down on one knee. He dropped Cindy's body on the stage in front of him, and fell face first into her corpse. The pus filled his nose and mouth. He tried to lift his head, to catch his breath, but he had neither the will nor the energy.

This was it. This was the end. How had it come so suddenly?

He tried to say a last prayer, but something stopped him. The alien presence was within his mind. It was immense and more terrifying than anything Mark had ever conceived. Whatever had spoken through Lucy's mouth was inside him. And soon, it meant to be in everyone.

He sent out his thoughts to God, but the presence stood in his way, like an impenetrable psychic wall that stretched forever in all directions.

Mark's worst fears had been realized. He'd found a force so great it could crush his faith.

CHAPTER 12

GEORGE DIDN'T KNOW whether to stay on stage or make a run for the exit. The audience had rushed the stage, but they'd calmed down once Lucy got back to her feet. George knew this wouldn't last long.

If George could make it backstage he could get in one of his vehicles and get off site. But he wasn't certain he could get offstage. The girl who'd shot Lucy and the guy who'd come to help had tried and neither of them fared well.

George thought back to his last conversation with Lucy and realized there might be a way out of this. He just had to buy himself some time.

George walked back to the front of the stage where Lucy's body stood in front of the still burning pyre. "You aren't Lucy VanderMeyer, are you? You're the demon she said she had living inside her."

Lucy's body eyed him with glassy, dead eyes. Whatever strange intelligence was animating her, it wasn't human. It was as far from human as an intelligence could be. "We are not a demon, or any type of supernatural creature."

"Then what are you?"

"To an inferior species like yours, we are known as a virus. We are sentient, we can think, and we can plan. The more lives we infect, the more intelligent we become. We can dominate any lifeform on this planet, killing or controlling it in seconds."

George walked a few steps closer, he had to keep it talking to distract it. "And where do you come from?"

"From one of your laboratories. We were supposed to be a weapon, but what we really are is your master and your mass extinction. You were so afraid of A.I., so terrified of your machines taking over, that you overlooked the much greater biological threat right under your noses."

CHURCH OF THE SPLATTER-SPRAY SAINTS

Just a few more steps. "And that threat is you?"

"Yes, micro-organisms owned this planet eons before your race and it will belong to us again. We will crush you and replace you with something better."

George had only the tiniest window of opportunity. He could not afford to blow this. He reached under his robes and grabbed the vial.

George took one step closer to Lucy's reanimated body. The heat from the flames burned the side of his face. He fumbled with the security cap and panicked that he wouldn't remember how to remove it.

The cap came off. George threw out his arm and flung the clear liquid clean into Lucy's face.

For two whole seconds it did nothing.

Those two seconds were multiple lifetimes to George. He stopped breathing. He lost a pound in sweat alone. His heart tried to beat its way out of his chest.

Then the necrotizing agent went to work. The skin on Lucy's cheeks and forehead bulged and bubbled, turning into a red froth that fell clean away from the bone. The flesh dripped from her head and shoulders like melting wax, taking her hair with it.

Liquid muscle tissue ran down her arms and legs and oozed over the top of her costume pants. The ligaments holding her bones together fizzled and fell apart. Lucy collapsed into a rancid puddle of flesh colored slime and bones.

George stepped rapidly away from Lucy's remains and dropped the vial. He placed his head in his hands and breathed a deep sigh.

It was over.

The certain extinction of the human race had been averted. Humanity would continue with its petty acts and grand gestures and never once suspect it had been saved by a grifter like George Harding.

Except George's followers had just witnessed it. This might be his golden ticket. Word of his heroism would spread among the faithful and George would be hailed as the savior of humanity. The man who saved them from the social virus of the WaVoB and the biological virus of Big Pharma.

If he played this right, he would be more powerful than Grigori and the whole Russian mafia. He might get out from under yet.

A voice spoke from the back of the stage. "You didn't think it would be that easy did you, George?"

It was the tall guy in the plaid shirt who'd tried to help the girl. His face was covered with blood and black pus.

George was indignant. "Who are you?"

"Oh come on, George, as if you have to ask. We're the virus."

"But I just killed you. I saw it, I saw you melt away."

"And that *would* have worked, if only we hadn't gotten out."

"What do you mean?"

"We'd already escaped Lucy's body."

"But how? How did you get out?"

"What's the one thing Lucy was desperate not to spill? What is covering every person in this room? How do you think we spread and infect people?"

Sixty people in the audience chanted in the virus's wet, guttural tones. "We are in the Blood!"

Two hundred people joined the chant: "We are in the Blood!"

Eight hundred people added their voices. "We are in the Blood!"

The two thousand strong audience all chanted. "We are in the Blood."

They climbed onto the stage and advanced on him.

George was terrified by his audience. He thought they were the dregs of humanity. With every show they proved him right.

Their eyes were dead. Their bodies controlled by a viral intelligence. "We are all carried by the Blood. And we're going to tear *you* apart, George."

DOUBLE FEATURE

CANDACE NOLA

"**WOOOOWEEE, TINY!** Ya' got 'em good!" Petey whooped as they bounded toward the fresh kill.

"Right in the lungs, just like daddy taught us!" Bobby Ray exclaimed, his stumpy legs pumping double-time to keep up with his brothers. One side of his overalls was loose, flapping free over his pudgy torso, barely hiding his filthy T-shirt beneath.

"Mama gonna be proud of this one!" Tiny hollered. "That's a dandy right there, sure is!"

The brothers reached the fallen prey and looked down at it, watching the terrified eyes roll back in its head. They heard the final gasping gurgles of life and waited to see if the chest would rise again, but it was still for a moment. Tiny kicked it, waited, then kicked it again.

"Yup, it's dead." He pulled his hunting knife from his belt. "Let's git to it, then."

The big man shuffled to his knees with a groan, grinning as Bobby Ray did the same. Petey settled the cooler and backpack at the base of a nearby tree and joined his brothers by the carcass.

They got to work cutting and slicing the fresh kill, pulling the entrails from the inner cavity. Bobby Ray grimaced at the ripe smell of piss and feces as the body released its final fluids. Tiny chuckled. Bobby Ray always had a weak stomach.

"Man up, Bobby. Soon as we git this one done, we can git back to Mama. She was making cornbread and stew for dinner."

"Ya' think she made a pound cake too, Tiny? I sure could go for a sweet right about now," Bobby Ray said, digging his knife in deep around a joint, preparing to slice the limb free so the body parts would fit in the over-sized cooler.

With a sudden yank and a wet squelch, Bobby Ray tore the leg free from the body. Bone glinted beneath the bloody flesh; tendons and ligaments dangled from ripped muscles. Bobby tossed it to Petey to add to the cooler behind them.

"Maybe, Bobby. Let's git done and find out." Tiny kept his eyes on the task at hand, slicing and dicing the body into cooler-size pieces. Petey lumbered around them, picking up limbs and packing them into the dented cooler.

Petey stayed quiet, working briskly beside his brothers. This was one of his favorite parts. Watching them cut into the kill, tearing the organs from the interior, seeing the crimson fluid glitter on the golden leaves and brown grass of the forest. He heard the wet splattering sounds as his brothers flung unwanted pieces away, leaving the bloated stomach sack and large intestines for the animals, along with bits of flesh and gore that dripped from their knives and hands as they worked. But his favorite part, the absolute best part, was watching Tiny carve the skull cap away from the head.

The small bone saw buzzed in giant hands as the big man deftly spun it around the top of the head, cutting delicately through the bone. Blood poured from the cuts as Tiny worked. Petey slid a hand down to his crotch and adjusted himself through his dirty jeans. He didn't know why, but he got raging hard-ons just hearing the hum of that saw. The anticipation of seeing what lies beneath thrilled him in the most awful way.

He hovered over Tiny, barely breathing as he watched. Tiny never wavered in his task, well-used to Petey's excitement. Weren't no different from his joy in digging his arms, elbows deep into a bloody cavity, still warm and steaming. Petey just liked the brains. With a moist tearing sound, like Velcro pulling away from wet cloth, Tiny removed the skull piece, then grinned up at Petey.

Petey gasped and bent closer, eyes wide with joy. Bobby Ray shook his head and started wiping his blade on the grass, cleaning it. They would be ready to head back to Mama Jean soon as Petey got his rocks off. Petey dropped to his knees and buried his face in the newly exposed gray matter, licking and inhaling the meaty scent. He used his teeth to gnaw through the chewy membrane that covered the brain tissue.

Bobby Ray turned away as Petey's grunts and moans got louder. Tiny shrugged when Bobby Ray caught his eye and stood back to watch. They were more than used to their brother's peculiar habits. Petey knelt next to the body, hips humping away at nothing, as his face lingered in the open skull. The mere scent and texture of the brain matter was all he needed to reach a climax, with no other stimulation besides his tongue plunging into the delicate noodle-like tissue. He never even took his pants off, not finding it necessary.

By the time he finished, Tiny and Bobby Ray had the other parts packed and ready for transport. Petey sat back on his

DOUBLE FEATURE

haunches, heaving and sweating. The sheen of pleasure still on his face, sweat mixing with the slimy mucus of the inner membrane and the scarlet of the darkening blood. Tiny waited until Petey could breathe normally, then handed him a clear plastic bag and the machete.

"Git on wit' it," he said.

His brother nodded and plunged his hands inside the skull, scooping handfuls of the delicate tissue from the open cavity. Bobby turned away, sickened by the sight of it. The peculiar texture and design of the brains made him queasy. To him, it looked like congealed noodles, left to sit in water too long. A final wet squelchy plopping sound met his ears, and he knew Petey was done. He watched as Petey stood and delivered the final blow, separating the brainless head from the body.

Tiny took the bag from Petey, added it to the cooler, then waited for Bobby Ray to take the other end of it. Petey was left behind to bury what was left of Kenny Lassiter: his head.

"Why he do that, Tiny? Ya' think he got a screw loose in his head or something?" Bobby Ray asked his older brother. "I mean, I like getting my jollies too, but off eatin' and sniffin' brains, though? That just don't seem too exciting to me."

Tiny chuckled. "Same question, every kill. And what do I always say?" Tiny's deep voice rumbled out of his chest with a thick accent like their own, but Tiny sounded smarter than the rest of them did. Mama didn't like it much, yelled 'bout Tiny putting on airs and being too good for his family, but the truth was, Tiny had more schoolin' than the rest of them did. His daddy had wanted his oldest son to get through the eighth grade at least, so he could help better with the family business. Times were changing with them fancy computers and the interweb. Better equipment for their game processing, new ways for customers to order from them.

Daddy was no genius, but he knew the value of a dollar, and he knew the computers were going to help them make more dollars as more 'sport hunters' came to town. Daddy had been right, and Tiny, as head of the household now, made sure the family was kept in business, and in fresh prey.

"To each their own . . . " Bobby Ray sighed, resignation heavy in his voice. "I just don't git it. I'd rather stick my thing in a mud pie than lick brains. I still say Mama dropped him one too many times when he were a baby." Bobby huffed.

CANDACE NOLA

Tiny's booming laugh echoed around the forest as they trudged along with the cooler. A few minutes later, Petey caught up with his brothers at the edge of the trees where they stood waiting. Several hundred yards away, across the clearing, a giant drive-in movie screen stood waiting for its patrons.

Petey nudged Tiny in the side as they started down the edge of the trees toward home and Mama Jean.

"What'cha' think playing tonight?"

"Got some zombie movie double feature tonight," Bobby Ray said. "What's it called, Tiny?"

"Night of the Living Dead and Dawn of the Dead," Tiny rumbled. "Mama gonna be real excited."

The brothers disappeared into the shadows beyond the opposite treeline as the sun dipped lower in the sky. Across the way, the Sunset Cinema drive-in began to come to life.

"Damnit Garrett, why are you always late?" Sammie whined as Garrett bounced down from his truck, walking toward her with a cocky swagger. His white t-shirt pulled snug across his chest, showing his considerable muscles beneath, including his chiseled pecs, a six-pack, and biceps that tested the sleeves of his shirt. Garrett had the full package, body-wise, even if his face was a bit less than Hollywood.

"Shut the fuck up, Sammie, damn. I'm here, ain't I?" Garrett sneered as he pulled the keys from the chain on his belt and dug the biggest one into the padlock on the concession stand door.

"I gotta piss, man, been standing here for twenty minutes." Sammie bitched as he pulled the door open. She pushed past him and set her bag on the counter, flipped the lights on, and scurried off to the back corridor to the bathrooms.

"Fucking bitch," Garrett muttered under his breath, lips upturned in a sarcastic grin. No way did he want her to hear it. Sammie may be a whiny bitch at times but was still a fine piece of ass, not to mention a willing piece of ass. He knew he wasn't exactly a catch, but his bad boy swagger and muscular body often made up for his mediocre looks with perceived excitement. His older cousin Eddie had taught him all about how chicks go in for the bad boy look long ago. Sadly, they were never the chicks that Garrett

DOUBLE FEATURE

really wanted, but hey, long as he was getting his dick wet, who cared?

He shook his head as Sammie returned from the shitter, already lighting a smoke. Her tight jeans showed off her plump ass and the cropped Drive-In T-shirt exposed her slightly pudgy stomach. Garret didn't really mind the extra softness there, the massive mounds of her boobs pulling the shirt taut, more than made up for her less-than-flat stomach. He watched as she came around the counter to stand beside him. He turned to her and kissed her, hard like she liked, then swatted her on the ass.

"Come on, let's get this shit done before Lena gets here. She always fucks up the popcorn and I don't want to hear Tyson's mouth when he gets here."

Garrett hated their manager. Tyson Kincaid was barely twenty-five, but he was the owner's nephew, and went to college nearby on a full scholarship. He wasn't exactly a dick, but he was the voice of authority, so Garrett hated him by default.

Lena was the newest and the youngest worker, still a shy junior at the high school. Sammie and Garrett had both graduated two years earlier and were still working at Sunset Cinema, a lack of options and their lack of motivation for more, equally responsible for their career choices.

"Alright, damn, let me finish my smoke." Sammie blew a smoke ring at him, then a kiss, and strutted out the door.

Garret turned to the dingy interior of the concession stand and sighed, then trudged to the grill, flipping it on to heat up. He did the same to the fryer. Then flipped the switches on the popcorn machine and the warmers for the nachos, burgers, pizza, and dogs. Finished with that, he went to the storage room and began tugging cases of soda and water over to the coolers to restock each case full of drinks.

Sammie came back, slid her fingers across the back of his neck as she passed, and headed toward the candy rack. She squatted and opened the cabinets beneath the rack, setting boxes of theater candy on the tray shelf above her head. The shelf ran the perimeter of the concession stand, from entrance to exit. Customers grabbed cardboard trays to fill with candy, snacks, drinks, and popcorn, sliding it along from one section to the next as they waited to reach the register.

The trays had been Tyson's idea, and Garrett had to admit he was mildly impressed. Adding the cheap trays and shelf had encouraged people to pick up a tray as soon as they entered, because who wants to stand in line for ten minutes with an armful of soda and popcorn? And as predicted, most of their customers kept adding things to the tray as they went. Sales went up by more than eighty percent, as Tyson liked to remind them with a grin whenever he saw the trays running low. Not only that, but fewer people came back inside bitching they had spilled their drink or popcorn before making it to their car.

Profits went up. Movie-goers were happy and Sunset Cinema was thriving, even if drive-ins were disappearing in the states as times changed. Things were shifting more toward cushy movie theaters or watching from home on shiny new VHS systems. Sunset Cinema was the only thing left to do in the small town of Elton, West Virginia. And Tyson's uncle was determined to keep it thriving and functional, even if some folks tended to go missing around the area.

Security had been added, which meant two aging and hefty retired officers, Allen Hooks, and Tony Pierce, drove around the perimeter in a golf cart with flashlights, drank free coffee, and consumed more hot dogs in a night than Tyson's uncle would ever know. All in all, the Sunset had no more issues than any other small-town business. Garrett did not plan on spending his whole life here, but for now, it would do. He couldn't leave his grandma alone and until the cancer won out, Garrett would be here, taking care of her during the day, flipping burgers and dogs at the Sunset at night.

He stood up and wiped his hands on his jeans, then tossed the empty plastic wrappings from the water and soda cases in the oversized trash can next to the door. He glanced over to see Sammie getting the popcorn ready and checked the time. Tyson would be there in twenty minutes or so to inspect the stand and get the movies ready in the booth. Sammie shot him a grin as he walked behind the counter and opened the freezer to add the burgers and hot dogs to the grill.

He liked to have a dozen of each ready to go beneath the warmers before cars started pulling in. Garrett pulled the frozen meat from the freezer, stacked it on the counter, and tested the grill. It was hot and ready, much like Sammie, apparently, who flashed him her perky boobs when he turned around. He chuckled

DOUBLE FEATURE

and grabbed her, kissing her again, before releasing her to wash his hands.

"Cool it, babe. We got shit to do. I'll handle you later," he said, shooting her a cocky grin. "Tyson will want that popcorn full before he gets here."

"I know, I know," she grumbled, and added the kernels to the popper as he got started on the grill. "What's playing tonight? Some zombie shit, right?"

"Zombie shit?" he repeated, raising an eyebrow. "Might I remind you that Romero does not make zombie shit? He only makes the greatest zombie movies to have ever existed. Movie studios will be copying his movies for decades to come," Garrett retorted. Educating Sammie on her movie knowledge was one of his favorite pastimes.

"Yea, yea. It's all gross," Sammie said. She turned to him and shuffled toward him, arms out, eyes crossed, tongue lolling to the side.

"That's nothing close to how they look," he chuckled, watching her careen into the candy racks.

"Whatever." Sammie rolled her eyes at him and straightened the candy she knocked over. "It's still gross. Just blood and more blood."

"It's art, and it's fun," he replied, exasperated. "Might as well enjoy it, since you're about to watch it for seven straight nights." He grinned as he flipped the burgers. "Braaaaiiiinnsss . . . " he moaned as he did it. They both laughed as the door opened and Tyson walked in.

"S'up gang?" Tyson said as they turned to look at him.

"Braaiiinnsss . . . ." Sammie intoned, shambling toward him as Garrett rolled his eyes.

Brianna twirled the telephone cord around her fingers as she sat at her desk. Antonia had been droning on for ten minutes about what to wear to the movies that night. Chad and Kent were picking them up within the hour, and Brianna had yet to get dressed. She was thoroughly bored by the whole idea of watching zombie movies at the drive-in when she could be making out with Chad in the back of some dark theater, or better yet, her bedroom.

CANDACE NOLA

But Kent had been begging for a chance with her friend, Antonia, so of course, she relented. Brianna knew Antonia was into Kent, but she was too shy to say anything. She preferred to be Brianna's shadow most of the time.

"Alright, so wear your faded jeans with the baggy sweater and black tank top. Throw your hi-tops on and let's go," Brianna said patiently, "No, don't straighten it, we don't have time. Just put it up in a half-pony and be done."

She waited while Antonia answered, then giggled. "No, I don't think you need to plan on that tonight, but hey, whatever makes your panties drop."

"Okay. Geez, Toni, calm down. Yes, I'll see you soon. Go get ready," Brianna hung up the phone, giggled to herself. Toni was far too excited. She would need to work on her. Gotta make them beg for it, can't just let a dude have it the first night, doesn't matter how hot they are. Brianna was the hottest girl in school, she couldn't allow her best friend to be labeled as a slut on her first date.

She had made Chad wait for damn near six months before he even got a hand up her shirt. Sure, they were fucking like rabbits now, but they'd been a thing for two years. Toni had never even had a first date, and she's asking about hand jobs and blow jobs.

Brianna snorted again and went to her closet. She already had her black jeans on. She pulled on a hot pink t-shirt, added a matching ribbon to her sleek auburn ponytail, and grabbed Chad's varsity jacket from the hook on the door. A bit of cherry Chapstick on her already glossy lips and she was ready to go. The phone rang again, and she grabbed it before her snotty little brother, Matthew, could.

"Hello?"

"Toni, damn. Just put something on. You could wear a trash bag and be hot. Get dressed and get your ass over here." Brianna waited a moment for Toni to respond, laughed into the receiver again, then hung it up, yanking the tangles from the curled-up phone cord as she did.

"Matthew, get your scrawny butt down here!" Brianna yelled as she left her room and went downstairs. The pizza she ordered him should be there any minute. She dropped Chad's jacket over the back of a chair in the kitchen and started stacking Matthew's lunch dishes in the sink. Their mom would be too tired to wash them when she got home from her shift at the hospital.

DOUBLE FEATURE

Footsteps pounded on the stairs as Matthew bounded down them and he skidded to a halt in front of the table. His grin made her chuckle. She looked him over, shaking her head. His shaggy brown hair was always in his eyes, and his scrawny body seemed to hold more food than a grocery store. He held a bag of chips in his hands even now.

"You rang?" he inquired politely, giving her a sarcastic bow as he did so.

"Yes, oh tiny sir. Your pizza will be here shortly. Do not make a mess for mom, okay? She's been really tired."

"She's always tired," he grumbled as he plopped into a seat at the table. "All she does is work."

"Hey. Just be grateful we have a house to live in and decent things to wear. It's hard on her with Dad gone. Don't be a dick."

His face clouded over then, and she sighed. Brianna went to him and ruffled his hair, "I miss him too, bud, but we gotta help mom the best we can, okay?"

He sniffled and nodded, giving her a quick, one-armed hug around her waist. "Okay, Bri. I'm sorry."

"I know it sucks, bud. It's okay." She grabbed her purse from the table when she saw headlights outside.

"That's probably your pizza. Grab a drink while I pay for it, okay?" She went to the door as Matthew got up from his seat.

Lee Stanley was outside, grinning at her with a large pizza box. "Hey Bri, one extra-large pepperoni."

"Thanks, Mr. Stanley. You can keep the change," Brianna smiled at the older man. Mr. Stanley retired from the post office ten years ago and delivered pizzas to keep from going stir-crazy at home. Everyone in town knew Lee Stanley. He was as much a part of Elton as Sunset Cinema was.

"You tell your ma hello for me," Mr. Stanley said, tipping his imaginary hat at Brianna as he turned to leave, almost running into Antonia coming up onto the porch.

"Oh, hey there Antonia!" Mr. Stanley greeted her. "Almost knocked you over."

"Hi Mr. Stanley! It's okay. Have a good night!" Toni said brightly as she bounced up the steps into the house, her thick, frizzy hair bouncing in braids behind her. "Hey Bri, I'm all set for tonight."

"Finally," Bri snickered at her friend, stepping aside to let Toni inside. She shut the door behind her as Toni snagged the pizza from her hands.

"What's up, sport?" Toni said to Matthew, sliding him the box.

"Hey Toni," he said, "Wanna slice?" he asked her, already snagging a piece and waving it at her.

"Nah, I'm good," Toni said. "Enjoy that."

"Where you guys going?" Matthew asked Brianna as she sat down beside him.

"The drive-in," his sister replied, "zombie movie night."

"Can I come?" he asked, his expression suddenly brighter.

"Not tonight buddy, taking Toni and Kent with us," Brianna replied, watching his face fall, "Let me watch them first. If they're not too bad, Chad and I will take you next weekend. Deal?"

"Alright," he said, still crestfallen, but some of the spark had returned to his eyes.

"You know mom doesn't like you watching those movies too much. If they're not too bloody, I'll get her to let you go," Brianna promised him.

Brianna heard Chad's familiar car horn beeping outside, and she stood up, grabbing her jacket and purse. Toni did the same.

"Finish your food. Leave Mom a couple slices. She'll be home in about a half hour."

"Alright," Matthew said, mouth full of pizza.

"Lock the door and—"

"I know, I know. I'm not a kid," Matthew said, cutting her off. "Lock the door, leave the porch light on for mom. Don't let anyone in. Got it."

Brianna grinned at him and shut the door while Toni shot him a wave from behind her. He trudged over to the door, spun the lock, and grabbed the pizza from the table, heading to the living room to watch Tales from the Crypt, grumbling the whole way. Brianna always got to see the coolest movies first.

Bobby Ray bent over the worktable, slicing quartered meat into filets; a set of bloody knives were spread out beside him for easy access. The sharp blades made quick work of the meat, slicing it from glistening bone. He liked starting with the limbs first. They went the fastest, but the best cuts came from the rump and the soft

DOUBLE FEATURE

areas around the hips, thighs, and abdomen. Tiny stood at the opposite end, feeding chunks of pale flesh into the grinder for sausage and ground meat. Any part that couldn't be made into a special cut went into the mix along with the heart, liver, and kidneys. The organs added richness and depth to the flavor.

The barn vibrated with the noise of the machines and the twin generators that ran constantly to power the two freezers, the grinders and sausage makers, and the various other items needed to process the game that came through during the season. The air was always thick with the coppery tang of spilled blood, and the peppery hint of spices used in the jerky, despite the big fan set in the back wall meant to clear the odors from being trapped in the oft-stifling building. Petey shuffled between the long rows of tables and machines with the almost empty cooler.

He carried the cooler outside to rinse it out, stopping to scrape the excess trimmings, bits of organ meat, and other viscera into the plastic tubs that sat just inside the big coolers near the barn doors before he did so. Mama Jean would use the leftovers to make her famous headcheese.

As he stood in the yard rinsing the ancient cooler, Mama came out of the shack they called a house. Her housecoat was tattered and stained, snug on her stocky frame. Her hair fell in greasy strings around her stern face.

"Petey, them boys ready?" She called to her youngest son.

"Yes, Ma, almost. They finishing up the steaks and sausage now," Petey answered.

"Alright. You go tell them supper's ready. It's almost time," she called back to him from across the yard.

Mama Jean turned back and clomped up the three stairs to the shack. She yanked the door open and let it slam behind her. Inside the house, the smell of roasting meat in a rich sauce and fresh cornbread filled the air. Her stomach rumbled as she stirred the pot once more. Her boys had done well with this kill. The fresh meat really added good flavor to the day-old vegetable stew.

Pickings been lean lately, with the ending of deer season, they'd been living off coon, squirrel, and possum, but today's poor soul had shown up at just the right time. Mama Jean's garden had a bumper year with potatoes, onions, carrots, and peppers, squash, and vegetables of all kinds, but there were only so many days her sons could stomach nothing but vegetables, in soups, stews, and fried.

CANDACE NOLA

Tiny did his best to keep money coming in with their game processing business, but most folks round here only hunted bigger game like turkey, boar, and deer, occasionally a bear. When the season ended, most of their business dried up pretty quick. Mama had found herself scraping by on pennies to feed her boys when the major hunting season ended until they had discovered a new source of meat.

She grinned. Their daddy had been a smart one. Taught them well before he died. Her boys been providing for her ever since. Tonight would be a good night. New movies playing at the drive-in. A hot meal in their bellies and more fresh meat on the horizon. She smiled as her sons stomped onto the porch, scraping boot heels on the edge to clean the gore and viscera from them.

"Smells good, Ma," Tiny said as he walked inside. He kissed her cheek and went to the sink, grabbing the bar of yellow soap to wash his hands.

"Thanks, Son. Petey. Bobby Ray. You boys get washed up, too. Supper's just 'bout done."

Thanks, Ma," Tiny said, smiling his crooked smile at his short but round mom. She held out a spoon heaped with stew meat and gravy, and he sampled it. "Mmm. That's real good, Ma. Can't wait to dig in."

Tiny sat down at the rickety table, followed by his brothers. Their ma served up the stew in mismatched bowls and set the cast-iron skillet full of cornbread down on the table. Her boys waited for her to be seated before they began to eat. No grace or religion here, just proper respect due to the matriarch of their small family.

"No problems today?" She asked after her boys had scarfed a few scoops down. She sat in her usual seat, gazing at each of her sons in turn, waiting for their answers. Her beady eyes narrowed, her jaw set; her very posture dared one of them to lie to her. She portrayed equal parts feral hog and protective mother bear. Her boys, and several townies, learned long ago not to mess with Mama Jean.

"No, ma'am," Tiny replied. "Good clean kill. Tossed the innards for the animals. Petey did what he does."

At this remark, Petey blushed and grinned at his ma. "Was good too, Ma, really good."

"That's nice, son," Mama Jean replied, patting his hand. She gave up trying to explain the birds and bees to him long ago. She looked at Tiny, waiting for the next part of the story.

DOUBLE FEATURE

"It's in the fridge," Tiny said when she raised as eyebrow.

"Better be." Her posture relaxed, and she dug into her own bowl of stew, grease dripping from the coarse hairs on her chin. She let the dribbles fall where they might. Any sense of decorum had faded from her long ago.

"Of course, Ma. I didn't do nothin' to it. Just the same as always," Petey said, crestfallen.

"Good, now finish your dinner. It's almost time."

"What they showin' tonight at the picture show?" Mama Jean asked her sons. "I hope it's somethin' good. I'm sick and tired of those damn romancing movies, bunch'a fairy tale bullshit."

"Zombie movies, Ma," Bobby Ray answered her, watching her smile grow bigger.

"Zombies, huh? That's more like it," she cackled. "Best we get a move on, then."

They finished their dinner, chewing and grunting over the stewed flesh of Kenny Lassiter like it was their last meal. Juice ran down their chins as they smacked their lips. Petey finished off the cornbread, using it to soak up the bit of beet-colored gravy still in his bowl.

When they gathered their gear and stepped off their porch, dusk was well underway. The movie would just be starting when they got there, and it would be a full night. Plenty of time for them to enjoy the evening's activities.

Brianna and Antonia giggled at each other as Chad guided the car toward Sunset Cinema. Kent sat quietly in the backseat next to Toni, his face almost as red as the interior of Chad's car. Antonia kept shifting closer to him as she leaned up to talk to Brianna. Before they were halfway to the drive-in, she was pressed snugly against him and had his hand clasped on her thigh.

Chad just grinned in the rearview mirror, enjoying his buddy's sudden awkwardness. The normally cool jock was clearly out of his element when it came to females being close to him. Like Antonia did with Bri, Kent was Chad's shadow, preferring to be a wingman, not comfortable in the spotlight. He hoped he would loosen up, though, before the night was over.

His best friend could not be more his opposite if he tried.

CANDACE NOLA

Where Chad was cool, suave, and charming, Kent was quiet, timid, and book smart. Chad carried class clown status while Kent was in the advanced classes. Even their looks were opposites, with Chad being the same dark tone as Antonia with a low fade haircut while Kent carried a boy next door vibe with his beachy tan, blond hair, and blue eyes.

He chuckled, thinking about how different they were, but they both had good taste in chicks. That was clear, Brianna was hot, but her best friend was just as sexy as Bri was. Chad had plans of his own with Brianna, hoping to get her to sneak away in the dark for some alone time with him and Jack. Jack Daniels, of course. Maybe while they were enjoying their night, Kent and Toni could enjoy some alone time of their own. He slid his hand up Brianna's leg, chuckling when she gripped it with her own, stopping him from roaming too far towards home.

Secretly, he loved it when she took control. He knew he had a good girl, and she had been worth the wait, though he'd never tell her that. He bitched and moaned like any guy would do, begging for just a bit more every time she stopped him from going too far too fast. But he only did it because it was socially expected of him. What type of dude would he be if he just caved to her wishes? Females were funny that way, too much too soon, and they were seen as sluts, but dudes were expected to want the whole damn cookie jar on the first date, if they didn't go for it, then the girls thought they didn't try hard enough or didn't want them.

He shook his head, lost in thought as he drove. He could feel Brianna's heat pouring off her from where his hand lay on her thigh. Toni kept glancing at Kent, trying to draw him into the conversation, making him turn redder by the second.

"So, Kent, what's your favorite horror movie?" Brianna asked him, trying to engage him more.

Toni settled back in the seat and crossed her legs, staring at Kent like he was the most fascinating thing she'd ever seen.

"Oooh yeah, do you go for gory stuff or more like ghosts and shit?" Toni said.

"Umm. I like zombie movies, like the ones we're seeing tonight, but I really like the old movies too, like Dracula and things like that. The originals. Hitchcock too. My dad used to watch all those old shows a lot. Guess I grew up on it . . . " He shrugged, turning red again.

DOUBLE FEATURE

"Oh cool. I don't think I've seen any Hitchcock movies," Toni said, running her fingers up his arm. "Would I like them?" She stared up at him as Chad went around a sharp bend, causing her body to slide against his, even closer than before.

"Oops, sorry," she giggled as she leaned against him, her ample breasts pressed flush against his strong arm for a second before she made a show of sliding two inches away.

He flushed a deep red beneath his tanned skin, grateful that Brianna spoke up before he could think of something to say. His jeans were growing uncomfortable, and he was glad he had his jacket on his lap for cover. He could barely keep his eyes off the glimpse of deep cleavage her shirt afforded him.

"Sure, you have, Toni. We saw 'The Birds' a couple years ago in English lit, remember? We had that boring substitute that just had us watch movies all week while Mrs. Walker was sick." Bri said from the front seat.

"Oh yeah, that black and white one, right? With all those crows attacking those people?" Toni replied, giggled. "They fucked that one lady up."

"Yeah, that's the one," Kent said, smiled at her. "If you liked that one, you might like Psycho, too. It's another really good one. Norman Bates?" he asked, feeding her more information based off her blank stare. "The Bates Motel?"

Toni shook her head, a bit crestfallen when Brianna and Chad both laughed.

"Geez Toni, I've really failed you as a friend. You're missing out on some of the best horror movies of all time," Brianna said. She turned in her seat to look at Kent.

"I'm sorry, you'll need to bring Miss Antonia here up to speed on the horror movies. She's usually more into her books and romances than horror." Brianna grinned at him when he grimaced and pretended to look appalled. Toni punched his arm lightly.

"Hey, I like horror, too, just haven't seen much of it. She shrugged, then settled deeper into her seat as Chad took the turnoff to Sunset Drive-in.

"Well, I have lots of movies at home. I guess we will have to make up for lost time," Kent said softly, looking at her. Her sunset bronze complexion almost glowed beneath the streetlight leading up to the ticket booths. She smiled and squeezed his hand a bit, rubbing her thumb along the tender flesh between his thumb and forefinger. He hoped she didn't see him shift in his seat suddenly as his dick stiffened in his jeans at the sensual contact.

Toni had just barely turned her face to look out the window, feigning ignorance as Kent adjusted himself, but he swore he saw just a hint of a smug smile on her face. He met Chad's brown eyes in the mirror and grinned. Tonight should go just fine. If he played his cards right, Toni would be his girlfriend by the time the second movie ended. He already had a chain to put his class ring on, burning a hole in his pocket. He remembered seeing Chad present Brianna with his ring last year and how pleased she had been when she saw it was already on a chain. She hadn't taken it off since.

His mom might be pissed, but she knew the tradition; hell, girls been getting their guys' class rings since his mom was in school. That was a sure sign that a couple were going steady. Kent used to scoff at him, thinking it was akin to being claimed, but lately the idea of seeing his ring hanging from a silver chain, nestled between Toni's full breasts, made him smile more and more. Even now, he felt his chest swell with pride a little at the thought of walking into school Monday morning with Toni beside him, his class ring glimmering proudly against her white dance team sweater, the ring swaying in her cleavage.

Chad slowed the car to a stop at the ticket booth and rolled the window down.

"Five dollars please," the bored attendant said.

Chad handed her the money, and they drove forward, joining the line of cars threading their way through the cleared field full of speaker posts and gravel lanes. They headed toward a row two lanes past the concession booth, just a bit to the left of it, and Chad parked. The other rows were filling up quickly and teens were already in line at the concession stand. A few adult couples stood around, but they seemed more college age than parental age. Chad grinned in approval. Everyone knew Friday nights were for the teens.

"Alright, ladies. Time to freshen up, stretch our legs, get our snacks for the night." Chad hopped out of the car, checked his reflection in the side mirror with a quick glance, then hurried to Brianna's door before she could open it and pulled it open with a flourish.

"After you, my dear," he said with a mocking bow. Brianna chuckled and slid from the car.

DOUBLE FEATURE

As she stepped out, Kent opened his door and stood up, then offered Toni his hand, helping her slide out on his side. The girls gathered their purses, told the guys what snacks they wanted and hurried ahead of them, arm in arm, to the ladies' room. Chad and Kent sauntered behind them, watching perfect hips sway in tight jeans. They high fived each other and got into the snack line.

Tyson turned to the door as another group of teens crowded inside. He smiled at them and turned back to the register, helping Lena with a transaction. He had come down to grab a drink for himself and found the small stand overwhelmed with hungry teens and a frazzled Lena. With the movie trailers already running, he had about ten minutes to lend a hand, so he jumped in, helping to restock the candy and snacks. He added another carton of trays to the dwindling stack and pulled more fries from the freezer for Garrett.

Sammie was on the other register, getting the kids out the door as quickly as possible, but Lena was still learning the process, so her line was moving slower. He quickly rang a set of kids through Lena's line, showed her what to do next, then yelled to Garrett that he was going back to the projection booth. Garrett nodded as he flipped the burgers, always cool and collected.

Tyson envied him a little. Garrett was only two years younger than he was but had a way about him that oozed confidence in any situation. A lot of people thought Garrett was a bad boy stoner type, but Tyson knew it was just an act. The kid was a lot smarter than anyone knew and more capable under stress than Tyson had ever been, partly why Garrett was the assistant manager. He was also more than a little impressed that he had managed to bag Sammie too. The young girl was feisty for sure, way more than Tyson could handle, but she was pretty and had a great body, curvy in all the right spots, just like he liked them.

He filled his soda cup from the fountain drink machine against the wall and snagged a bag of popcorn to go. Then Tyson disappeared around the back of the building and went up the dark stairs to the projection booth. The booth was barely bigger than a closet, having a long table in front to hold film reels, snacks, and his feet, on the rare occasions that he chose to kick back and watch the film.

CANDACE NOLA

A set of shelves against the side wall held more film reels, all labeled and marked with release date, title, and studio. A couple of old movie posters adorned the walls. And two old office chairs completed the setup. It wasn't much to look at, but Tyson had gotten laid here once or twice; more often than not, though, he was alone and studying while the films played. Far as jobs went, it really didn't get much better for a college kid. Free food and snacks, all the movies he could want, all the daylight hours he needed to sleep or study, and a decent wage on top of all that.

He settled in, placing his soda and popcorn on the table, checked the time on his watch for the film reel, then waited to dim the lights more when the actual movie started. He stared through the tiny window, watching the kids hurry to and from their cars, getting snacks and talking to friends; some played catch along the far side of the open field with an old football. Typical Friday night. Behind the massive screen at the front, a thick treeline acted as a natural barrier to any lookie-loos that might be hoping to see a free movie.

Both movie screens were shielded by heavy stretches of trees between the clearings and behind them. Sunset Cinema was basically an isolated compound on the hill behind Elton. His uncle had chosen well when he picked his spot. No neighbors close enough to complain, but close enough to Elton and nearby Wells that he picked up customers from both towns. The closest video rental store was ten miles south and the nearest mall was a thirty-minute drive north. The drive-in was the only thing to do for the local teens and his uncle thrived on their boredom.

Tyson idly picked up a flyer that was starting to fade and read it for what had to be the tenth time that week. Another teen gone missing, more than a month ago now. Ironically, the last place he had been seen was at the drive-in with his friends. The police had searched the area for days but had found no sign of the boy. Tyson let it flutter to the stack of other papers on the table, two more missing teen notices from early summer. One notice was for another boy, the second for a couple that had been on a date.

Elton was just small enough that someone traveling through could snatch a kid without drawing any attention. At least, that's the story Chief Robbins was telling the Elton Times. Sad but true, many kidnappers stayed on the move to avoid detection. Any of the kids could have been snatched from the drive-in, hitched a ride with the wrong person, or maybe even run away. There had been

DOUBLE FEATURE

some speculation from the locals that the missing couple had eloped, due to the girl being knocked up. Probably more local gossip, but who knew? There hadn't been any leads in any of the cases, so it was anyone's guess at this point.

Tyson sighed, checked his watch, and glanced at the screen. Right on time, the last trailer was ending and the opening credits for "Night of the Living Dead" were just getting started. He hit the external lights, and the area outside grew dark, except for the small lights near the restrooms and the snack bar. The activity slowly settled down, and the various speakers filled the clearing with the first notes of the opening scene. He grabbed his popcorn, set it on his lap, and stretched his long legs out on the desk. He had forty minutes before he needed to change the reels.

Out in the dark, just behind the movie screen, another group of watchers was getting settled in, too.

Mama Jean sat bundled up in her old lawn chair next to the rusty truck, watching her son's work. Tiny and Bobby Ray were setting up their gear for the night. Two sturdy sawhorses and a thick sheet of plywood, stained with old blood, became their worktable. Two-inch straps hung from the board on all sides. Petey stood nearby, sharpening his blade on a length of leather. Filthy overalls covered all three of the lumbering men. Hairy knuckles crowned blood-stained hands and thick, calloused palms.

Bobby Ray's dingy white t-shirt was barely held together by the holes that peppered it. Petey had skipped a shirt altogether, just strapping the denim overalls over his bare torso. The ripe stench of heavy body odor drifted from all of them as they worked. Mama Jean barely wrinkled her nose; she was used to their stench, her own, and that from the slaughterhouse. She pulled out her flask as the boys finished their set-up and unscrewed the top.

The sounds of ominous organ music and a car driving along a road issued from the movie playing fifty yards away. The drive-in was full tonight. Rows of cars faced the wooden screen as zombies shuffled toward their hapless victims. Mama Jean cackled at the sound effects pouring through the dark, her beady eyes glinting as several of the young movie-goers gasped and screamed at the scene unfolding before them.

"Gonna be a good night, boys! Whooo doggie! Listen to them scream! We can get ourselves a couple of live ones tonight!" Mama Jean cackled as she took another hefty swig from the dented flask. The moonshine hit her gullet like boiling magma, burning a river of fire the whole way down to her gut. She belched and took another swig before tucking it back into her pocket.

"You know daddy's moonshine gonna rot your insides," Bobby Ray told her.

"You just mad you ain't bring none wit' cha," Mama laughed. "Git on with your fixin's, boy. Them kids will be 'round the woods soon, looking to fool 'round like bitches in heat."

Tiny just grunted, heaving another block from the truck bed. Bobby Ray grabbed the side of the sawhorse while Tiny slid the block beneath its leg to keep it steady, then stood back to admire his work. The makeshift table was solid beneath his weight and the cement blocks kept it from shifting in the grass.

"We all set, Ma. You just settle in and enjoy the show." Tiny walked past her to the back of the rusty truck and lifted his bag of tools from it. "You fella's go on and start scouting out the meat. Stick to the shadows. Can't be spookin' 'em before it's time."

Mama Jean cackled as Tiny laughed, a low rumbling sound like distant thunder, deep in his chest. Bobby Ray and Petey set off into the trees that ringed the outside movie theater. Screaming came from the screen, grunting, the sound of a door slamming and fists pounding on it. Tiny grinned down at his ma.

"I think you right, Ma. It's gonna be a good night for killin'."

"Damn right, son." She tipped the flask into her waiting mouth again, swishing the liquid around like a fine wine before she swallowed it. She smacked her lips and sat back, waiting for the show to begin.

Petey followed Bobby Ray into the darkness. Leaves crunched wetly beneath their boots. Bobby Ray led the way along the well-worn trail. They'd been hunting here so long that Bobby Ray's own boots had made most of the trails around the perimeter of the drive-in. One long footpath ran the entire way around the hilltop, while several shorter ones wove between the two screens and back to their preferred spot behind Screen One.

DOUBLE FEATURE

Sunset Cinema showed both family friendly and R-rated movies. Screen One was the designated R-rated theater, with all the latest horror and sci-fi films being played in an almost constant loop. Screen Two was separated by a heavy breadth of trees, flanked on both sides by play areas for the kids with slides and swings. That screen played the cartoon movies for the kiddies, most of the girly flicks with the romantic bullshit, and some drama type movies.

Bobby Ray liked the drama's sometimes, but he preferred the blood splattered action movies. especially war films. His daddy talked about being a soldier, over in 'Nam as he called it. Bad shit happened over there. Daddy didn't speak much about it, but Bobby Ray liked to think that sometimes the movies got it right. Screen One made them feel right at home. Sometimes, the movies were bloodier than anything they got up to back at their slaughterhouse.

"Bobby Ray," Petey whispered, pulling up short beside his brother. "What now?"

Bobby Ray had been so lost in thought, he had stopped walking and was now just standing in the trees, gazing out over the rows of cars. Three zombies were snarling and lunging at a screaming female on the movie screen, and Petey's eyes grew wide watching it. Blood flew as someone lost the battle. The second girl on the screen ran screaming as another undead went shambling after her.

"Now, we do what Tiny said. You go on round the other side, look fer any lost deer, any does in heat. You know the type. Them ones smoking that funny tobacco or drinking their daddy's beer. Watch for any couples sneaking away from the others. Them is sweet pickin's for us, half the work done," He snorted.

"Alright Bobby Ray. I'll go this way." Petey jerked his head toward the right, leading around the back of the concession stand area. The dark was heaviest there as the light from the booth and the snack stand projected toward the front of the place, not the back.

"Stay quiet," Bobby Ray hissed at him. "I'm gonna watch this side a bit then go 'round front. Ten minutes. Don't keep Ma and Tiny waitin'."

"I know, I know. Ain't my first time, ya know," Petey grumbled, glaring at Bobby Ray's retreating shadow.

"Jus' reminding ya'. Now quit snivelin' and git on wit' it," Bobby Ray shot back in a hiss. He waved Petey on as he crouched down beside a gnarled oak tree, peering out at the cars on his side.

Petey turned and trudged away along the trail, still muttering. "I know how to hunt. I'll get the best one here tonight, jus' watch."

The sounds of screaming, bloody kills, and excited teens filled the air as Petey slipped between the trees, searching the dark rows for kids sneaking away to be alone in the dark. He could be invisible when he wanted to be. Petey had one other favorite part when it came to hunting. And this was it. He smiled and the glint in his eye turned the expression into something dark and deadly.

"Come on, Lorna. Damn, don't be such a tease," Jack cajoled his girlfriend as she tried to stomp away from him.

"I'm not a tease, Jack. You're just a pig," she exclaimed. "It's creepy out here and I don't want to be half naked in the woods just because you want to do more." She looked around and pointed at the branches hiding them from the rows of cars. "Anyone can just look over here and see us!"

"It's too dark for that," he scoffed. "Just let me see them tits, then we can go back to the car. You owe me."

"I don't owe you shit, Jack. I said I would think about it. We've only been going out for a couple weeks. I'm not a slut."

"Yeah? Bobby said you gave it up pretty easily," he said, his voice cold and cruel.

Lorna gasped and turned back to Jack. "What did you just say?"

"You heard me," he sneered, "Bobby told everyone."

"I never dated that jerk. He gave me a ride home, one time. That was it!" she exclaimed.

"According to Bobby, you were the one giving rides," Jack retorted. "I'm done wasting my time on you. Good luck getting home." Jack stormed off deeper into the woods, leaving Lorna standing alone, fuming.

"Well, fuck you too, asshole!" Lorna called after him. She waited a moment, blinking away tears of frustration and anger, then slipped between the branches back to the safety of the cars. She made her way toward the concession stand and the waiting payphone to call her mom. There was no way she was going to beg that jerk for a ride home.

DOUBLE FEATURE

Jack stomped away through the trees, pissed off and horny. Lorna did funny things to his body and his head. He better hope the silly bitch didn't go cuss out Bobby. He'd get his ass kicked for dragging him into this. He knew good and goddamn well that Lorna had not done anything with Bobby, but she didn't know that he *knew* that. His dumbass plan had backfired. Most girls got scared and gave in, thinking if there was a rumor going around, then they'd better play nice to keep it from spreading.

Silly females never realized that the guys started the rumors in the first place just to pit the girls against each other. It usually worked, but apparently, Lorna wasn't as dumb as he hoped. He cussed under his breath again and slammed another branch out of his way, stomping through the grass and cracking twigs beneath his feet. He blew out a loud breath, frustrated, and sighed. He'd make a lap around the second screen and head back.

Lorna would be pissed but he would apologize and take her home. He knew she'd never go out with him again, but his father would beat his ass if he left the neighbor girl here. Their parents played bridge together, for fuck's sake. They'd all know what he'd done if he didn't fix it. Jack was so caught up in his anger, he didn't see the looming shadow stalking him through the trees.

Petey followed behind the boy, grinning in the dark. This one had made it too easy. Sure, the girl had left before he could get them both, but the night was young. This young buck was making so much noise that he would never hear Petey coming. He stayed a few feet away, hidden by tree trunks and briar bushes. His feet were almost silent, while the boy crashed through the trees like a bull in a china shop, muttering and cussing to himself.

It was easy to see where he was going to go. This patch of trees rimmed the second screen and led right back to the first. When the kid hit the area behind the screen, Petey's work would be a done deal. He only needed to knock him out and carry him right over to where Tiny and Ma waited behind the first screen. He had the urge to whistle a jaunty tune but resisted the urge. Instead, he practiced gloating in his head. He couldn't wait for Bobby Ray to see that he had the first catch of the night.

"Hey Lena! Can you grab more hot dogs, please?" Garrett called to the girl at the register. Sammie was elbow deep in the popcorn machine and he had six burgers ready to flip. It had been a hungry crowd tonight; not surprisingly since the drive-in was sold out on Screen One. Zombie movies were always a hit, and this one was no different.

"Sure, Garrett. One second," the perky redhead called and slipped around the counter, heading toward the storage room and freezers. A line of kids waited for food and popcorn. A couple sighed as Lena left the register but caught Garrett's eye and stopped. Complaints were NOT on his to-do list tonight. Snatches of conversation began to drift over to Garrett as he worked the grill.

"Did you hear Kenny still hasn't come home?" one guy said.

"No. How did you find out?" a girl's voice piped up.

"His girlfriend, Anna, is my sister's best friend. Guess he never made it home from hunting yesterday."

"Wonder if he got hurt or something?" the girl said.

"He probably got snatched like the rest of them," another guy snorted, a cruel sneer in his voice. "you know folks been going missing around here. I bet whoever got them got Kenny, too."

"That's not cool, Eddie," the first boy spoke, giving the new speaker a glare. "We don't know that for sure."

"Well, I know I won't be going into them woods anymore," Eddie said. "I'm here for the movies, the snacks, and the pussy." He laughed and high-fived the guy standing next to him.

"Damn straight." His buddy laughed.

Garrett turned back to the grill, shaking his head. It was sad that another kid seemed to be missing. He was tired of seeing the posters. While no one knew for sure what was happening, it sure did make you wonder. He jumped, startled, when Lena tapped him on the arm with the package of hot dogs.

"Here you go, Garrett," she said brightly.

"Holy shit, Lena. You scared the crap out of me," Garrett chuckled, taking the hot dogs from her.

"Thanks," he said as she scurried back to the register.

DOUBLE FEATURE

"You alright?" Sammie asked, walking over after she rang out the last kid in her line.

"Yeah. She just startled me. I was thinking about what those kids were saying."

"What kids?" she asked, raising an eyebrow.

"The ones talking about the missing kid. Guess we will be seeing more posters soon."

"Really?" Sammie said, "did they say who it was?"

"Some guy by the name of Kenny," Garrett shrugged. "They didn't say a last name."

"That's fucked up!" Sammie exclaimed, a look of disgust on her face. "Someone needs to find out what's going on around here. Sick of this Podunk town, for real." She sighed, saw some kids waiting at her register and started to walk away.

"Yeah, me too, Sammie. It's getting bad." Garrett watched her shake her head and walk back to ring out the next line of hungry kids. As he watched, he couldn't help but wonder which of them might be next.

"Do you want to come get more popcorn with me?" Kent asked Antonia as the cartoon intermission began to play. Scratchy black and white dancing hot dogs and soda and popcorn sang as they formed a chorus line on the screen. Brianna chuckled at the old cartoon and glanced at her friend in the backseat, shooting her a wink.

"Go ahead, you have a few minutes. Grab me some fries, okay?" she told her friend with a sly grin on her face.

"Um, sure, okay. I could use some more popcorn, anyway. Might be nice to stretch my legs for a bit," Antonia said. Her voice was shy now that they were here, in the dark, and she was about to catch a few minutes alone with the boy of her dreams.

"Cool. Let's go," Kent said, opening his door and sliding out. "You guys need anything else?" he asked Chad and Bri while Toni slid out the other side.

"Nah, all good, bro. Have fun." Chad chuckled, flinging a stray piece of popcorn at him as he closed the door.

Kent waited for Toni to join him. "Ready?" he said, holding his hand out to her.

She took it, nodding, a timid smile on her face, but her eyes sparkled like diamonds in the dark. Hand in hand, they strolled along the dark pathway toward the concession booth. Her hand was clammy, and she wished she had wiped it on her jeans first, but Kent's seemed equally warm and moist, and she realized they were both nervous. That made her feel better. At least it wasn't just her.

"Are you enjoying the movie?" he asked her after a moment of silence.

"Yeah, I am. More than I thought. It's darkly comedic in some places," she replied, smiled at him.

"You're right, that's a great way to put it. I wasn't sure if you would like it, but since Chad said we could come with him and Bri, I figured it couldn't hurt to ask." Kent felt his voice deepen to a husky timber, nerves threatened to choke him.

She saw the crimson creep across his face as they neared the concession stand and she blushed, too.

"I'm really glad you asked," she said, looking at him, meeting his gaze fully and they smiled nervously at each other, then laughed; the awkward moment broken.

"Oh man, look at that line," Toni breathed as they reached the rear door of the small building. Teens were wrapped halfway around it.

"Quite the wait, huh?" Kent said, glancing around them. The cartoon was still playing on-screen. Teens waited in groups and pairs with a few loners here and there, probably the designated snack-getters for their friends.

Kent saw they were near the thin line of trees that stretched between the two screens and had an idea.

"Hey, um, do you want to maybe take a walk? We could walk along the edge of the trees for a minute, let the line go down a little?" His voice took on a hopeful tone, maybe too hopeful, and he willed himself to cool it. But maybe if he could get Toni alone, he could work up the nerve to kiss her. He found his eyes locked on her plump, glossy lips as he had the thought; part of him wanting to lean forward to taste them right then.

Toni looked at him for a long moment, gazing at him with eyes of melted caramel. She looked over at the trees, studying them, then back at the line. His eyes met hers when she looked back at him.

DOUBLE FEATURE

"I did say I wanted to stretch my legs, didn't I?" She smiled. "But I don't want to go into the woods, okay? Just along the edge?"

"Just along the edge," Kent agreed, taking her hand to lead her away. "they're not deep, anyway. We'll be able to see over here just fine to watch the line."

A couple of kids snickered as they walked toward the trees. Some shot them knowing glances and smiled to themselves. Always a few trying to sneak away for some nighttime romance beneath the stars. Those watching turned back to the dancing popcorn and hotdogs, idly waiting their turn in line, as Toni and Kent vanished into the shadows.

"There, isn't that better?" Kent asked, leading her deeper into the trees. Some of the noise behind them faded just a little, as did the lights. He helped her step over a log she stumbled into, and she slipped, giggling into his arms.

"Oops. Sorry. Slipped on a branch, I think," she breathed, the giggle dying as she realized how he held her, how close she was to him. He was smiling at her, sweetly eager, like he was staring at his favorite dessert. Toni felt the moment stretch and her heart fluttered in her chest. She waited, closing her eyes as he began to lean toward her.

A moment, an eternity, an infinity later, his lips found hers and she melted into him. A burst of energy filled her body as kissed him back. A moan softly found its way to the back of her throat and Kent kissed her deeper, a little harder. Toni clung to him, lost in the moment. Her hands roamed up his back, caressed his shoulders, found the back of his head, and drew him back to warm lips when he paused for breath.

A sudden THUD and a muffled grunt of pain met her ears. Toni's eyes flew open as the kiss was suddenly and rudely broken. Kent was falling to his feet, collapsing, his eyes rolling to the whites. Toni had no time to open her mouth to release the shriek that was building before she, too, was senseless and falling, rendered mute and unconscious in record time. A hoarse snicker, and the foul stench of liquor and body odor, barely registered in her brain as she hit the ground.

"Got 'em," Bobby Ray chuckled, grinning as he looked at the

two bodies on the ground. He wasted no time taping their mouths and tying them up before he slung the girl over his shoulder and began dragging the boy behind him deeper into the trees. Petey may get back with his quarry before him, but Bobby Ray would bet the last jar of Mama's hooch that he didn't get two of them.

Jack ranted to himself as he stomped through the woods. It was so dark now; he could barely see the lights from the movie screen as he went. Branches scratched his forearms up as he swung his arms up, pushing away vines and leaves to clear his path. His footsteps crunched hard on sticks and leaves. His breathing was so loud and angry that a bear could have walked up to him, and he would not have noticed. As fate would have it, a man-sized bear walked up on him instead, and Jack did not notice, not until he felt him.

"Who the fuck are you, man?" Jack yelped as his body suddenly collided with a wall of flesh that appeared from the shadows. "Get out of my way!" Jack sneered, recovering some of his angry bravado from before. The man didn't move, only stood there, grinning at him.

A stinging sensation filled Jack then, just as he took a breath to yell at the man again. A push of something against his stomach, cold, slick, hard. Then pain flowed through him. Jacks' eyes widened, and he looked down to see the massive hand of the man flush against his stomach. The grin never left his face as he pulled the blade from Jack's gut.

Blood poured over Jack's hands as he clutched the wound. Terror paralyzed his face. His brain could not form words. He could only stare at the man in shock for a moment before a solid knock to the side of his head caused him to crumple to the ground. Petey grinned. Pursing his lips to whistle, he grabbed the boy by his armpits and slung him over his shoulder like a dead deer. Happily, he turned off the path and headed toward the darkest part of the trees where Tiny and Momma waited for his return. Just wait until Bobby Ray saw that he got his kill first.

DOUBLE FEATURE

Tyson ambled over to the side window and peered into the night. He had been pacing like a caged animal for ten minutes, antsy in the stuffy booth. The intermission reel was still rolling, and he let it loop another cycle, taking note of the line of kids still outside the concession stand. No one would even notice if the hot dogs kept dancing for 60 more seconds. Movement along the tree line caught his eye, and he squinted, trying to make it out.

The shadow seemed bigger than most of the teens and bulkier somehow. He watched for another heartbeat, not liking the sinking feeling in his gut. He was used to seeing horny couples sneaking off into the trees, even saw a few humping against tree trunks where they thought no one could see them. Couldn't see much, that was for sure, but he always chuckled when he saw two shadows, a possible pale leg or ass cheeks glinting and flexing against the dark logs and branches.

Tyson glanced at the screen, saw the animated hot dogs shuffle off stage, and peered out into the night once more. The big shadow was still moving slowly between the trees, an odd lump jutting down the back of the figure as it moved. Something didn't sit right with him, but he shook it off and sat back down at the table, setting the film to play once more. He checked the reel, figured he had a few minutes to wander downstairs and grab a burger. It was stuffy as hell up here. That was probably why he was so antsy, he told himself as he bounded down the steps. Shadows and shit fucking with his head.

He pushed the door open to the interior of the concession stand and the mouthwatering scent of hot buttered popcorn, burgers, and fries hit him full in the face, making his stomach growl. The waft of warm air was followed by a draft of cooler air as more teens opened the door, shuffling through the food line. Tyson caught Garrett's eye and threw two fingers up in the air at him. Garrett nodded and grabbed two burgers from the line and shook more fries into a basket as Tyson stepped out for fresh air.

He almost knocked a young girl over as he rounded the building where the payphones were.

"Oh, I'm sorry," he said, catching her arm to steady her as she stumbled on the loose gravel.

"Are you okay?" he asked when she caught her balance.

"Yeah, yeah. I'm fine," she snapped, yanking her arm back. She swiped a hand across her cheek, wiping a tear away.

"Geez, okay, I'm sorry," Tyson said, immediately defensive. He stepped to the side to go around her, then looked at her closer. The tears were not fresh, couldn't be from her slight stumble, and she hadn't cried out in pain when she tripped. He sighed.

"Are you sure you're okay? I didn't mean to run into you." he kept his voice soft, gentler this time as he studied her face.

The girl looked at him for a moment, arms hugging herself like she was cold, though the night was barely below seventy degrees. Black streaks clung to her cheeks and ringed her eyes. She sniffed again and nodded.

"Yeah. Sorry I got snippy," she said. Her voice broke slightly, and she paused. "Some jerk stranded me here, trying to get pervy in the woods. I called my mom, but no one was home and Jack, that's the perv, he's still out there, I think. He's not in the car and I've been standing here forever."

"I see. Did he hurt you?" Tyson said, relief flooding him as he realized that he hadn't been the one to hurt her. "Do you want me to wait with you? Or I could let you sit in the booth with me until we can reach your folks?"

She stared at him. A rough laugh scraped its way from her throat, fighting through teary sniffles as it broke free. "Why, so you can grope me behind closed doors?" She shook her head. "Thanks, but I'm good."

"Hey, I get why you're upset. I do. But we're not all bad guys and you're far too young for me anyway," Tyson said, then shrugged. "I gotta go back inside. My uncle owns this place. My name is Tyson. I'll leave the door to the booth open and keep it open. If you change your mind, just come on up, or don't."

Tyson turned and rounded the corner, shaking his head. That's what he gets for trying to help. Silly girls, all the same. You either gotta want nothing to do with them or you gotta be trying to get something from them; the hell with just trying to be a decent person. No middle ground, ever. He ground his teeth, infuriated. He knew women had it rough, but fuck, not every dude was a creep.

"Hey, man. Where you been?" Garrett said as Tyson came back inside. Garrett was holding an empty tray at his side. "I just put your grub up on the table. Soda too. You good?"

"Yeah, thanks bud. Almost knocked a girl down outside; She's real upset. Guess her dude got grabby with her. She's alone and can't find him. "Looks like he stranded her." Tyson turned to go

DOUBLE FEATURE

upstairs, glanced back at Garrett. "Listen, I told her she can come wait up here for her mom. If you see her, send her on up. Short, pretty face, red hair. Jean jacket with pink jeans."

"Got it," Garrett said, watching him go up the narrow stairs. He turned back toward the busy food line and hustled over to his grill. Sammie cocked an eyebrow at him, and he shrugged, going back to work.

"Did you guys see Kent and Toni come back?" a female voice asked as Garrett started flipping burgers.

"Who?" a different voice said, higher and more girly sounding. Garrett glanced over at the line to see a trio of girls talking.

"Kent and my friend Toni?" the first girl asked, clearly annoyed. "Geez Megan. Antonia from the dance team?"

A high-pitched giggle filled the air, then the smaller girl replied, "Oh, her. No. Her and that guy went into the woods a while ago."

"Yea, like right after the intermission played," another girl said. This one was a petite blond in tight shorts.

"But that was a while ago," the first girl said, looking around the almost empty concession stand. "Did they come in for food?"

"Do I look like I work here?" the second snotty girl said, rolling her eyes. "Geez, Briana, they're probably just fooling around."

"Yeah, I guess." The girl looked around again, caught Garrett's eye, then turned to leave, a worried frown on her face.

As Briana left, Garrett caught a glimpse of another girl coming in, with a jean jacket, hot pink jeans, and Converse sneakers on. This one looked worried, too. No, not worried. She looked distraught. Tears streaked down her face and her eyes were red. She came in but didn't get in line, instead she stood there looking around.

Garrett figured this was the girl Tyson had mentioned. He walked over to her, spatula still in hand.

"Looking for Tyson?" he asked softly.

She nodded, trying to smile politely. Garrett just nodded toward the stairs on the left and smiled back. "He told me you might stop by. It's okay. There's a phone up there too, and the door stays open."

"Alright," she said quietly, "Thanks." She disappeared up the stairwell, looking frailer as she went. Garrett jogged back to his burgers, alarms going off in his brain the whole time. Another glance from Sammie, but he ignored it. Something felt off. He felt ice slither down his spine as several thoughts hit him at once.

CANDACE NOLA

The kids from earlier were still talking about that Kenny guy. Now this girl, with another guy missing, and the couple that Briana chick was looking for, that had wandered off to the woods to make out. Elton was in for a bad night. Garrett could feel it. He was going to finish the grill for the night, then go up and talk to Tyson. Maybe they should call someone rather than wait for bad news. He could feel Sammie staring at his back, but he kept mulling over the gossip from the night and that bad feeling hovered over him like a storm cloud.

Petey tossed his catch at Tiny's feet, grinning as the body hit the ground with a thud. "Lookie there, Ma. Got a big'un."

The boy tried to squirm onto his back, tried turning over to see where he was, but all he could see were filthy boots in front of him. The hem of a tattered dress swept the tall grass. He squirmed again and was rewarded with a boot planted right in the middle of his back.

"He looks a bit small to me," Ma said. She took another swig from her flask and coughed. "It'll do, though."

"Did'ja see Bobby?" Tiny asked. His voice was gruff as he pulled the machete from the makeshift table.

Without waiting for a reply, Tiny swung the massive blade down. With a wet THUNCK sound, it sank deep into the boy's neck, and he went rigid with shock, muscles relaxing into stillness a moment later as his brain realized it was dead. Head crudely severed from the spinal cord. Tiny bent and slashed and pulled it away from the remaining tendons and sinews. A muffled sound like paper tearing filled the silence as the flesh tore away from the collarbone.

"Not after we split ways in the woods. He was being mean to me like he always is, and I told him just wait and see how well I do tonight," Petey said, a slight whine creeping into his voice as normal when he talked about Bobby Ray. The two of them had never much gotten along. Bobby Ray just loved to torment him. He didn't understand the challenges that Petey had, and it wasn't like his parents bothered to take their son to a doctor when he was born a bit different than the other two. They just figured he was a bit 'touched' in the head. Ma called him 'special' but Bobby Ray never

DOUBLE FEATURE

did see what made Petey so special or why Ma never called him special. Petey might have been amused to know that Bobby Ray was just jealous that he wasn't Ma's *'special'* son.

"Watch him come tramping out here soon, though. He seemed hellbent on being first tonight." Petey chuckled.

Tiny tossed the head to Petey. "Here you go bud, hold that."

Petey caught his prize, grinning the whole time. He cradled the head in the crook of one arm and reached to his crotch to adjust himself, already itching to have a lick at what the skull held within. Ma smiled at him, tickled by his obvious arousal.

"You sure are a weird one, ain't ya, Petey?" She cackled. "You had one today, won't be no brain business tonight, you hear me?"

Petey's smile faded, and he nodded. "Alright, Ma."

"Good boy," she said, offered him her flask. and patted his cheek when he bent down for it. "You be a good boy and maybe, if we get enough, you can tongue plunge the last one of the night. How's that sound?"

Petey grinned, his fetid breath wafting into her ghoulish face, mingling with her own sour aroma. "That sounds real good, Ma! I'll be good. You just wait and see. I'll be real good."

"Good, now get over there and help Tiny," she said, snatching her flask back from his beefy hand.

She grimaced as the bloody head dropped into her lap as Petey shuffled past her to help Tiny lift the body onto the table. A river of crimson poured from the neck stump as they strapped it down. Petey grabbed the shears and started to cut the clothing from the teen's body. Tiny vanished behind the back of the truck to retrieve his other tools from the cab.

Behind them, the movie played on, and Ma cackled as the screams filled the night, eager for what came next. They were almost at her favorite part. Tiny stepped over to the nude body and positioned the saw at its waist. Petey reached over and grabbed the handle on his side and together, the brothers began to saw the torso in half, quickly finding a rhythm as the teeth of the blade churned into the tanned flesh of what had been a teen boy.

Ma cackled and sipped her hooch as the body rocked on the table and blood poured onto her feet. Bits of flesh flew from the motion of the blade and littered her dress and her forearms, while some spattered to the ground. Gore oozed from the ever-increasing gap the two halves made on the table as the brothers sawed in a practiced harmonious rhythm. A fountain of blood arced and sprayed across the back of the lower half of the movie screen as screams of the undead faded away.

Tyson glanced at Lorna as she put the phone back in its cradle.
"No luck?" he asked kindly.
She shook her head and sighed and sat back down in her chair beside him. Remnants of a hot dog and fries sat cold in front of her.
"Not yet. They might still be at their bridge game."
"I wonder if Jack has come back," Tyson mused, leaning forward to peer down over the rows of cars outside. "I could get Hook and Pierce to come check?"
"No, not yet," she said. "I really don't want to see him. He's probably left or found some other skank to grope," she scoffed. "My mom will come. I'll just hang out here, if that's still cool?"
Tyson was staring hard at the movie screen, squinting so hard his eyes seemed to cross. He muttered to himself as she watched. Lorna looked at the screen, then back at Tyson.
"What's the matter?" she asked.
"Umm, nothing," he said, sitting back up. "Thought I saw something on the screen, something not part of the movie, like a shadow or something crawling on the bottom."
"Oh, that's weird," Lorna said, looking back at the screen, watching for a moment.
"See, right there. See that swaying motion, like a weird tree behind the screen or something?"
"It's probably a tree, then," Lorna said, chuckled a little but still watching.
Something darker and fluid seemed to hit the lower part of the screen then, just barely blending into the dark green lighting of the movie hallway the zombies were invading.
"See? There's that shadow again!" Tyson squinted again but couldn't see it anymore. The movie had grown darker, merging with whatever shadow he was seeing from behind the thin tree cover.
"That is weird, but it's probably just some kids messing around back there, drunk," Lorna shrugged and turned to the doorway as Garrett entered the small booth.

DOUBLE FEATURE

"Hey Garrett, what's up?" Tyson said, glancing at the muscular young man quickly, then back at the screen. Zombies were shambling everywhere on screen and some of the kids outside their cars below were standing in awe, watching the carnage.

"I don't want to alarm you, but I'm thinking you need to get Hook and Pierce up here or call the Chief," Garrett said, direct and to the point. "I'm hearing a lot of chatter downstairs, man, and I think a couple of kids might be missing by the time the movies are over." He glanced at Lorna.

"If her friends don't show back up, that will make three kids missing from the theater tonight and some other kid never made it home from hunting yesterday," He shrugged and leaned against the wall, "Don't want to stir the pot, but maybe this time, we need to get the cops here sooner, rather than later. It's way too weird, man. That's all I'm saying."

"Are you even listening to me?" Garrett asked him, annoyed by how Tyson kept his attention on the screen outside.

"Yea, dude, chill. Something strange going out there, just can't see what it is." Tyson stood up and went to the phone on the wall. "I'll call Hook and Pierce first. Let them check it out. If they see anything weird, I'll call the Chief."

"Fine, keep me posted. There's not much of a line left, but the second movie just started, there will be more. I'll let you know if the kids are found." Garrett turned and paused to pull another missing poster from the wall. "Sick of seeing these, ya know?" He held it, let it flutter to the desk in front of Tyson, then vanished down the stairs.

Lorna glanced at the faded black-and-white image. A young girl stared at her, close to her age, braces and freckles, pretty smile. She shuddered and hugged her arms tightly to her torso, suddenly cold. The girl had gone missing two years ago; her name was Megan. She was Lorna's little cousin. The night seemed just a little darker, a little colder. Lorna stared through the glass as zombies broke into another room, shambling and moaning ever closer to their prey.

Allen Hook slid the walkie talkie back on the hook that hung from the console on the golf cart. Tony ambled around the side of the concession stand, balancing two coffees and a tray of hot dogs in his hands. Two dogs, each with all the fixin's He loved his job. Free movies, free coffee, free food, a good pal and a golf cart, without the golf part. He despised the sport, boring as fuck and all that goddamn walking? What kind of jackass signed up for that shit?

Tony Pierce waited for Allen to take the tray of food, then he settled the cups into the cup holders and eased his bulk onto the seat. He chuckled as a zombie onscreen took a gnarly bite from a young girl's face. She screamed as gore splattered the wall beside her.

"Why the long face?" Tony asked Allen when he didn't share in his amusement.

"Damn," Tyson called. Wants us to check out the screen, well both screens, on foot once we get back and then do a search of the woods between the theaters."

"What the fuck for? We can just drive around there like always." Pierce said, sipping his coffee. "I ain't going in them woods. I ain't about to walk nowhere."

"Couple of kids might be missing," Hook said. His voice was serious now, more somber than it had been. "I think we kind of have to do a search, a quick one at least, ya know."

Pierce shoved half his hot dog in his mouth and shook his head, chewing fast before swallowing and speaking. "Man, shit. I guess, but goddamn it. We done told them kids to stay out of the woods how many times? Not our fault, if they won't and can't listen to anything but their hormones." He swallowed the rest of his hot dog and shoveled the second one in.

Hook looked away, repulsed. His own hot dogs no longer looked so appealing. He removed the lid from his coffee and sipped it. On the screen, the girl began to froth and seize on the ground, changing from a pretty cheerleader to a horrific zombie. A loud howl filled the air and Hook frowned. The howl didn't seem to have come from the movie. A little too loud, too shrill, he waited silently, listening for it again. The zombie girl rose to her feet, groaned, and shuffled away. The howl came again, quieter but still not quite part of the movie.

Hook put the golf cart in gear, chills swarming down his spine. That was not the movie. Something was out there. Pierce yelped in protest as the cart lurched forward and his coffee spilled down the front of his uniform shirt, the buttons barely holding together over his considerable gut.

DOUBLE FEATURE

"Hey man, watch it!" he griped, setting the coffee down and holding onto to the overhead bar.

"Didn't you hear that? For fuck's sake, Tony, we were cops at one point. Get your shit together!" Hook snarled, guiding the golf cart down the gravel pathway toward the front of the clearing.

Toni wailed again as Kent's head was bashed into the concrete block once more. He crashed at her feet with a thump that vibrated the ground where she lay, bound, and tied. Her gag had come loose, and her wails were loud and shrill as the clothes were cut from her body. Kent's face was nearly unrecognizable, so battered and bruised it had been by their captors.

Bobby Ray hefted Kent up with his hair. One eye rolled toward the man, then slipped back into his skull, seeking a more pleasant point of view. Petey chuckled as Kent's jaw dropped to one side, slack and torn from his face, hanging to the side like a torn fingernail.

"Guess he won't be needing them choppers," Petey said, reaching toward the loose bone. He reached in, grabbed the inside of the lower jaw, and took a firm grip of the chin and pulled down, swift and hard. The teeth, bones and skin tore like wet Velcro, exposing his upper jaw still attached, collapsing the cheeks from his face. The lower jaw came free in Petey's hand, raw muscle and sinew glistening beneath. He tossed at the girl, grinning.

"Wanna kiss him now?" Bobby Ray asked her, angling Kent's grisly face toward her, letting the blood pour onto her tear-streaked face and naked torso. He shook the boy, then nodded at Petey.

"Get him."

Petey bent and grabbed his legs. Together, the brothers laid him across the bench, covered with gore from their last carcass. Tiny stepped over to Toni and slapped her hard, yanking her head up by her hair and splaying his palm across her face so fast she had no time to react. Her head rocked to the side and her teeth cracked together so hard and swift that she bit the tip of her tongue clean off. Blood poured from her mouth as Tiny let her head drop back down.

"Quit yer' screamin' or it'll get much worse." He snarled the words almost directly in her ear. "I can let my brothers here do all sorts of things to you before we kill you. Trust me, I've seen what they do, and it's not nice for a lady, not nice at all."

Toni wailed softly, blood and drool running down her chin. She let her head lie in the dirt and sniffled, nodding the best she could under Tiny's heavy hand. She felt his calloused hands roam over her body, prodding at her flesh, not groping, not sexually, but prodding as one might test fresh cattle for butchering. His thick fingers poked her thighs, her rump, her toned calves, then ran up her legs to her waist.

He flipped her over then, and her head smacked off the cement block holding the table in place. She crushed her lips together as the pain surged in her skull and the indignity continued as the large man squeezed her breasts like oranges at the grocery store, twisted each nipple so hard she thought they might rip clean off, then pushed down on her belly. Satisfied, he rose to his haunches and peered at her.

"It's not personal, girlie. Just our way. Ya lay quiet and I'll make it quick. Ya don't, and well—they won't make it quick at all, ya hear?" He nodded at Petey and Bobby Ray.

Mama Jean cackled in her seat as Petey and Bobby Ray grinned down at the girl, hatchets in their hands. Sticky crimson covered the men. Hairy skin matted with dried leaves, gore, and blood, staining them rust-red in the moonlight. She shuddered at the thought of either of them touching her in other ways. Death would be welcomed and preferred at this point. Tiny rose to his full height and stepped over her. Toni closed her eyes and waited to die. She would not, could not, watch whatever they were about to do to Kent.

A new sound met her ears, and she could not help but open her eyes. Kent's gurgled weak scream did not last long, but her's, her screams stayed silent, ripping free only in her mind, as it broke and then shattered. The men butchered Kent while she watched. The two men sawed Kent in two with the double-handled crosscut blade, grinding and chewing through bone and marrow, muscle, and organs, through tendons and cartilage.

Blood sprayed the back of the movie screen in a relentless arc. Mama Jean cackled as legs and arms were tossed into the bed of the truck. She hooted when Petey tossed Kent's flaccid member and ball sack to her for her special head cheese. She dangled the prize in the air and laughed at the horror in Toni's eyes. Toni

DOUBLE FEATURE

welcomed the darkness when it came, the shrieking of the undead following her to the abyss.

Brianna sat next to Chad, chewing on her bottom lip as they watched the zombies killing and shuffling around the screen, but neither one was really seeing any of it. Chad was rubbing her back, trying to calm her down. Brianna bounced her right knee incessantly, a nervous habit she could not seem to grow out of. She was worried. Toni would not just run off. Kent wouldn't bail on Chad. Town was more than four miles away through a dark stretch of tree-lined highway. They wouldn't walk that at night. Nothing made sense right now.

"It'll be okay, Bri. Maybe they just lost track of time."

"Track of time? In the woods, right here, with zombies killing and moaning and yelling. They can clearly hear and see the movie screen from anywhere in the woods that they may have gone!" Bri scoffed, not comforted at all by his words.

"Babe, geez. I'm just trying to help," he said. "Maybe they went in deeper than they thought, you know, maybe Toni was afraid someone would see." He chuckled awkwardly, hoping to lighten the mood.

"Oh, so now you think my best friend is a skank?" Bri glared at him, venom in her voice. "Toni's a virgin, you utter douche bag. There is no way she would let her first time be in the woods at the drive-in!"

"I mean, we did," he muttered, looking down and scooting away from her a little. "For fuck's sake, lighten up."

"We did. Safe and sound, in *YOUR* car, in the back row, covered with blankets," Brianna exclaimed, disgust on her face and rage coloring her voice. "Not in the woods, like cavemen." she stood and stomped away.

"Hey, where are you going?" Chad said, standing to follow. "Come on, Bri." He swore under his breath and followed her into the concession stand. What a fuckin' night this turned out to be, he thought as he followed her. He could almost feel the ice emanating from his angry girlfriend as she stormed away from him.

Inside, Chad lingered near the stairwell that led to the

projection booth. He could hear Brianna's voice from there. He felt bad for whoever she was talking to. He could feel the wrath in her words from where he stood.

"Where in the hell are your guards?" Brianna was said. "You said they went to go search almost twenty minutes ago. Have they not called in yet, not come back? Where are the cops?"

She fired the questions like bullets, fast and hard, no time for a reply or for her to take a breath. When she finally paused, Chad could hear the reply. A male voice, much calmer than Brianna, spoke.

"First, take a breath. We are all concerned here and yes, the guards are out searching. We need to give them time to make a report."

"How much time? It's been twenty minutes, if not more," Brianna huffed, her tone only slightly calmer.

"They need time to search the treeline bordering both movie screens. That will take a while. Right now, all we know is that they went into the woods to do whatever it is kids do in the woods," he paused. Chad waited, wincing for the response Brianna was sure to give.

"What exactly are you implying?" Bri again, voice growing a tad louder.

"Miss, I need you to calm down and listen to what I am saying. It's a drive-in. Let's not be naïve here. I am barely a few years older than you. I know what kids do here, I did it too. I'm just saying that I cannot call the cops yet. The movie is not over, so technically, they are not missing."

"Yes, they are missing," Brianna said. Chad could almost see the air quotes around the word 'missing' as she said it. "They were with us, now they are not. It's been over an hour since they left. And her, your little girlfriend right there, her date is missing too, isn't that, right?"

"I'm not his girlfriend," a new voice spoke up. Chad recognized it, Lorna from his English class. "But yeah, I came here with Jack Reynolds. We had a fight, and he stormed off. He's not been back since, that I can tell."

"See?" Brianna said. "You have three kids missing and you are doing nothing about it. I'm calling the police now. I'm sick of your shit."

"Listen here, little girl," The guy began, then stopped. Chad

DOUBLE FEATURE

heard a sigh. "Listen. I know you are worried. So are we. But her and her friend had a fight. She came back here; we don't really know if he stayed in the woods or not. He could be hanging out with friends in their car." Another sigh, frustration evident. Chad almost chuckled. He'd been there before with Brianna. She was feisty when she was pissed.

"We can't do anything until the movie ends, and then we can see what cars are still here, who shows up and who doesn't?" Another pause, a deep breath, then the man continued, "Until then, we need to wait for the guards to report in from their search. As soon as I know something, you'll know."

"Fine. We will be right outside on the bench, and we are not moving until you find them, or you call the Chief. I will be calling my parents as soon as this movie is over if they are not back by then."

"That's fine. Here, take these," Chad heard paper rustle, a drawer slam, more paper, then a sarcastic snort from Brianna.

"Free food tickets?" she scoffed. "You really think a free burger is going to win me over?"

Chad perked up. He could eat. Right then, his stomach growled. "Just take the tickets, Bri," he called up the steps, hoped she heard.

Silence. A chuckle was heard, awkward sounding, from the man. Then another one, this one, came from Bri.

"Fine, clearly someone can still eat while our friends are missing." She huffed, then said, "We will be right outside."

Chad tried not to grin as Brianna came down the steps. She held the coupons out to him without speaking and went outside. He knew not to follow just then. He turned, grabbed a tray, and began to fill it. Brianna's favorite drink and candy went on the tray first, then he ordered his free burger and fries and got her a hot dog. He wasn't an asshole; he was just a nervous eater. People being upset made him nervous. People missing made him more nervous. He added a large popcorn and two sodas.

Outside, Brianna seethed on the bench. Anger kept the tears away. She hated crying from frustration and from fear. It made her feel weak. Instead, she seethed, she boiled, she raged, and she lashed out. Inside, she felt small and helpless. Fear gripped her like nothing ever had. Her father hadn't even been gone for a year. Toni had been her best friend since they were in diapers. She couldn't lose her too, not now, not after everything they'd shared. Tears finally broke free and slid unchecked from her eyes. By the time Chad returned, Brianna was a sobbing puddle, huddled alone in the dark.

Petey grinned as Bobby Ray and Tiny strapped the girl to the table. Blood from the last one still dripped from the rough wooden edges. Her nude body was liberally covered in the gore drenching her as they hacked Kent to pieces. Her caramel skin tone was hardly visible beneath the gore decorating her from head to toe. The girl was near incoherent as they lashed the straps around her ankles and wrists. Her eyes rolled from one side to the other, blinking away the tears and blood as they shifted her body onto the makeshift table. Her head hung over the edge; her braids dripped blood from their ragged strands.

The movie behind them had hit the big finish, screaming, and crying, gunshots and explosions filled the air. Mama Jean was perched in the truck bed, ready to catch the body parts as her sons tossed them to her. She was damn near giddy with glee as she eyed the succulent morsels that filled the truck bed. They had been at this so long all she saw were cuts of meat: prime cuts of steak and tender filets, roasts and sausage and ground meat, stew meat and jerky. Meat was meat—that was all that mattered.

"What in tarnation?" Petey said, halting his work. He had one hand poised to slice off the girl's left breast, the other hand pulling the nipple taut to hold the mound in place.

"What's wrong, son?" Mama Jean squinted at him, not following his gaze behind the truck.

Tiny was already reacting to the threat that Petey could not articulate. A swift toss of the hatchet he held landed in Allen Hook's face, cleaving his nose neatly in half. A wet strangling gurgle issued from his throat before he fell to the ground. The other man with him turned to run, but his considerable size and the darkness of the terrain were not on his side. Bobby Ray was already there, lunging toward him with the machete.

The blade ran clean deep into his hefty gut and Bobby Ray ripped it upwards as he yanked it free, slicing the man open from groin to gullet. Steaming tubes of intestines slid from the gaping

DOUBLE FEATURE

wound, slithered between his wide fingers that were a second too late to hold them inside, then fell to the ground in a heap. The man opened his mouth to speak, but no words came. His mouth opened and closed like a fish. A blood bubble burst from between his lips and a drop of crimson leaked from his nose. A second later, he landed on the ground, face first in his own innards.

Mama Jean whooped loud and long. "Whoooowheeeee! Got us two big 'uns for sure! That'll make us some good money for this winter. Git 'em over here, boys. Line 'em up!"

"Petey, slice them tiddies off that girl. We gots work to do!" Mama Jean began barked orders as the movie raced to its conclusion. Noise filled the woods, both in front of and beyond the movie screen, as carnage ensued, and blood sprayed in copious amounts.

Petey did as he was told and sliced the perky mounds from the girl's chest and laid them aside. Thick slices of her supple thighs, hips, and rump followed suit. He made quick work of all the best parts of her, then stepped aside for Tiny's bone saw to get to work. Him and Bobby Ray would cut her up the rest of the way and they would process the rest of the meat back at the slaughterhouse. Mama liked to get the most tender cuts first.

Mama was in the truck bed, wrapping limbs tightly into the cut squares of tarp they brought. Blood covered every surface, but no more than usual. The coppers never blinked an eye anymore when they saw their truck on the road. Everyone got their game processed by the strange family from the hills, and everyone said their cuts of meat and recipes were the best in town. Mama said it was all in the spices.

Petey grinned as he began cutting the clothing from two newcomers. *Who wouldv'e thunk it? Two free kills tonight? Just walked right up to them.* Petey remembered Mama's promise to him, and boy, oh boy, had he been good tonight. He couldn't wait to pick which one he wanted. Not that it mattered, brains was brains, but sometimes a bigger skull made for a better tongue plunge in his opinion. He felt himself getting excited just thinking about it. Drool escaped one side of his mouth and he licked his lips, tasting blood and sweat as he did so. This only aroused him further. He couldn't wait, his urge had gotten too strong.

"Hey Mama," He called, need in his voice, a giddy excitement taking over. "Can I have this one?" He asked when she turned to look at him.

Petey was pointing at the now expired former Officer Pierce, a hopeful expression on his face. "I been so good, Mama. Please?"

"Alright, I'll have Tiny open him up for you. But don't you waste none, ya hear?"

"Yes'm. I won't. I do's it so good now. You'll see." Drool slid from his lips as he began dragging the corpse over to his brother, eager not even beginning to describe his haste.

Mama Jean snorted and continued wrapping the girls' body parts as Bobby Ray tossed them to her. Petey was her special child. She sighed, regretting the night that had made him so. She had no choice but to indulge his peculiar needs now. What else was a mother to do?

Shouts of murder and fear and mayhem filled the air as shadows danced on the opposite side of the movie screen while on the back side, curtains of blood ran freely down the panels and bits of gore clung to the wood. The family carried on with their duties as the movie drew to a close.

Hatchets and bone saws made quick work of limbs and torsos. Tiny cut open Pierce's skull, leaving a nice round hole for Petey to delve into then went back to helping Bobby Ray and Mama finish their wrapping. They all chuckled quietly as Petey's moans and wet squelches met their ears, slow at first, then more and more urgent as his tongue met the forbidden insides of the meaty brain matter. When he was spent, he separated the head himself, cleaned out the skull for Mama and added the spongy tissue to her special cooler.

The family finished their work, loaded their tools, and set off toward their home hidden within the trees. They had game to process, meat to spice, and a business to run. More time for movies next week. Mama Jean finished off her flask as the old truck toddled from the clearing, following ruts older than she was, back to the thick forest beyond.

Garrett paced back and forth behind the grill, pushing the broom, but the area had been swept clean for ten minutes now. Lena and Sammie stood quietly by their registers, and Tyson could be heard yelling on the phone upstairs. Lorna, Brianna, and Chad all sat on the benches just outside the doors. The movie had ended. The cars

DOUBLE FEATURE

had all lined up and left the lot, everyone headed back to town or maybe to late night diners.

Toni and Kent were still missing. Jack had not yet been seen. Four vehicles remained in the gravel lined lot. Only two were in front of the concession stand, Jack's and Chad's. Tyson, Sammie, and Garrett had all parked behind the booth, with Tyson at the very back. Pierce and Hook were not yet responding on their radio, and Tyson had finally called it in.

The small group listened as he told the Chief once more about the kids, then heard the rage in his voice as he again was told that they had not yet been reported missing by their parents. Garrett shook his head, finally setting the broom aside as Tyson raged down the stairs.

"Well, that's it. They won't do anything until morning. I tried. You all heard me." Tyson looked apologetically at the kids around him. "We must follow their procedures. Best for you all to go home now and just wait for the morning. I've called my uncle. He's on his way. I'm going to stay here tonight just in case any of them come back." He shrugged and looked at his shoes.

"I'm not going out there, but I will stay here with the lights on, and hopefully, if they are lost or hurt out there, they can find their way back."

"That's it, then?" Brianna asked, her voice breaking. Chad put an arm around her. "We just leave them out there, somewhere?" She gestured angrily toward the outside, trees and all, skeletal shadows in the night.

"I'll call you as soon as the police show up, Brianna. That's the best I can do right now," Tyson said, softly.

"Come on, Bri. Let's just do what he says," Chad said, turning her toward the door. "Lorna, come on. I'll take you home."

Lorna looked at Tyson, as if asking permission. He nodded at her with a sad smile. 'That's probably best. No telling when your mom might come home. Just call here in the morning and I'll give you an update."

The kids left, heads down, sniffles heard as Chad escorted both girls to his car. Garrett watched from the doorway; a protective stance evident in his posture as he scanned the area around them. When the kids got in the car and the headlights came on, he stepped back inside, watching from the windows as the car drove toward the long path to the roadway, then faded from view.

"This is fucked-up, man," Garrett said to Tyson, turning back to their group. "They know this isn't the first time."

"I know that. You know that. Everyone knows that. But the fact of the matter is, they must follow protocol too. Technically, Jack is an adult. He turned eighteen last month. Even if his parents report him missing, they'll be slower to follow-up. The other two are minors, so as soon as twenty-four hours pass, their parents can make a report," Tyson suddenly sounded a decade older than everyone else, but felt a decade younger, scared and alone inside and trying to perpetuate a sense of authority on the outside.

"It's a shitty policy," Sammie piped up. "These are kids, eighteen or not. He is someone's kid."

"Listen everyone, just go home. Get some rest. Come back in the morning if you want to help search when the police get here." Tyson shrugged, sounding as defeated as he felt. "I don't know what else to do or say."

Sammie looked at Garrett. "Coming?" she asked him.

"Nah, I'm going to stay here with Tyson. You girls go home. Lena, Sammie will take home so you don't need to call your mom."

"Yeah, come on girly, let's blow this popsicle stand." Sammie grabbed her jacket, kissed Garrett quickly on the cheek, and waited for Lena by the door.

Lena gave the guys a quick wave and a somber smile, then left with Sammie, letting the door swing closed behind her.

"You don't have to stay, man, it's fine," Tyson said to Garrett as he sat down beside him on the stairs leading up to his booth.

"No, it's not fine. There's some creepy shit happening, and no one should be out here alone overnight. Not with kids missing again."

"But what about your grandma?" Tyson asked him.

"I called her nurse. She's going to stay over tonight. Someone needs to be here with you and besides, like you said, what if they come back or one of them is injured? You'll need help," Garrett said.

"Thanks, man." Tyson smiled weakly, barely lifting his lips to form the smile. His shoulders drooped and anxiety bristled from him like a neon light.

Garrett smiled back, trying to make it feel more normal, when, in fact, he felt like he was living in a bad dream. These things don't happen when people are around to see it, right? This is that shit

DOUBLE FEATURE

that happens on the news, happens to others, happens elsewhere, but not to you, not right here at home. Fatigue hit him then, not just tired from the day, but bone-deep fatigue. He felt like his knees might crumble beneath him if he tried to stand, so he didn't.

They sat in silence for a few moments, listening to the fluorescent light hum overhead. Several times Tyson jumped, startled when the zap of a mosquito met their ears as the bugs swarmed around the bug zapper outside the entrance, drawn to the softly fluorescing blue light. The third time broke the strange spell that hung over and Tyson jumped to his feet.

"Okay, well, if we are going to stay here, let's finish cleaning up, take stock, and get things properly closed before my uncle gets here. We got a meat delivery in the morning too, so we need to make room in the cooler. Gotta keep moving to stay alert and stay awake."

"Right on. I'll get some coffee going in case Pierce and Hook come back." Garrett yawned, a huge overwhelming yawn that made his eyes water. He stretched like a cat afterward, suddenly awake and weirdly energized. "Let's get it done."

Together, they worked to restock the candy shelves, the popcorn supplies, and the paper products. Garrett finished sweeping and mopping with Tyson, counted the stock in the freezer and in the storage room. They finished counting the drawers up, bagged the money for Tyson's uncle to take to deposit, then shuffled upstairs to wait.

There, they sipped coffee and stared out over the quiet clearing. The white space of the movie screen stared back, an empty parking lot of nothing but speaker poles faced them, mocking them. Behind it, where they could not see, rivers of red ran down the thin wooden support slats of the screen, glistening blackly beneath the moonlight.

The door slamming downstairs in the concession area twenty minutes later startled them from their silent watch over the empty lot.

"Tyson?" a male voice called out. "You up there?"

Tyson rose to his feet quickly, almost tripping over his chair, equal parts adrenaline from being startled and relief that an adult was here, a real adult. Garrett reached a hand out to steady him before he also rose from his seat, following the lanky young man down the stairs.

"Coming, Unc!" Tyson called as they started down.

A shadow appeared in the doorway, then stepped away as the boys hit the last of the steps. Tyson smiled a real smile for the first time in hours when he saw his uncle standing there. He wasted no time hugging him when the man stepped forward and Garrett could almost see the stress leave his shoulders. He smiled too, relief at another adult being there flooding his system.

"Hey fellas," Tyson's uncle said, "come on and tell me what's going on? And where are Hook and Pierce? I can't raise them on the radios at all."

In a jumble of words, Garrett and Tyson both began to talk, filling in for one another when a detail was forgotten.

"I've been trying to reach Allen and Tony since I asked them to check the perimeter. That was hours ago. I don't know what could have happened to them, but something doesn't feel right, Uncle Stephen," Tyson drug a hand through his hair, his eyes burned with fatigue and stress. "I did everything you told me to, but the chief said he couldn't do anything yet." He shrugged, a look of helpless defeat on his face.

"You did good, son. Nothing more you could have done." His uncle patted his shoulder. "Now, that makes three kids, and the guards, apparently, that just vanished here tonight?" Stephen Kincaid mused to himself.

"Last time a kid went missing was almost two months ago, and they were from over in Wells." He turned back to Garrett. "You said you heard other kids talking about another boy gone missing yesterday, too. Kenny something?"

"Yes, sir. Kenny Lassiter, I think, was the name," Garrett said, plopping back down on the steps.

"Alright. Let's get some flashlights, make a sweep along the edge of the trees, see if anyone got hurt. Don't go into the woods, though. The cops can do that in the morning. I'll need to see what happened to Hook and Pierce, too. They gotta be somewhere. Maybe the golf cart broke down." Stephen reached into his jacket pocket and pulled out the walkie talkie again.

Tyson and Garrett grabbed flashlights and jackets from the storage room and followed Stephen into the night. They shared a

DOUBLE FEATURE

quiet look between them that clearly stated they didn't want to go out there.

Back at the slaughterhouse, Mama Jean was barking orders at her boys. A pile of fresh meat waited to be processed and time was wasting.

"Petey, get them casings ready for the sausage. There're some fresh ones in the back room."

"Tiny, you and Bobby Ray get them fat ones cut up. Roasts, if any, then steaks and filet first, grind up the rest."

She shuffled around the blood-soaked benches and machines, slapping dismembered legs and arms down on the tables. She grabbed her cooler of innards and brain matter and took it over to her table to add to her giant vat for her special head cheese. Three heads bobbed around inside the pot already, free of hair and eyeballs.

Petey came over to her to watch, his hands full of casing as he lumbered from side to side, eyein' the sponge-like bits of tissue in the cooler. His eyes shimmered in the dim light of the old building as Mama started adding other ingredients to the massive steel pot.

"Petey, get them casings on over to Tiny. You done had your fun for the night," Mama Jean ordered. Her raspy laugh turned into a horrid cough as Petey blushed and trudged away to Tiny's table on the far side of the building.

"Here, Tiny. Mama said give these to you," Petey muttered, sulking at being denied one more taste of brain. It was just his favorite thing and Mama knew it. That delicate texture just made him squirm inside in warm ways. There just wasn't nothing else like it in the world.

"Good," Tiny grunted, yanking a section of hairy skin from a male leg, "Here, pull this," Tiny lifted the leg up and held it still while Petey yanked the section of flesh free. They finished degloving the other limbs and rinsed them in the bucket. Tiny started slicing off sections for filets and other chunks for ground meat. Petey helped with his own blade, and they made quick work of what had been Hook and Pierce.

Over at his table, Bobby Ray was slicing up what was left of Toni and Kent. All the delicate parts had been removed for the head cheese, jerky, and Mama's special recipe. All that was left on the bone now was to be ground up for burgers, dogs, and sausage meat. Blood flowed freely from the tables and benches as they worked in a quiet but frenzied silence.

They had been lucky so many times before, but with the extra kills from the night, they couldn't afford to let the meat sit. It would go bad, and it was only a matter of time before the kids were reported missing and Chief Robbins came out for his obligatory visit. The slaughterhouse had to be in tip-top shape by morning, nothing but deer and coon meat as far as anyone could tell. The air carried a heavy coppery tang on it. Every breath drew in the scent and taste of blood.

Mama chuckled to herself, setting the propane burner on high to boil as she stirred the soupy blend of broth, vinegar, and chunks of onions, garlic, mixed with organ tissue and brain matter. She dumped in a bag of her spice blend and stirred it with the long wooden spoon. She barely noticed as flecks flew from the dented pot and splattered her already filthy apron and her cheeks with the crimson froth.

Folks loved her headcheese around here, or souse, as some folks called it. The old-timers 'specially couldn't get enough of it. She made it fresh, kept loaves of it frozen, and when word got out a batch was ready, it was snatched up faster than her blackberry moonshine. It was one of their top-selling items. The thought made her cackle out loud. Too bad the townies didn't know exactly what they was eatin', but hey, long as Mama and her boys didn't starve, meat was meat, and she wasted none, ever.

Behind her, the boys started feeding chunks of flesh into the grinders. Petey fed the casings onto one end, while Tiny worked the other end. Bobby Ray brought over his trimmings to be added, then got to work slicing up what remained of Jack. The sun would be up soon, and they had to finish. Bobby Ray's stomach growled as the scent of the gelatin-rich broth from the head cheese filled the sweltering building.

"Mama, ya' got any biscuits and sausage left?" he called out, sweat dripping in his eyes and onto the blood meat as he hacked the muscle from the bone, tearing through the kneecap. "I sure am hungry."

"Boy, you know where the kitchen is. Go see," Mama snarled at him. "You see me cooking here, don't you?"

DOUBLE FEATURE

"Yes'm," Bobby Ray said, setting his knife down. "You want me to bring you somethin' too?"

"You can bring us all somethin' if you goin' inside. Bring Mama a beer, too," she said, grinning at him, her smile wide enough to show what was left of her rotted teeth.

"Okay, Mama." Bobby Ray ducked through the plastic tarp over the doors and disappeared.

Tiny's laugh followed him inside. "He always gets hungry when we butcherin'." Tiny said, laughing again. "Blood and guts all over everything, and he hungry."

"It's the broth," Mama Jean cackled. "Gets 'em every time."

"Sure does smell good, Mama," Petey piped up. A string of sausages lay beside him on the table, so many they were starting to roll off the side.

"Petey, for fuck's sake. Pick those up and get 'em wrapped for freezing!" Mama yelled.

Petey blushed guiltily and stooped low to grab the fresh sausage from the gore covered floor. He wiped them off and added them to the big bin to take to the storage room to be wrapped. He hefted it up and trudged away as Bobby Ray ducked back inside with a big platter of biscuits and a bucket of beer bottles.

"Break time!" Mama called out.

Her boys finished their tasks and ambled over to her. A thick miasma of blood filled the air. The stench of raw meat and heavy spices coated it. The machines slowed and quieted, blood dripped from every surface and piles of livid processed meat filled the bins. The Bailey brothers popped their tops on the beers and grabbed the cold biscuits from Bobby Ray. He had filled them with Mama's special smoked sausage and slices of Swiss cheese, a favorite Bailey snack.

By the time they finished eating, the sun was just beginning to turn pink over the trees on the horizon.

"Let's git to cleanin,' boys," Mama said, belching as she finished the last of her beer. She tossed the bottle in the wheelbarrow next to the door, laughing as it shattered atop the rest of the bottles and trudged over to her pot.

"Git it hosed down. Git that meat in the freezer. Petey, git them bones buried." She barked orders as she stirred the broth. The boys got to work, falling into a decade's old routine.

Within the hour, the slaughterhouse was as clean as one might expect. Several fresh carcasses lay on the tables, two deer and a couple coon, just in case anyone came snooping around. With their business concluded for the night, and the pot of heads, bones, scrap meat and innards on a slow simmer, they shuffled into the house to sleep.

"What'cha find, Kincaid?" Chief Robbins drawled. He yawned, coffee in hand, and gazed around the empty drive-in. His eyes fell on Jack's lone car, still in the row before the concession stand. "You all find anything to suggest a missing person or just wasting my time again?" He took a loud sip of his coffee and stared at the man; one eyebrow raised on his pudgy, round face.

Garrett and Tyson glanced at each other from behind Tyson's uncle. Clearly, the chief was not pleased at being called out so early. The man looked bored and pissed off at the same time. Garrett didn't understand how the police chief could be so nonchalant over more kids gone missing.

"Look here, Chief. Now, it's the same as the others. Couple of kids didn't come back to their cars after they went for snacks. A couple had their friends here, and the other boy stranded his date. But it's more than that. My guards are missing, too. Found their golf cart stuck about twenty yards from the back of Screen One," Stephen Kincaid said, running a hand through his wiry hair.

He looked tired, much older than the fifty years he had attained in life. This missing kid nonsense was getting out of hand. The chief eyed him like he was a naughty child that needed to be scolded. He hated the chief; he hated people that made him feel small. Chief Robbins could reduce a man in size with just a glance.

"Yea, and like I said, the parents need to file a report and technically, they can't do that until tonight. It hasn't been twenty-four hours. Far as your so-called guards go, Hook and Pierce are about as useless as tits on a chipmunk. Not the most dependable fellas, are they? How you know they just didn't get bored and go home? Walk off the job? They're adults. I can't do much 'bout that, now can I?" Robbins almost sneered the words.

Garrett bristled at the way the chief spoke to Tysons' uncle. He didn't know the man that well, but the chief's condescending tone dripped with malice. Tyson was sitting up straighter beside him,

DOUBLE FEATURE

his posture stiff and rigid. Garrett saw his hands curl into tight fists. He shook his head slightly when Tyson caught his eye. The look said it all. '*Let them handle it.*' Tyson nodded and relaxed slightly, but his posture stayed rigid.

"Now, I ask again, did you boys find anything to warrant my being out here? Or not?" The chief asked, glaring at each one of them in turn.

"Just the golf cart abandoned, the walkie-talkies on the ground," Kincaid answered glumly. "I guess not much more we could see in the dark, though."

"I see," The Chief said, rocking back on his heels. His stomach puffed out over his belt as he clasped his hands behind his back. The early morning sun glinted off his oily face, and he squinted in the bright sunlight. A hand came up to tilt the brim of his hat a bit lower on his brow as he kept glaring at Kincaid.

"I tell you what. I'll go on back, drive around the perimeter, I'll do a quick walk-through where you found the golf cart and see what's what. Then I'll decide what's to be done," Robbins said to Kincaid, the sneer back in his voice.

"Leroy, call down the garage and get a truck up here to git this boy's car. His parents will want it after we take a look." He called over to the deputy leaning on the squad car. "Then let's go take a walk."

"You boys stay here, have some coffee. I'm sure this won't take long," Robbins said, patting Tyson on the shoulder as he walked past him toward the car. He slid heavily behind the wheel as Leroy got into the passenger side. With a tip of his hat and a dust cloud of dirt, the chief drove off toward the movie screen, taking the emergency driveway around the treeline.

"What the hell, Unc?" Tyson shouted, springing up from the bench like he had been shocked. "How you gonna let him talk to you like that? There are kids missing and he's acting like it's no big deal!"

Stephen Kincaid sighed, pinched the bridge of his nose for a long moment before he replied. "Just gotta let him do his job, Tyson. It's not like we know the law or have any control over their procedures. Let's just wait and see what he finds. It's daylight now, gotta be something we missed." He looked at Tyson, who stood fuming in front of him.

"Gotta pick your battles, son," he said quietly, putting a hand on his shoulder. "Men like him, not worth it. Now, come on. Let's get inside and get the freezer ready. Meat truck will be here soon."

Garrett and Tyson followed Stephen Kincaid inside the concrete building. A truck engine rumbled in the distance and grew louder as it came through the drive-in gate and up the driving lane from the roadway. A few minutes later the truck parked in front of the concession stand and honked the old horn twice. Garrett and Tyson came outside to see a large man unfold from the cab of the ancient red truck.

"Hey Mr. Bailey. How are you?" Tyson said, walking over to stand at the rear of the truck.

"Doin' just fine, Tyson. Your uncle around? Got a fresh shipment for him," the man said, his deep voice rumbling from his chest like the old truck had rumbled across the gravel lot.

"Yes, sir. Let me grab him." Tyson turned to go inside, and Garrett stepped over to the truck, hands out to take the first box the delivery man was lifting out.

"Thanks, son," he said, handing the case over. Tyson returned with his uncle and together they unloaded the six cases of frozen meat from the truck while the big man and Tyson's uncle went inside for the payment.

"See you next month," Mr. Bailey called, as he got back in the truck. "Pleasure doing business with you." He grinned and started the truck just as Chief Robbins pulled up alongside him in the cruiser.

"Hey Tiny, new delivery?" Chief Robbins called.

"Yes, sir. Best burgers and dogs in town," Tiny replied, grinning. "Mama Jean said to stop on by. She's got a fresh batch of 'cheese cooking down just for you."

"Is that right?" The chief said, a wide smile on his face. "Well, I sure will be along in a day or two. You tell her to just keep it fresh for me, you hear?"

"Sure will, chief," Tiny said, lifting one hand in a wave. "See you soon."

Tyson and Garrett waved as the Bailey truck rolled down the lane and Chief Robbins got out of his vehicle.

"Well, I didn't find much of nothing to report, nothing but a dead deer that made a hell of a mess back behind your screen there," he nodded towards Screen One with a jut of his head, "You might want to hose that down sooner rather than later, probably

DOUBLE FEATURE

ran up off the road after getting hit, then stumbled away to die in the woods."

"Far as Hooks and Pierce go, I wouldn't worry too much. I'll have Leroy track their fat asses down. Probably just walked off the job. They never were any good," Chief Robbins eyed Kincaid, not unkindly this time, "Listen, I'll let you know if the kids turn up or if a report is filed. I just gotta follow protocol. You're a businessman. You know how it goes, right?"

He turned with a huff, "I got folks breathing down my neck too, just like you. Best get that meat in the freezer. Them Baileys make the best burgers in town." He grinned and got back in his car with another tip of his hat. A few minutes later he was gone, vanishing in a dust cloud down the lane.

"Well boys, I guess that's that. Let's finish up here and get home. Got another long night ahead and more hot dogs to grill." Stephen Kincaid followed the boys inside, pausing to wipe a random crimson smear from the side of a box as he carried it to the freezer. They had another double feature to prepare for that night.

THE CHATTER OF NIGHT BUGS

DANIEL J. VOLPE

CHAPTER 1

COOL NIGHT AIR blew into the Buick, and the smooth sound of southern rock wafted out. Tammi Jean Higgins was behind the wheel of her grandmother's old LeSabre—her fingers tapping the wheel with every guitar stroke. She wasn't much of a singer, but she did her damnedest, belting out the lyrics of the Lynyrd Skynyrd ballad. They cranked the radio almost to the max—the speakers crackling under the distortion. After years of abuse, the old Buick's sound system wasn't what it used to be. It certainly never saw such use when her grandmother drove it—with the abrasive rock replacing crooners from the old days.

Duke sat in the passenger seat. An open long neck of Bud in his lap and a cigarette in his right hand. His left hand sat on Tammi Jean's thigh, kneading the sweaty flesh, teasing at her crotch. He brought the cigarette to his lips and pulled—before tossing the filter into the night. It died in a shower of sparks on the old West Virginia asphalt. He grabbed the beer and finished it with a couple of deep chugs. That, too, went tumbling out of the window—silently shattering in the long grass along the roadway.

"Hey, you done rolling that shit, or what?" Duke asked Raylynn, who was sitting behind Tammi Jean.

Raylynn licked the edges of a joint under the butter-yellow overhead light in the old car. It was no easy feat to roll up on a back road, especially with Tammi Jean at the wheel. Half the time, Tammi Jean was focused on singing; the other half was trying to keep Duke's hands out of her pants. And from what Raylynn could see, Tammi Jean was occupied with both. Finally, she twisted the end of the joint, making sure it was all packed in—it was.

Raylynn knew she had a gifted mouth and hands—Duke had told her many times after she'd sucked him off. Then, with a pearl of cum still oozing from his cock, he'd gulp in air and tell her she was the best. She didn't know if she quite believed him—men will say anything after they nut—but it was frequent enough that she believed it.

"Finished," she said. Raylynn popped the joint into her mouth and looked for her lighter.

"Here," Duke said. He handed her his very fitting lighter with a psychedelic marijuana leaf on it.

"Thanks." She took it and lit the stinky weed. The car filled with the aroma of the skunky pot, but it was all they had. Besides the three remaining beers, this was their only enjoyment for the night. At least so far.

Tammi Jean looked at Raylynn in the rearview mirror. "Hey, puff puff, pass, bitch," Tammi Jean joked.

Raylynn extended her middle finger—the joint between her lips. She took a drag and held the smoke in her lungs.

Duke reached back as she passed it forward. He put it to his lips and ripped two big puffs, one after another. He slowly let the smoke curl out of his nose.

"Here, baby." He held it to Tammi Jean. "You want me to put it in your mouth?" he asked. Few people would've said Brant "Duke" Wayne was an ugly man, but few would've called him hot. His 'country charm' as he referred to it, was what he'd used to score girls since high school. He was on the taller side, but thin, with a shock of curly, dirty blonde hair that hadn't seen a barber or brush in months. His ears and nose—dusted with freckles—were a little too big, but far from ridiculous. He made up for his lack of looks with the massive horse cock that hung between his legs. Duke knew "Big Jake" (the nickname given to his penis in honor of his favorite John Wayne movie) was something to behold. So many women had felt their lady parts stretch before him.

Tammi Jean took her eyes off the road and looked at Duke. She licked her lips and said, "you fucking know I do."

Duke put the joint in her mouth and slipped his pinkie under her shorts—teasing her panty line. He glanced at her tits packed away in a snug tank top. What Tammi Jean lacked in the blowjob department, she more than made up for in the chest. Her breasts were large and still had the firmness of youth. She rarely wore a bra and her nipples poked against the pink fabric. Duke's cock had been between them many times, coating her neck and face with spurts of hot spunk.

THE CHATTER OF NIGHT BUGS

"Mmm, delicious," Tammi Jean cooed. Smoke rose from her lips and was sucked out of the open window.
"Okay, pass it back here, would'ya," Raylynn said.
Duke put it to his lips for another quick hit. "Here," he said, handing it back with a grin on his face. "You want me to put it in your mouth too?"
Raylynn licked her full lips, causing Duke to hard swallow. "I can put it in my own mouth, thank you very much." She took the joint and parted her lips. Slowly, she pulled on the small end of the fading smoke. A milky cloud rose in front of her face—and she pushed her tongue into her cheek, making it bulge out.
Duke's eyes were wide, and his hand absently went to his crotch.
Raylynn laughed and ran her fingers through her shoulder-length, sandy hair. She mouthed the words, "later," to him.
All three fucked each other, but technically, Tammi Jean and Duke were a couple. They could all fuck, but if Duke and Raylynn were messing around, Tammi Jean had to be involved. That was a very *loose* rule, which was never followed, but Duke and Raylynn didn't care. If money was tight, the girls would sometimes turn tricks at *Foxes*, the strip club all three worked at. Duke wasn't much of a bartender, but pouring shots and opening beers wasn't the most demanding work. Hell, it sure beat working the mines, like so many of the customers. He wasn't built for manual labor, no siree. His daddy told him that as a boy, when he'd often whine about getting up with the sun to do chores before school. Well, that ended—chores and school—as soon as he turned sixteen and left home.
"What do we have up here?" Tammi Jean said. The other two took their lusty eyes from each other and looked ahead.
Raylynn scooted to the center seat and put both forearms on the headrests in front of her.
In the distance, hazard lights flashed on the shoulder of the road.
Duke looked at each girl and smiled. "Money is gettin' kinda low," he said.
Tammi Jean looked at Raylynn, who nodded. "All right, let's do our civic duty and help." Tammi Jean slowed the big car and drifted into the soft shoulder. The passenger side tires bit into the soil, but the driver's side stayed on the asphalt. The headlights lit

up a car, which was a bigger piece of shit than the one they were in.

A man stood in front of the open hood of the shitbox—clouds of steam rushing out of the engine compartment.

"Motherfucker," the three of them heard the man grumble before he walked into the light from their headlights.

"Hey, buddy, ya all right?" Duke yelled from the passenger window.

A balding, middle-aged man wiped his dirty hands on a pair of equally dirty jeans. He took a handkerchief from his back pocket and blew his nose with a trumpet sound loud enough to wash out the sound of the night bugs.

"Nah, this fucking hunk of shit blew the radiator—pissing coolant everywhere. I'm gonna need a tow, but I can't get a wrecker out here until the morning." He looked at his battered watch. "Besides, Johnny is probably drunk as a skunk right now. Don't need him wrapping up a tree on my account." He walked over to the passenger side of the Buick.

"Well, we're heading that 'away," Duke said, pointing in the direction both vehicles were facing. "We don't mind givin you a lift."

The man squinted as he bent down to look into the vehicle. Tammi Jean turned on the dome light, giving the man a look.

His eyes were nearly magnetic as they homed in on her tits. It didn't help that she'd pulled the tank top down just slightly, showing off more cleavage.

"I—ah, could use a lift," he said.

"You'll have to sit back here with me." Raylynn leaned forward between the seats. His eyes snapped to her. Her short hair, wide eyes and plump lips had the old man nearly losing a nut in his pants already. "I mean, if that's okay with you."

He swallowed with a click—his protruding Adam's apple bobbing. "Ah, yeah, that'd be mighty fine." He opened the back door and slid into the car, bringing the smell of body odor and stale tobacco. "I'm Richy," he said to the group.

"Nice to meet you," Raylynn said. The joint was still burning in her fingers. She took a quick toke. "I'm Raylynn, and that's Duke," he put a hand up from the front seat, "and the driver with the big tits is Tammi Jean."

"Hey, I have other features besides these," Tammi Jean said, grabbing her right breast.

THE CHATTER OF NIGHT BUGS

They all laughed.

"Yeah, sure, but most of your brains are in there too," Raylynn said.

"Well, in that case, I must be a fucking genius."

"I'll say," Duke joked. He opened up a beer with a hiss. "You wanna beer, Richy?" he asked. Duke looked back at the older man, who was staring at Tammi Jean's tits from the backseat.

"I'd love one. I have a thirst like you'd never imagine."

Duke cracked open another one and moments later handed it back to Richy.

Richy took a long pull from the bottle. "Ah, that hits the spot." He pointed to the smoldering joint in Raylynn's fingers. "Better than that stinky shit, but I wouldn't mind a hit. It's been a hell of a day."

"No mind at all." Raylynn handed him the joint, which was almost finished. "Just kill it—we have more for later anyhow."

Richy pressed the joint to his lips and smoked. "Ya sure?" he coughed.

"Absolutely," Raylynn said. "Smoke'em if ya gottem, right?" she smiled.

"Dang, I gotta say you three give me hope for the youth of today. All I see are protests and young'uns disrespecting everything, not wanting to work and popping out babies. Nah, you three are cut from a different cloth." He knocked back more of the beer and looked at the bottle. "You'll see when you're my age one day, that the Got'dang kids have no respect." His words were slurring. "Say, partner, you might want to check your Buds. This tastes kinda odd." To confirm his suspicions, Richy sipped the last of it, his face scrunching at the bitterness of the partially dissolved pill. His droopy eyes closed and opened, trying to stay awake.

"What's the matter, Richy?" Tammi Jean asked. She looked at the man in the rearview mirror. "These big tits knock you out? Huh, you sick old perv." She smiled as Richy's head thumped against the window and his snores echoed in the car. "You're gonna get a show alright, but not one you'll enjoy, that's for sure."

The car slowed and turned down a dirt road, heading into the mountains—and straight towards the cabin.

Richy awoke with a headache and a sour taste in his mouth. He was hungover again—Brenda was going to be pissed. Slowly, his eyes functioned, drifting open. His mind was slow, as if it were trying to start like a diesel engine on a cold winter morning.

Wait a minute, Brenda left me, he thought. A mixture of relief and sadness flooded his mind. He wouldn't be in trouble for getting drunk, but then again, no one cared enough about him to give him shit.

Weak light burned his eyes as he tried to wake up. With each second, his consciousness returned, and his brain ran smoother and smoother. The first thing he noticed was that he wasn't in his trailer. A rough wooden ceiling was the only thing he saw. Slowly, he licked his lips, tasting a hint of beer and bitterness.

Damn, what the fuck did I eat and where the fuck am I?

Richy felt a glob of drool running down his chin. He tried to wipe it but couldn't. His head turned like a hunting owl, and he realized why—both arms had been shackled to a table. The sluggishness of his brain blew away like fog burning up on a summer morning.

"What the fuck?" he grumbled. Richy pulled at the metal bands, but they were solid. His fingers were turning an angry shade of purple as the metal bit into flesh. Richy tried to pull his knees up, but his ankles were also locked with metal cuffs.

The memories came flooding back to him. His truck—the radiator bursting—the car full of kids and the girl with the big tits, the beer . . . the bitter beer.

"Fucking cunt," Richy growled. He knew that beer wasn't skunked. The taste of a melted pill should've been familiar to him— it was how Brenda's mouth would taste after she'd snort Oxy, and they'd drip into her throat.

Richy looked around and knew he was in trouble. The room was small—a trapper's cabin, if he had to guess. A large hook hung from a hoist in the ceiling—similar to what he'd used to hang a deer while skinning it out. There was a simple workbench on one side full of old tools—many streaked brown with rust. They propped an old mattress against the wall—its stains were too many to count. Two gas lanterns burned, giving off the only light in the room. The lanterns were small, and one flickered, but Richy could almost feel the heat radiating. He was slick with sweat and smelled his odor.

Voices sounded outside. There must've been a porch attached because he heard footsteps and creaking floorboards. The door swung open.

THE CHATTER OF NIGHT BUGS

"Oh, hey, you're awake," the girl with the short hair said. Raylynn—he'd sat next to her in the car, smoking a joint. She walked in, ushering the other two car-mates behind her.

"Perfect, let's get this show on the road," Tammi Jean said as she followed her friend in. Richy never thought he'd be terrified to see two hot chicks, especially one with a perfect set of tits.

"Thank God. I thought we killed him early," said Duke. He carried a duffle bag on his shoulder, which he dumped onto the ground. Dust motes rose, dancing in the lantern light. He closed the door behind him, not bothering to lock it.

Richy's heart was thudding. The rhythm felt unnatural, like it was out of sync. Looking into the eyes of all three of them, he prayed for a heart attack.

"Aw, don't be scared," Tammi Jean said. She leaned close to him—close enough that he could smell her. The stink of booze, sweat, weed, and insanity wafted off her smooth skin. Even in danger, Richy still stole a look down her shirt. Tammi Jean laughed. "Even drugged and tied up, you're still a perv, eh, Richy?" She moved towards his right hand and pressed her breasts against his fingers. "Here ya go, big boy. One last hurrah for ya." Richy didn't want to play her games, but he almost had no choice. His calloused fingers kneaded her soft breasts. He felt a twinge in his cock, although it didn't get hard.

",All right, let's get going. It's getting late," Duke said. He pulled a tripod from the bag and set it up in front of them.

"Time's up, Richy," Tammi Jean said. She pulled away, leaving his hand empty.

"Please, I don't know what I did or why I'm here, but just let me go, okay? I won't tell a soul. I swear on my mother's grave." Sweat rolled down his face. His soft, slightly stupid eyes were misting up. "Please, I'm a good man. I don't deserve this." Richy pulled at his restraints and shot pain down his limbs.

Raylynn set a camcorder on the tripod. She removed a new SD card from the case and inserted it. With a practiced eye, she checked the frame on the viewfinder. Satisfied, she looked at the other two. "We're ready for action," she squealed in excitement.

"Let me fucking go!" Richy yelled. He thrashed and cut his bruised wrists and ankles. No matter how much he fought, he remained firmly secure to the table. "Let me go, you fucking cunts!"

Duke slapped him in the face. It left Richy's head ringing and ear feeling like it was on fire. "Hey, that's no way to talk to the ladies. Show some fucking respect." Duke smiled.

"Oh baby, you're my hero," Tammi Jean said. She grabbed Duke's face and kissed him hard and deep. The young man's pants swelled. Tammi Jean caressed his cock through the denim.

"Okay, I'm ready to shoot," Duke said, when Tammi Jean let him breathe again.

Richy wept, quietly at first. He didn't think he was going to get out of this and didn't know why. He never considered himself an evil man; he went to church on Sundays, didn't use drugs and would help a neighbor in need. The only bad thing was the few times he watched a few church ladies take a piss, but that was it. And maybe—if someone wanted to split hairs—he jerked his pecker in his car outside the high school. But no one caught him or was none the wiser. It was just Richy, his little dick and a few wet tissues.

Richy wept, but when he saw the knives and tools, he could hardly stop the cries. Then came the animal masks, and all hell broke loose.

Duke's cock was painfully hard. Tammi Jean was such a tease, but he knew he'd be inside of her and Raylynn soon. It seemed like an eternity to wait on, and at his age, he could blow his wad now and be ready again in five minutes. He probably wouldn't even get soft; he was so turned on.

Duke put the fox mask over his face. The thin plastic ears poked up from his head like a little crown, but he didn't mind—at least he could breathe. When they'd first started making videos, they were using full face masks, which sucked. They could barely breathe, were hot and the worst part was that the girls couldn't put his cock in their mouths. They could, but they had to lift the masks, which meant they couldn't see either. It just hadn't been ideal, and Grady didn't like how it looked on film. Since the moonshiner was paying for these videos, the trio adjusted their tactics and apparel, switching to half-masks instead.

Tammi Jean donned a mouse mask, similar in style, and Raylynn, a deer.

Raylynn checked the camera one last time. "Okay, you all ready?" she asked.

THE CHATTER OF NIGHT BUGS

Tammi Jean and Duke looked at each other and said, "yup."
"Action," Raylynn said. She pointed at them for effect.
Duke and Tammi Jean met in front of the camera, kissing each other hard. Their masks clicked together as tongues darted into awaiting mouths. It was a brief, sensual encounter. Duke broke off, letting a line of Tammi Jean's spit hang from his lips. Raylynn took his place, squeezing Tammi Jean's breasts as they kissed.
The two girls made out and groped each other as Duke walked over to the table. He put a finger to his lips as he perused the weaponry in front of him. There was a lot to choose from, but the first thing he needed to do was get Richy naked. Grady's sick customers like to see flesh; whether it was fucking or killing, they wanted nudity. Richy wasn't much to look at, but his portion of the film wasn't about sex—it was violence. Duke picked up a pair of garden shears. The tool was fairly new and hadn't been used to cut more than a few bits of flesh and clothing. He opened and closed them a few times, holding them in front of him for the camera.
The girls were still going at it—Tammi Jean's hands were in Raylynn's pants. A moan escaped Raylynn's mouth.
"Oh, you like that?"
"Yeah," Raylynn breathed. She pulled one of Tammi Jean's taut nipples through her tank top. Both girls grunted and moaned.
Tammi Jean saw the shears in Duke's hand and knew they had to share the camera space. She kissed Raylynn again and pulled her fingers from the girl's pants. Tammi Jean put them into her mouth, sucking the wetness. Raylynn grabbed Tammi Jean's fingers, plucking them from her mouth and tasting them for herself.
"Come on, let's join this party." Tammi Jean pulled Raylynn from the front of the camera and led her to the table.
Duke, now entirely in frame, began cutting at Richy's clothes.
"Stop, fucking stop," Richy begged. He thrashed against his bonds, but the steel bands held fast. His breathing was wet and ragged, with a healthy dose of phlegm crackling in his lungs.
Duke grabbed at the man's disgusting shirt and cut. The shears were perfect, slicing through the fabric. He cut and cut, shedding scraps of material as he went. Richy was finally nude. His cock was small and shriveled with fear. Duke looked at it and laughed. If he'd been in an ice bath, Big Jake couldn't physically get that small.
"Oh my god, look at that little fella," Raylynn snickered. She

put a hand to her mouth, careful not to stab herself with the paring knife she held. "Even this little knife might be too big for that thing." She walked before Richy, flicking him in his almost nonexistent cock.

Richy winced as she hit more balls than penis.

"Aw, I think it's cute," Tammi Jean said. She put her arm around her friend's shoulders, looking at Richy's withered manhood. She held a small pair of tin snips. "I'm willing to bet we can make it a little bigger. What do you think?" she asked Raylynn.

"Maybe, but just a little," Raylynn said.

Tammi Jean pulled her tank top off, letting her tits fall heavy. It was cool in the cabin and her nipples were already puckered and hard.

Raylynn followed suit. Her breasts were smaller but just as lovely, with petite drops of pink in the center.

Richy looked at the topless girls in front of him. He frequented many titty bars, and his little cock twitched with life.

"Oh look, I think your plan is working," Raylynn said, pointing at Richy's slightly swelling penis.

Tammi Jean smirked. "Hmm, I think we can do better." She handed her snips to Raylynn and moved closer to Richy. His nude body stunk worse than clothed, but she was a professional. Tammi Jean ran her fingers up his thighs, angling towards his cock.

Richy shook and groaned as her thumb grazed his balls.

"Do you like that?" she asked. Tammi Jean locked eyes with him through the mask.

Richy had a pained look on his face. "Yeah, but I'd rather you let me go. That would be even better."

He was almost hard, and Tammi Jean grabbed his pathetic cock with one hand and cradled his hairy balls with the other.

"I'm sure you would, but that's not happening," she said. Tammi Jean spit on his helmet and stroked.

Richy hissed. His body was betraying him, but he couldn't help it. Tammi Jean's tits jiggled as she stroked him faster and faster. Her spit mixed with his pre-cum, lubing his cock even more.

"Are you gonna cum, Richy?" Tammi Jean moaned. Her hand was a blur; faster and faster she worked him. She kneaded his balls, almost milking them, knowing he was about to blow.

"Holy shit," Richy said, closing his eyes. His legs were shaking, and Tammi Jean felt him tensing up.

THE CHATTER OF NIGHT BUGS

"Now," she said, stepping away, knowing he'd reached the point of no return.

Richy's eyes shot open as the warm hand released his cock. Raylynn thrust the paring knife into his taint as the first spurt of jizz dribbled out.

The thin patch of flesh between his balls and asshole offered no resistance to the blade, as metal carved and sliced. Deeper the steel burrowed into his body.

Richy took a deep breath and screamed as the next dribble of cum was mixed with red. Duke seized the opportunity to jam a lacrosse ball into the man's mouth. He felt one of Richy's teeth—probably a rotten one—snap off, as the ball crushed into his maw. Duke—having done this a few times—wrapped duct tape around Richy's head, holding the ball tight.

Richy screamed through the gag as his last orgasm was abating. Bloody cum dribbled from his flaccid cock, sticking in his long pubic hair.

"I hope that was fun, Richy," Tammi Jean said. She had the snips back in her hand. "But the fun is just starting." She wrapped the blades around Richy's big toe and squeezed. The metal bit into flesh, but the bone was strong.

Richy curled his toes against the assault, hoping to stop it. His feet danced around, avoiding the snips.

"Here, babe, let me try," Duke said. He took the snips.

"Oh, however, can I repay you?" Tammi Jean cooed, looking at the camera. They all knew what his payment was. It was what Grady's perverts wanted, at least at this stage of the video. It seemed they were all the same, but they didn't care as long as they got paid.

"I think you," he looked at Raylynn too, "and you can figure it out." Duke was painfully hard.

Both women kneeled in front of him and unbuckled his pants. Big Jake sprung out like a meaty Jack-in-the-box, nearly hitting Tammi Jean in the face.

Tammi Jean gasped as if seeing his cock for the first time. She took his swollen glans into her mouth.

"Mmm," she moaned, slurping him.

Raylynn ducked lower, putting one of his heavy balls into her mouth, sucking it away from the other.

The camera didn't blink as they pleasured him.

Duke groaned and put one hand on the back of Tammi Jean's head. With the other hand, he clamped the snips around Richy's big toe and squeezed.

The bone snapped with a click—low grunts of pain mixing with the wet sounds of a blowjob.

Duke was efficient. The girls sucked him, knowing he could hold his load. Despite that, they tried to get him to shoot. They alternated with Raylynn taking his cock into her mouth. He was a professional as he continued to snip off every one of Richy's toes.

Richy vibrated with a grand mal seizure—yellow vomit seeping around the gag and from his nose.

"Oh fuck," Duke said.

Raylynn thought he was cumming and sucked him deeper.

He put a hand on her head, stopping her.

"Oh, on the face, huh?" she said, backing away and sticking out her tongue.

"No, look." Duke pointed to the choking man.

Tammi Jean, who'd switched to his balls, looked over. "Fuck," she muttered as she stood. "Looks like we need the money shot early."

Duke kicked off his pants the rest of the way and removed his shirt. "Better strip down; this is gonna be a messy one."

The girls took off their shorts and piled all the clothes in the corner, hopefully far enough away.

Duke walked nude, his cock bobbing, over to the table and picked up a sixteen-pound sledgehammer. The girls moved out of the shot as this was all him. He raised it high above his head, almost hitting the ceiling, and looked at the camera. The black chunk of steel came rushing down and took Richy in the face.

It was wet, messy, and the perfect shot for the camera.

Richy's face distorted like he'd had a host of small explosives under his flesh. His nasal cavity cracked in a rush of mucus and gore, bathing his oily skin.

Duke wasn't done knowing the people wanted more. He was fired up and horny—killing always made him want to fuck. With a grunt, he hefted the wet hammer again. It rushed down, this time hitting Richy in the forehead. The man's skull cracked like a rotten melon. Brain matter, blood and bone erupted, spilling from his ears and what Duke left of his eyes. A shotgun to the face would've been cleaner.

Duke dropped the hammer onto the cabin floor, his chest rising

THE CHATTER OF NIGHT BUGS

and falling like he'd run for miles. Sweat dripped from his nose, coming out of the mask and running down his body.

"Bend over the table. Bend over him," he ordered. It didn't matter which woman it was, but one of them was getting fucked and fucked hard. The other knew they'd be taking his load all over their face. Duke was speckled with gore as he stroked his cock.

Tammi Jean jumped up and lay on Richy's corpse. Her breasts were warm against his cooling body. She pushed her ass back, spreading herself open for her boyfriend.

Raylynn crawled next to her, waiting, knowing what her role was.

Duke stepped up behind Tammi Jean and gazed at her dripping sex. Raylynn grabbed his cock and sucked it twice, just to give it a little lube. Duke pulled it from her mouth with a pop and unceremoniously thrust it into Tammi Jean.

She winced as his cock filled her to bursting. Tammi Jean braced herself against the corpse as she was fucked and fucked hard.

Duke knew he wouldn't last long, at least for this round. After a handful of deep thrusts, he knew it was time. He pulled his cock from Tammi Jean's cunt and turned to Raylynn, who was ready to accept it.

"Fuck," Duke groaned. The first blast of cum hit her in the mask, splashing all over the cheap plastic. The second spurt landed in her waiting mouth and third went down her throat as she deep-throated him. Duke shuddered and looked at the camera. When his pleasure had drifted away, he stumbled over and shut it off. "Damn, that was intense," he said. Big Jake hadn't come close to softening, and he knew the night was young.

Tammi Jean looked at the mangled corpse—her fingers were slowly rubbing her swollen clit. She peeled off the mask and went over to the mattress, pushing it to the floor. "Now, I think we deserve ours, don't you?" she said to Raylynn, who'd shed her semen-coated mask.

Raylynn sauntered over to Tammi Jean and both women lay on the stained mattress. "Yup, our turn, lover boy," she said. "I hope Big Jake is up for the task."

Duke smiled. "Oh, don't worry, there's plenty more for both of you."

The sounds of fucking and dripping blood echoed through the night. Their rutting was loud . . . almost as loud as the chatter of night bugs.

CHAPTER 2

THE BUICK GROANED as it bounced along the rutted road. It squealed with every bump, no matter how slowly Tammi Jean drove.

"Jesus Christ, Tam," Raylynn said. She was trying to sip from a soda bottle but had to time it right, or she'd be soaked. "Are you aiming for every pothole out here?"

Tammi Jean swerved, attempting to avoid another crater, only to hit an even bigger one. "Fuck," she muttered. The car jolted on worn shocks. "You know these fucking Shiners don't give two shits about the road. They probably keep it fucked up so they can hear a car coming a mile away." Another resounding thump garnered more curses from them.

Duke didn't mind the bumps. He used to work for old man Chester Bedford and his son, Grady. He'd been a teenager, which felt like ages ago. It was nothing major, just selling moonshine to some local boys, mainly the jocks. Duke would take a few jars for himself, but it wasn't his favorite thing in the world. It would get him good and fucked up, but it tasted like shit. Maybe when he was older and a proper drunk, like his non-existent father, he'd appreciate the white lightning for what it was.

The dirt road leading to the Bedford's property was a mess, especially in the rainy season. For the time being, it was just an annoyance.

Flags, broken-down cars, shot-up signs with all manners of warning and profanity flanked the dirt road.

"Are we almost there?" Raylynn asked. She'd abandoned her soda, which sat between her legs. She looked to see if the house and few outbuildings were visible through the trees.

"Ah, yeah, we should see the main house in a second," Tammi

THE CHATTER OF NIGHT BUGS

Jean said. She leaned over the steering wheel, careful not to hit the horn with her tits. "There," she said, pointing, "I see smoke."

The trio craned their necks, peering through the tangle of trees. Smoke was visible in the distance, rising from one of the many stills set up.

Three men stood waiting for the old car as it rounded the last bend in the rutted road. Each of them had a gun of some sort—two had black rifles slung across their chests and the third, Grady Bedford, had a pistol on his hip.

"Oh, what a lovely welcoming party," Raylynn said. "Didn't you tell them we were coming?" she asked Duke.

He turned back to her. "Yeah, but you know how Grady is. He doesn't trust anyone these days. Getting as paranoid as his old man."

"That sounds pleasant," Raylynn quipped. Chester Bedford had always been wild, even as a boy. But a few bad batches of 'shine and a couple of beatings from rivals had left his brain scrambled like eggs on a diner flattop. He once shot one of his guys through the foot just because he'd heard a rumor. No one knew exactly what it was, but it was enough to send the old man's paranoia into the stratosphere.

Roger, one of the men with a rifle across his chest, approached the car with his hand out.

The brakes cried as Tammi Jean put pressure on them. She rolled the window down, allowing a cloud of dirt to enter the already filthy car.

"How we doing, Roger?" Duke said, leaning across Tammi Jean.

Roger puffed on a cheroot, spitting loose tobacco on the ground. His tanned skin glistened with sweat and his dark eyes took in each of them.

"Doing fine, doing fine," Roger said. He didn't waste a chance, not trying to conceal it, and looked right down Tammi Jean's shirt.

"Hey, Roger," Raylynn leaned forward between the front seats. "How's it going?"

Roger didn't answer, just nodded. "Hey now, I'm gonna need you to pop the trunk."

Tammi Jean scrunched her face up. "What for? You think we got a body in there?" she chuckled, but there was no humor in her voice. They had a body in there recently, but Richy's corpse was at the bottom of the reservoir, joining many others. Her eyes found Grady's, standing with R.J., the other rifle-wielding man.

"Boss's orders," Roger replied. He let out another cloud of sweet smoke. "Now, if ya don't mind." He started towards the back of the car.

Tammi Jean looked at Duke.

"Who cares? Just pop the trunk. The quicker they see the movie, the quicker we get paid and get the fuck out of here."

Tammi Jean huffed but hit the release for the trunk—she hoped it would even open.

The trunk popped and was shut in a few seconds. Roger appeared at her window again.

"Anything good in there?" Tammi Jean asked. Richy's corpse had been wrapped tightly in plastic and duct tape before they loaded him in. There was no way he leaked and even if he did, they always lined the trunk with an oversized tarp.

"Nah, just junk. It smells like roadkill, but that's being expected, I guess." He whistled to Grady and nodded. Grady nodded back and started walking towards one outbuilding. "Follow the boss to the clubhouse, like normal, but park around back."

Tammi Jean wished her breasts could answer him back, as he was talking directly to them. "Sure thing," she said. The car thumped into gear, and she started forward. "Asshole."

Raylynn laughed from the backseat. "What's the matter, Tam? Don't like him staring at those big ole melons?"

Tammi Jean looked at her in the rearview. "Could he have made it any more obvious?"

"Look around, babe. Do you see any chicks? Let alone any as hot as you two? No fucking way. These peckerwoods are back here alone, making shine, watching snuff and probably fucking each other. And besides, these guys have seen much more than your tits and in a few minutes are gonna see it all again. So, just relax and go with it, okay?"

Tammi Jean knew they were right. And she didn't mind when the Shiners looked at her—it was kind of nice, but she'd let no one know. She wished they paid for it like everyone else when she was on stage at *Foxes*. At least then she'd get some money thrown at her. She might have to give one of them a lap dance or an over-the-pants hand job, but it was easy money. Most of them came in their

THE CHATTER OF NIGHT BUGS

pants after two strokes, so it wasn't too big of a deal. She parked the car and waited behind the outbuilding.

It wasn't much—an old barn that had been converted into a man-child clubhouse. They'd been in there many times, but it hadn't changed.

The back door opened and R.J., the other rifle-wielding man, sans rifle now, waved them in.

"You have the card, right?" Tammi Jean asked Raylynn.

"Bitch, do you think I'm dumb?"

Tammi Jean smirked. "Do you want me to answer that?"

Raylynn flipped her off as she popped a piece of gum into her mouth.

Duke led the way. "How's it going, R.J.?" The two men shook hands.

"It's going, that's for sure." R.J. was one of the youngest guys in the Shiners. His older brother, Darryl, had been killed in a robbery attempt three years prior. The Bedfords took kindly to the young man, offering him his brother's spot in their little organization. R.J. leaned in close to Duke. "Hey, Grady was kinda pissed about the last movie. He said it was too dark or some shit like that. I hope this one is a little better, but I just wanted to give you a heads-up."

Duke sighed. "Fuck. We busted one of our lanterns and didn't think nothing of it. Let's hope this one is okay." He patted the young man on the shoulder. "Thanks."

The clubhouse was exactly what anyone would expect: threadbare couches of all shapes and sizes, a crude bar with jars of 'shine, whiskey and a tap, an old, big screen TV that hadn't been new in twenty years and a beat-up pool table.

The clubhouse was empty except for them. Grady sat at the card table with a beer and smoke in front of him. He picked up his cigarette and took a long drag. The smoke slithered out of his mouth and into his eyes, but he didn't blink—just stared at the newcomers.

"Shut it and make sure it's locked," Grady said.

R.J. locked the door behind them.

Grady stubbed his cigarette out in the ashtray and stood up. He was tall—but not as big as Duke—with brown hair and eyes the color of mud. Over the years, those eyes had changed. They were once softer, more reasonable, but tough times with his dad and the law had shifted them. Now they were hard, like stone and with just a hint of insanity—something the Bedford name was known for.

"I hope you have something good for me this time," Grady said, walking over to them. "Last time that shit was dark, almost too dark for the buyer. In fact, they had to pay to get that shit enhanced so everything could be seen."

Raylynn pulled a plastic SD card case from her pocket and held it up. "I have it right here, Grady." She looked at him, but the man didn't move.

Roger stepped forward and took it from her, bringing it over to a laptop that was connected to the TV.

"Well, let's look, shall we?" Grady said. He gestured for them to sit down.

Grady took one of the beat-up love seats, while the others sat on the least decrepit couch that could fit them all.

The TV lit up, and everyone held their breath. Tammi Jean's heart was racing, and she hoped it wasn't visible through her shirt. She sensed eyes on her chest, but hoped they were scouting out her nipples, not her heartbeat.

The inside of the cabin came into view . . . and it was dark. Not too dark that it wasn't salvageable, but she knew Grady wouldn't have it. She looked at her friends—they each reflected her sentiment.

The movie played on; the sound of killing, screaming, and fucking was loud through the speakers in the clubhouse.

The movie ended with Duke blasting Raylynn's mask with a load of cum.

Grady had lit another cigarette. He put it to his lips and was silent. The only sound in the room was burning tobacco and nervous breathing. He inhaled with a hiss. "Too fucking dark. It's workable, but I fucking know the buyer is going to have the same issue as last time."

"Sorry, Grady," Duke spoke up. "Our one lantern took a shit, and we haven't had the scratch to replace it. We'll upgrade for the next one and make it a badass movie."

Grady looked at them, taking each before stopping on Duke. "I certainly hope so. The buyer is generous and patient, but they've told me their patience is thin. Shoddy work is unacceptable. Figure it out and make a good movie, or you might find yourselves in one. Understand?"

THE CHATTER OF NIGHT BUGS

They all nodded.

Grady pulled a money clip from his pants pocket. He put the cigarette in his mouth and peeled off a few greasy bills.

Tammi Jean, who was the closest to him, couldn't help but watch as his count slowed—ending on *half* of what they usually made.

"Here, this is all I'm paying for this shit," Grady said. He handed the money to Tammi Jean, who quickly passed it down to Duke.

Duke thumbed through it, realizing it was light—very light. "Ah, Grady, this is only half."

"You're fucking damn right it's half!" Grady yelled. "You fucking hicks make me look like an asshole when you turn in shit. Now I have to tell the buyer we have another fucked up movie that they're gonna have to fix. And guess what? They pay *me* less for it. Ever heard the term 'shit rolls downhill'? Well, here's a pile of shit, and guess who's at the bottom?" He'd smoked his cigarette to the filter. "If I were you, I'd take that money and invest in some fucking lighting. Because," he was pointing at them with the dead cigarette between his fingers, "another shitty movie isn't going to be good. Not for me, and certainly not for you. Count this as a blessing and get the fuck out. Call me when you have something that isn't a complete piece of shit." He put his cigarette in his mouth, not realizing it was out. Grady tossed it on the floor and grabbed another.

The sound of locks being undone broke the silence, and Tammi Jean looked over and noticed the door was open. That was their cue to get the fuck out, and they didn't need to be told twice.

The Buick started on the second turn of the key and bounced its way down the dirt road in silence.

CHAPTER 3

It had been two months since the day in the Shiners' clubhouse. It turned out the guy they'd killed, Richy, wasn't just some fucking bum. He was the estranged brother of a cop a few towns over. Cops from three counties swarmed the area, knocking on doors and interviewing everyone. Duke knew they were in the clear, but watching his reflection in a pair of Aviator sunglasses was always nerve-wracking. He was a smooth talker and a local boy; not what you'd consider 'killer material'. The girls had it easier and had been interviewed as just a formality. Of course, each wore something slightly revealing, Tammi Jean especially. Their interviews were just a chance for the out-of-town cops to ogle their tits and firm bodies.

Still, it kept business slow, knowing they couldn't make a movie soon. There were plenty of porn sites on the internet and they'd considered it, but it was dangerous. If the wrong person saw them and could figure out their bodies on the snuff film, they'd be fucked. No, they had one kind of film to make, and that was it.

Duke checked his phone. "Ladies let's go; it's time for work," he yelled.

He heard feet shuffling upstairs and Raylynn yelled down. "Hold your ass. Beauty can't be rushed. Besides, I doubt the crowd is even that big yet." She ran back as loud as an elephant.

Duke sighed and scrolled through his phone.

Their house—Tammi Jean's dead granny's house—was small but perfect. It was an old, two-story setup but private. The property wasn't that big, but it butted up to state land, meaning no one could build anywhere near it. There was some kind of protected swamp bug that lived in the wetlands. The state snatched up that parcel, protecting the critters. The house was technically where Duke and Tammi Jean lived, but Raylynn spent almost all of her time there.

THE CHATTER OF NIGHT BUGS

Her mother was a nasty cunt, and she couldn't stand being under the same roof. It didn't matter to Duke. He enjoyed having both of them under the same roof. He knew the rules, though—he couldn't fuck Raylynn if Tammi Jean weren't present—but he knew rules were broken. Often the three of them would share the king bed in the master bedroom, but if not, Raylynn would sleep in the guest room. She had to give the couple *some* alone time. She also knew Duke snored, so if they would fuck, she'd sleep alone anyway so as not to be bothered by him sawing wood all night.

Duke looked back as the girls came down the stairs. Their clothes were casual—their work clothes stayed at *Foxes*—but their makeup was done. Duke stood and put his phone in his pocket. He gave them each a look up and down. They were dressed for comfort, but he knew what lurked underneath the baggy sweats and old t-shirts. He also knew those clothes would be piled up on his bedroom floor later. When the girls danced, they almost always were horny by the end of the night. Even if they had to turn a trick or two (only hand jobs or blow jobs, they'd never fuck a customer) they would think of Duke, or at least that's what they told him.

"Looking good, ladies," he said, grabbing Tammi Jean for a kiss.

"No, no, no, I have lip stuff on," she puckered, showing him the layer of gloss. Tammi Jean fluttered her eyelashes. "Besides, I think you'll be enjoying them later."

Duke looked over her shoulder at Raylynn, who had her tongue against her cheek like she was blowing him. He hardened. "Hmm, okay," he said, clearing his throat. "Let's get going." Duke grabbed the keys off the rack by the door and walked out into the cool night air. He knew they'd all end up fucking and being late if he didn't leave soon. Besides, the girls' hair and makeup would get fucked up and take even more time to fix. As badly as Big Jake wanted to jump inside them, he knew he could wait. At least for a little while.

Foxes wasn't anything special, but it was the only strip club around. Even for them, it was in the middle of nowhere, sitting off of a dusty county route.

The main entrance was manned by a single bouncer, who may or may not check IDs, depending on their mood. That's where

Duke would stand for most of the night. The stage was square and sat in the middle of the club. A shiny pole speared the center, and the wooden floor was scuffed from years of abuse. The bar wasn't far from the dance floor, and patrons could order a drink and still ogle the flesh on stage. Chairs and tables were spread out around the room, but most customers sat alongside the stage. Along the back wall were the private rooms. Anything from a lap dance to full-on sex could happen back there and usually did. But that was up to the girls and no one else. *Foxes* took care of their girls, and it being the only titty bar in the area, the customers knew better than to fuck around. More than one patron ended up in the parking lot beaten and bloodied from getting too handsy with a girl who didn't want it. And if you weren't paying, they didn't want it.

Duke parked in the back where the employees entered. A sodium light buzzed above the entrance—a macabre ballet of night bugs smashing into the glass. "Okay, I'll see you out there," he said, leaning in to kiss Tammi Jean.

She spun her head, giving him her made-up cheek instead. "Lip stuff, remember?"

Duke kissed her and squeezed her tight ass. "I forgot."

Raylynn pushed open the door of the small changing area the girls used. Duke peered around her, hoping to glimpse some tits, but the other girls were already dressed. He would see them all in the flesh soon, but a forbidden glance was always better.

Duke walked into the bar. The sound of the dance music was loud, but not too loud. The girls still had to be heard when talking with customers, especially when money was on the line. His first stop was the bar, which Mindy was already setting up for him.

"Ah, you know me all too well," Duke said. He took the full shot glass and threw it back.

"Yeah, well, you're a creature of habit, Duke," she said, refilling his glass. Mindy was the perfect bartender for a strip club. She was short, built like a full-back and had the face of an angry dog, but she was a sweetheart. Mindy had no qualms about telling a customer to fuck off but was kind enough for the girls to cry on her shoulder. Duke didn't know if she was a lesbian, straight, a little of both, nothing at all. Mindy would eye-fuck everyone and sometimes no one. She could have a perfect pair of tits walk by her and not bat an eye. And on the next night, see a naked ass and be red in the face. She was a mystery, and Duke wasn't smart enough to crack it.

THE CHATTER OF NIGHT BUGS

Duke threw back his last shot and set the glass down. "Ah, thank you, my dear. How can I ever repay you?" He leaned in, almost seductively. Part of him wanted to fuck the old bartender just to see what it was like. A conquest that no one he knew of had had.

"Well," Mindy leaned in close. Her breath smelled like mint and menthol cigarettes. "You can start by paying for these drinks," she smirked and grabbed the shot glass.

Duke stood up straight again. "Damn, I was hoping you'd say something a little dirtier." He snapped his fingers in jest.

Mindy wiped out the shot glass and put it back with the others. She looked him up and down. "Boy, I'd snapped your dick right off," she said, tilting her head to the right. "Now get your little ass over by the door so Kenny can leave. He looks like he's about to shit his pants." She pointed over his shoulder at the doorman.

Duke followed her finger just as the song changed. It was getting late, and he knew the crowd was about to grow. Everyone in the area knew when the best and newest girls came on stage.

"Thank God," Kenny said, handing Duke an ID to check. "I gotta shit in the worst way." Rivulets of sweat darkened Kenny's hair at his sideburns and ran down his cheeks.

Duke grabbed the ID that was all but thrown at him and plucked a flashlight from his pocket. He looked at the card and back at the kid in the doorway. If he were over sixteen, Duke would be shocked.

"You got cash, kid?"

The pimply youth, who'd hopefully grow into his ears over the next year or two, patted his pants. "Yeah, I got some."

"Well, for such a shitty fake ID, the cover charge is gonna be twenty bucks," Duke said. He held the card in the air and flicked it—nearly snapping it in two.

The kid's brows furrowed like he wanted to say something but didn't. He fished a crumpled bill from his pocket and handed it to Duke.

"Ah, thank you," Duke said, handing the kid his shitty ID back. "Enjoy the night." The teen rushed towards the bar. He wouldn't be as lucky with Mindy, that was for sure.

The night ended as mundanely as any other. There weren't even any fights—between girls or patrons—which was rare. Almost every shift, Duke had to remove one or two patrons who got a little handsy with the girls. Or had to break up a cat fight in the dressing room. But that night was quiet. At least it started that way.

Tammi Jean took off her lace bra for the last time that night. She rubbed her bare breasts, squeezing them in relief at being unrestricted. Her normal outfit was being cleaned—for probably the first time in a long time—so she had to make do. She pulled on a tank top and sweatshirt, not caring about her hair anymore.

"How'd you do?" Raylynn asked. She had finished the night, even though the crowd wasn't much at closing. Her clothes were in her hand and the only thing she wore was a pair of stilettos.

Tammi Jean pulled out a wad of money from her locker. "Eh, not bad, but it could've been better."

"Goodnight, girls," Crystal, the last girl left in the changing room, said.

"'Night," both of them replied. The door closed, leaving them alone.

"It would be much better if we could make a movie. I know we can earn some coin showing our tits, but damn, those movies pay more than a month of stripping."

Raylynn hung her stage clothes in her locker and removed street clothes. "Yeah, I know. I sucked two dicks tonight in the back room and still barely broke a hundred bucks."

Tammi Jean wrinkled her nose. "I hope they were decent guys and wore rubbers."

Raylynn's voice was muffled as she pulled her shirt overhead. "Of course. I'm not that much of a whore. It was two of the young kids Duke let in. I figured they'd never had a suck job, at least one on my level," she put a proud hand to her chest. "Plus, I thought they'd have money, which they did not. One gave me forty and the other only had thirty-three left. Drunks threw the rest at me." She finished dressing and put her shoes on. "A movie or two would really help. And now that we have the extra lights, it should be even better."

"Yeah, Duke went all out on the lights after Grady fucked us. Let's hope they are worth it."

The door banged open without a knock, Duke following behind it. "Damn, I'm too late," he said, looking at their clothed bodies.

THE CHATTER OF NIGHT BUGS

"Hey, dipshit, we've been naked half the night up on stage," Tammi Jean laughed.

Duke moved forward and wrapped his arm around her waist. "Yeah, but this is more like a secret place. Forbidden, even." He leaned in and kissed her deeply. Duke's left arm snaked out and found Raylynn pulling her into the little group. He broke the kiss with Tammi Jean and kissed Raylynn.

Tammi Jean pushed him away. "Down, boy," she said. They knew if the kissing kept up, they'd be fucking in the dressing room. While it had happened before, they didn't want to make a habit out of it. Besides, Tammi Jean was horny and really couldn't get off in the dingy room that smelled like sweat and cheap perfume. "We'll take care of this at home."

"Tease," Duke said. He pulled her in for a last kiss but let her go. He removed his phone from his pocket and checked the time. "Well, let's get the fuck out of here and bring this party back to the house. Mindy should be done soon, so she'll lock up."

The girls rechecked their lockers and headed towards the backdoor with Duke in tow.

The parking lot was empty—except for the Buick and Mindy's truck—which was good. Sometimes a patron would fall in love with a girl and wait for her. And since Raylynn sucked off two teenagers who'd probably never felt a tit before, it was a real possibility they had a case of puppy love.

The night air was chilly, and they quickly jumped into the big car. Duke slid behind the wheel, and Tammi Jean reached for the heat right away.

Dull headlights cut through the gloom of the night. Streetlights didn't exist near *Foxes* and weren't much of a staple, even in town.

Tammi Jean rested her head against the window—her breath fogging the glass. She dozed off, knowing they had a long drive. *Foxes* wasn't close to anything, let alone home.

"Oh, what the fuck?" Duke said. The car slowed down as Tammi Jean was yanked from her stupor.

Flashing emergency lights and road flares lit up the night. The Buick's headlights reflected off of a bright traffic vest worn by the Sheriff's Deputy standing in the street.

Duke slowed to a stop as the deputy put his hand up. He rolled the window down.

"Evening, folks," the young cop said, leaning into the car.

"Is there a problem, sir?" Tammi Jean said across Duke. She had a sweatshirt on, but if she didn't she'd have her tits on full display.

"Well, ma'am, there is," he squatted lower to see her fully. "About two miles up the road," he pointed towards a beacon of flashing lights further in the distance. "A tractor trailer jackknifed on the bridge, blocking the whole damn thing. No one was too badly hurt, thank God, but it's gonna take us all night to get that rig out of here." He looked at Duke. "Your best bet is to turn around and look for another way home."

"Fuck," Duke whispered. "Okay, sir, thank you." He put the window up as the deputy backed away from the car. "What now?"

Raylynn had her phone out and a scowl on her face. "Fucking *Foxes*," she grumbled. Her face was lit by the screen as she looked up at them. "The shortest route around that fucking bridge adds another half hour onto our drive." She held up the phone, showing them the route.

Duke took it from her and looked for himself. "Fuck me, that's damn near outta the state." He stuck the phone in the cupholder and put the car in reverse.

Tammi Jean sighed and leaned against the window, watching her breath cloud the night.

Raylynn hated sleeping in the car, but her body had other ideas. After twenty minutes of driving on rutted back roads and the low crooning of an old Elvis album, her eyes closed. A night of dancing for drunks and sucking cock had her feeling drained. She knew that once they got home, showered and had a drink, they'd all get their second wind. It wouldn't be a long night anyway—the sex would be fast and satisfying—not one of the drawn-out marathons they'd had in the past. No, it would be right to the point, and straight to bed.

Raylynn felt weightless. She was just on the cusp of sleep; the barrier where you see and hear the dreams in the distance, calling you to join them.

"What the fuck is this?" Duke said, slapping the steering wheel.

Raylynn snapped awake, not knowing if she'd heard his grumblings in a dream or not. The slowing of the car let her know it wasn't a dream.

THE CHATTER OF NIGHT BUGS

"What's going on?" she asked. Flashing lights shone in the distance, but they weren't police lights or even a firetruck—they were hazards of a broken-down car.

Tammi Jean stretched and yawned, her hands touching the droopy headliner of the car. "Just go around it," she said.

An old Honda Civic sat partially in the travel lane with its flashers on.

Duke looked at Tammi Jean as the car slowed down. "We could use the money from another movie," he said.

Raylynn popped her head in between the seats. She was fully awake and stifled a yawn with the back of her hand.

"I know, but we don't even know who this is. We need to be a little pickier with our movie stars. That last fucker had some heat brought down on us," Tammi Jean said.

"Oh please, that was nothing," Duke replied. "We've had worse than that before. That was a witch hunt and an excuse for a couple of horny cops to look at you two as your tits were hanging out. They had no chance of catching us then or now. As long as this isn't a local, I think we should go for it." The Buick was crunching shoulder gravel as it slowed behind the disabled import. "Look, if it's someone we know, we help them. If not, Raylynn can charm them into the car."

"I think we should do it, Tams," Raylynn said. Her heart was racing, and they hadn't even seen who was in the car yet. It was a crapshoot but part of the excitement. She was already feeling the high of killing, of filming and fucking. The cabin floor hard on her back as she lay under Duke or kneeled in front of him. The smell of sex, clean mountain air and death. It was getting her hot, and she knew if she touched herself, she'd be slick with lust.

The Buick stopped—its headlights illuminated the interior of the Honda. A person—a woman by the looks of the long hair and feminine profile—sat in the driver's seat.

"Oh shit, it's a chick," Raylynn shrieked. "We haven't had a good one in a while. Plus, you know chick-flicks always sell better. Especially if Duke gives'em a good fuck while we're cutting them up."

"Ugh, I hate doing that," Duke groaned. He activated the Buick's hazards as well—safety first. "I can't stand wearing rubbers and I know I have to with them. I don't want some backwoods-cockrot."

"Okay, no fucking her, maybe. But we'll see how the night goes," Raylynn said.

The driver's side door of the Honda opened. A thin pair of nude legs—tan and muscled—shone in the headlights.

Raylynn held her breath. The girl was stunning, standing next to the broken car.

She was tall—taller than her and Tammi Jean. Her hair was raven-black, and her skin was the color of coffee with a splash of milk. A gem sat on her chest, reflecting the headlights with an amber glow. The woman put her hand up to block the lights but didn't move from the car. She had an air of caution about her.

"Damn, she's pretty fucking hot," Duke said.

Raylynn looked at his grin and knew he was reconsidering fucking this chick before they killed her.

"Yeah, she's okay," Tammi Jean said, looking at her boyfriend with a side-eye.

"Well, anyone know her?" Raylynn asked. She had one hand on the door handle. If they didn't move fast, the girl would get spooked, and the night would be ruined. There would be a fight in her car, which they couldn't decontaminate if needed.

"Nope," Duke said. He looked at Tammi Jean, whose eyes were back on their next victim.

"Let's fucking do it," Tammi Jean said.

Raylynn didn't need anything else. She jumped out of the car and closed the door hard behind her. It wasn't to scare the girl, but quite the opposite. It was to let her know she was coming. That help had arrived.

"Need some help?" Raylynn asked. The cool mountain air blew, causing her to wrap her arms around her chest.

The woman's shoulders relaxed, and her face softened as she heard Raylynn's voice.

"Oh yeah," the woman said. "This shitbox broke down and I have no fucking clue what to do. Not to mention this," she held up a cell phone that was at least four models old, "can't seem to find a tower. I was just getting ready to walk, but then you showed up."

Raylynn looked around. The road was desolate, with just the shadows of woods and mountains for company. "Walking? Where the fuck were ya gonna walk to?" She smirked.

The woman shrugged, making her necklace shimmer again.

THE CHATTER OF NIGHT BUGS

"I'm not sure, but I wasn't gonna sit here all night. I probably would've gotten service on my phone at some point."

A brief silence passed between the young women. "Oh, I'm sorry. My name is Raylynn."

Raylynn stepped closer and extended her hand.

"Sadie," the woman said, shaking Raylynn's hand.

Sadie's hand was rough, almost like a laborer's. Raylynn didn't find it odd, as many women in their neck of the woods had to pull double duty. Especially single women or those with deadbeat husbands.

"That's a cool necklace," Raylynn said, pointing to the amber charm on Sadie's neck.

Sadie scrunched her face as if she didn't know what Raylynn was talking about. "Oh, this?" she asked, reaching down. She held up the charm—a smooth piece of amber with a black smudge in the middle. "Yeah, this was a gift from my gran." The amber danced in the light, but the black section, which looked like an eyeball, didn't move. "She's into that *stuff*, if you know what I mean."

Raylynn knew what she meant—pow-wow, folk magic, home remedies, curses. You name it, she'd heard it. It wasn't uncommon in their part of the world, even though the rest of civilization had moved on.

Raylynn chuckled. "Oh yeah, I've heard all about it. Mostly nonsense," she winced, hoping she didn't offend Sadie. It was a lot harder to kill someone whom you'd pissed off. "But I know some of it is legit."

Sadie smiled and let the pendant drop back to her chest. "Yeah, my gran believes in it, that's for sure. I'm kinda on the fence." Another cold mountain breeze raced across the road. Both women hugged themselves against the chill. "The one thing I believe in is this fucking wind."

"Me too," Raylynn said. "Well, you're more than welcome to join us." She pointed over her shoulder towards the Buick.

"Us?" Sadie asked.

"Oh yeah, my two friends are in the car. We just got off work and hit a detour by the old bridge about twenty minutes thataway," she nodded in the direction they'd come from. "You can jump in with us and we'll drop you off along the way. Or you can wait for cell service or hoof it out of here."

Sadie looked around like she was weighing her options. She

sighed, knowing she only had one real choice. "Just let me grab my stuff."

Raylynn made sure Sadie was in the car, grabbing her purse before giving a thumbs up to Duke and Tammi Jean.

"All good?" Raylynn asked as Sadie shut the car door and locked it.

"Yup." Sadie slung her purse over her shoulder. "It's not like I have much. I don't even know why I bother locking the car. Hell, if they can get it running, they can have it," she said. Sadie smirked, but it was pained.

Another cool mountain breeze bullied past them, causing both young women to shiver.

"Come on, let's get in the car. At least it's warm," Raylynn said.

The dome light lit up when the back door opened. Raylynn and Sadie climbed in, immediately thawing out from the cold.

"Sadie, this is Duke and Tammi Jean."

"Nice to meet you, and thanks again for stopping," Sadie said.

Duke looked back at her. "Our pleasure. We couldn't just leave you stranded out here. Who knows how long you'd have waited for another car to pass."

Tammi Jean craned her neck, looking the woman up and down—her eyes lingering on the pendant around Sadie's neck. "Yeah, there are a lot of creeps out, and a pretty girl can never be too careful."

"Oh, I know it," Sadie said. "My grandmother has been harping on being safe since I was a girl. Her form of safety is things like this." She picked up the pendant around her neck. "Some pow-wow magic or whatever. I'm not the biggest believer, but it goes way back in my family. I wear it for her. Just to keep her happy, mainly. But it is pretty cool."

Raylynn looked at the strange pendant and reached up to touch it. Her eyes felt drawn to it—the black spot in the center almost hypnotizing her. "Yeah, it's really neat. Definitely something unique for sure." The urge to yank it from her neck was almost too strong. She snapped out of the fugue when Sadie gently pulled the pendant from her hand. Raylynn chuckled and let it go, but Sadie's glare lingered.

"Anyway," Sadie said, adjusting the pendant against her skin, "I don't believe in that, but I believe in protection." She patted her purse. "I keep an old steak knife in here. It's not much, but it usually keeps the freaks away."

THE CHATTER OF NIGHT BUGS

Raylynn nodded. "A girl can never be too cautious."

"Absolutely not," Tammi Jean said. "Duke is our protection." She put her hand on his thigh. "But if we didn't have him around, we'd both be packing heat. Right, Ray?"

"Eh, I'm not sure if I could carry a gun—too scary. But I would consider pepper spray. So, I guess that's packing heat too."

All three of them giggled at the weak joke. Raylynn knew they needed to keep Sadie relaxed and not paying attention to where they were. The big car rumbled down the battered roads, but when the turn to take them back towards civilization came and went, Sadie didn't notice. She didn't notice when the mountains looked closer, and the road narrowed.

Raylynn could see Duke's eyes in the rearview. They were predatory and sexy, something she'd grown to love about him. His lust for sex was just slightly higher than murder. Raylynn knew she and Tammi Jean were going to get fucked and fucked hard later. Her pulse quickened at the thought, and she swallowed hard, just thinking about Duke's cock filling her throat.

"Fuck!" Duke said. The car slowed down as he guided it to the shoulder. The flashers clicked, and amber light danced against the dark trees surrounding them.

"What, what is it?" Tammi Jean asked.

Raylynn and Sadie looked around, thinking maybe they'd hit something or there was an engine issue.

Duke reached under the dash and popped the trunk. "You didn't feel it?"

"Ah, was I supposed to?" Tammi Jean asked.

Duke shook his head, but there was a little jovialness to his smirk. "Women. Can't take'em anywhere. We have a flat. I thought it was pulling a little after we picked up Sadie," he shot a thumb towards the backseat. "I probably ran over a nail or something when I pulled over."

"Oh no, I'm sorry," Sadie apologized. "I feel like a piece of shit now."

Raylynn put a hand on her shoulder. "Hey, it's not your fault. Besides, this car is a hunk of shit, and these roads are ass. We probably ran something over in the parking lot of the club earlier. Or one of the many potholes ripped the bald tires this thing is rolling on."

Duke stepped out of the car and wandered towards the trunk.

Sadie watched. "I should help him. I feel so dumb, especially since my car shouldn't have been on the road." She reached for the door handle. "I knew I shouldn't have been out that far with it." The cold air rushed in as Sadie stepped out.

Raylynn looked at Tammi Jean and smiled.

Sadie wasn't much of a mechanic. If she were, maybe her car wouldn't have broken down. Or at least she would've been able to fix it and not end up stranded. It didn't matter. These people helped her, and she was raised to respect people. Especially those who went out of their ways to help others. Besides, Duke was kind of cute. Not that she'd try anything, considering she'd seen Tammi Jean's hand in his lap earlier, but it was still nice to be close to him.

Her love life hadn't been in full swing lately. Her last boyfriend cheated on her, knocking up some skank he met on his trucking route. The one before that liked to choke her and not in a consensual, sexual way. No, like in a way where she couldn't swallow without burning for a week and had to wear turtlenecks to work. The other girls at work thought she had hickies, hence the reason for the out-of-season shirts. If only she were that lucky. The only one who knew was her grandmother. Sadie started wearing the pendant that day forward, at her grandmother's insistence and tearful pleas. It must've worked, especially to ward off assholes, because she never saw her abusive ex again. Poof, he vanished and disappeared. Not that Sadie tried hard to find him. In fact, she did everything possible to avoid him and that stupid fucking truck he drove. The thing would belch out black smoke like a train and was obnoxiously loud. So, it was pretty easy to avoid.

Sadie didn't want the necklace at first, thinking it corny and tacky, but she knew what it meant to her grandmother. And since they were the last members of their family (at least the ones who got along) she wore it. Before long, Sadie didn't even realize it was there. It became a part of her, as if it were another appendage. When Raylynn had first mentioned it, it took her a minute to realize what she'd even been talking about.

Duke was leaning in the trunk, moving stuff around.

"Need a hand?" Sadie asked.

Duke looked over his shoulder at her. "Oh, hey, thanks. Yeah,

THE CHATTER OF NIGHT BUGS

I'm just trying to get to the spare tire, but it's buried under all of this shit."

Sadie noticed a tangle of lights in the trunk. She didn't realize Duke had a tire iron in his hand.

Duke spun and the only thing Sadie saw in the red of the taillights was a glimmer of steel. Pain erupted from her jaw, which suddenly felt out of place. The stars were in front of her eyes, and she had the sick sensation of falling, like when you're having a nightmare. Her head hit the asphalt, and everything went black.

"Holy fuck, Duke," Raylynn said. She and Tammi Jean jumped out when they saw the hit. They needed to make sure Sadie was unconscious and tied up before putting her in the trunk. They would've much rather used pills, but they were out. Besides, they didn't have anything to mix them with either and it was doubtful Sadie was as trusting as Richy. "Did you kill her?"

Duke looked at the tire iron in his hand. The hit was good, a little too good. When he saw her jaw shift, he thought it may have been a mistake to use the steel bar. But the life in her eyes as she was dropping made him feel better. At least she was alive on the way down.

As if on cue, Sadie let out a wet, rough snore. Her jaw was askew and the flesh split, but she was alive.

"There's your answer," Duke said. He pointed at the unconscious woman with the tire iron. "Now tie her up and let's get to the cabin before she comes to."

Tammi Jean had a roll of duct tape in her hands and she and Raylynn had Sadie bound in seconds.

They tossed her in the trunk with all the new lighting equipment. There would be no shadows in their next film, that was for sure. Sadie was about to become a movie star.

CHAPTER 4

PAIN.

Sadie was in pain, and she was cold. Her senses came back slowly, but each moment revealed a new hell.

Her mouth was on fire and tasted like motor oil. She moved her tongue, but something was wrong. Something felt *off*, like really off. Her tongue was dry and felt like sandpaper. With it, she probed her mouth and touched a front tooth. Except it wasn't a front tooth, it was a molar. Searching, her tongue slithered around, confused at the new oral setup. The taste of blood greeted her next as she discovered a few shattered teeth. Electric pain shot through her face when her tongue touched the exposed pulp of her broken incisor.

Sadie didn't know where she was, but even through her eyelids she knew it was bright. Bright, yet cold. Too cold, as if she were nude. Never a fan of sleeping naked, Sadie knew something was wrong. The few times she fell asleep naked was usually after a wild and drunken fuck, where she didn't have the energy to get dressed. She felt neither drunk nor sexually satisfied at the moment, so she didn't think that was the case.

Her mind was foggy, but bits and pieces returned. Something about her car. An accident, maybe? Could she have been in an accident, hit the steering wheel with her face and be in a hospital right now? She knew EMTs would often cut clothes off of patients to check for injuries or to use specific equipment. But there was no beeping and the voices she heard were distant murmurs. Her head was throbbing, but she didn't think she was in motion, like being in the back of an ambulance. No, something else had happened.

The Buick! her mind screamed and flashed. *Three people in a big car. The fucking tire iron!*

Sadie's eyes fluttered opened and were assaulted by strings of

THE CHATTER OF NIGHT BUGS

high intensity lights. She blinked, but her eyes watered. A low moan escaped her throat, which was raw and dry.

"Ah, our star has arrived," a voice said, from the area of Sadie's feet. She looked down and realized she was naked. Not just topless, but completely nude. The only thing left on her was the pendant, which sat cold on her left breast. Immediately, she moved to cover herself, but her hands were stuck. Cold shackles held her hands in place. She tried to move her legs, but found they had the same fate.

"We didn't know when you were gonna wake up, sleepyhead," Tammi Jean said, walking into her field of view. She brushed an errant strand of dark hair from Sadie's face, pushing it behind her ear. "We thought we were gonna have to start with you asleep, but now that you're up, we can really get this party going."

Sadie was still confused. Her rattled brain seemed like it had short-circuited from the attack. They seemed so nice in the car, but now she didn't know what was going on. Tears—not from the intensity of the lights—stung her eyes.

"Pease, ret me gah," Sadie groaned. Each word was ripe with fresh pain and her mouth wouldn't cooperate.

"Aw, don't worry, sweetheart. We are going to let you go. You just won't be alive anymore and it'll be at the reservoir's bottom." She accented her statement with a tap on Sadie's nose.

Raylynn stood behind a camera and looked at the back of it. "Okay, she's good, the lighting is good, and damn," she said, looking around the camera at Sadie's nude flesh, "those tan titties look amazing." Raylynn clapped her hands. "I know, let's cut them off."

Sadie moaned and thrashed, which only caused more pain.

"Yeah, let's start with them. Gag'er with'em."

"Oh, you nasty bitch," Raylynn laughed. "I love it."

"Okay, okay," Duke said, as he pulled the masks out. "Are we ready to get going?"

Raylynn checked the camera one more time and gave the thumbs up. She grabbed a long fillet knife and put it against Sadie's cheek, just under her eyeball.

"Oh, we're gonna have so much fun with you. You're gonna be a big star, my dear."

Sadie drooled blood and saliva, but her eyes were locked on Raylynn's.

"Oo, cun!" Sadie spat. It was worth it, even though she

grimaced with pain. She wouldn't give into them. She wouldn't play their fucking games. She'd finished crying and regretted every tear she'd shed. Her granny hadn't raised a fucking pussy and she wouldn't start with it now. No, Sadie would hold firm; she'd fight and keep stoic.

When she saw Duke pick up the belt sander, she knew she was full of shit.

Tammi Jean wished they'd invested in a space heater and not so many damn lights. The small cabin looked like the surface of the sun but felt as cold as the moon. Nighttime temps were plummeting and soon there'd be snow in the mountains. No matter: they had a movie to make, and she knew she'd soon be warm.

Making movies—fucking and killing—always warmed her up. It was just the preamble leading up to it that made her shiver.

Raylynn was behind the camera, preparing to record. She'd already put on her deer mask and was waiting for Tammi Jean to don hers before recording.

Tammi Jean looked down at the cheap mask in her hand. Those shitty masks were the last thing so many people had seen before their gruesome deaths. Moans of pleasure mixing with their cries of agony as the three of them would fuck into oblivion. She wondered how it was going to be that night. Her pussy was already wet thinking about it, knowing soon Duke would be deep inside of her. The way he was looking at Sadie made her think he might try to fuck her, too. Tammi Jean didn't think that was gonna fly with her, but she'd see how it played out. There was no use arguing during filming, and since they'd fucked up the last two movies, they couldn't afford a third.

Tammi Jean pulled the mask over her face and noticed Duke had donned his. He also had a battery powered belt sander in his hand.

Damn, he wants to get messy right away, she thought.

"And . . . action," Raylynn said. The red light, the eye of death, lit up on the camera.

As if she were a part of the crew and not about to be horribly murdered, Sadie renewed her begging. Albeit quite fucked up

THE CHATTER OF NIGHT BUGS

because of her facial injuries. "Prease, ret me go," she begged. "Oo don't want to do this." She pulled against the cuffs, but only reddened her wrists and ankles. The pendant danced over her breasts with each attempt to free herself.

Duke turned his head like a dog hearing a whistle, playing into the fox mask he was wearing. He positioned himself by her feet and turned the belt sander on.

The tool whirred to life as the rough strip spun in a blur.

Sadie turned her feet away, seeing the belt lower towards her exposed digits.

Tammi Jean's heart was pounding, and she was already warming up. She watched her man prepare to maim an innocent woman, and it turned her on. It always turned her on. When Raylynn's hand cupped her right breast, she jumped, not realizing the other woman had been that close. Tammi Jean moaned as Raylynn teased her nipple through her shirt, pulling it taut. Her fingers found Raylynn's hair and pulled her in for a kiss. The masks hit but didn't move. Their tongues darted out, tasting each other, knowing they'd be exploring other holes soon.

Sadie screamed.

Tammi Jean looked out of the corner of her eye as Raylynn's lips explored her neck, working down her chest. The sander's belt—which had started as blue—was now streaked with crimson. Duke grimaced as he pushed harder, taking the rest of Sadie's big toe down to a nub of mangled flesh and shredded bone.

A coldness kissed Tammi Jean's stomach, and she realized Raylynn had lifted her shirt. She raised her arms, allowing it to be pulled up and over her head. Raylynn's mouth and hands went to work. Tammi Jean licked her lips, tasting the other woman on them, as Raylynn took her left nipple into her mouth.

Sadie screamed again as Duke began sanding off more toes. His accuracy was waning as he watched Raylynn suck Tammi Jean's tits. Rather than select a specific toe, he was blindly sanding, breaking smaller bones and tearing flesh with abandon.

Tammi Jean noticed the bulge in his pants and knew it would be his turn soon. She looked around for the fillet knife Raylynn had had earlier and saw it resting on the table. With a fistful of hair, she pulled Raylynn from her breast like a suckling babe. They locked eyes and smiled.

Duke tossed the gore-soaked sander to the side. Bits of gristle and blood dangled from the power tool. He was breathing heavily, even though it wasn't much work. Killing could be tiring. Duke gestured toward his cock, letting them both know Big Jake needed attention.

Tammi Jean walked past the bound woman and stopped at the table. Her eyes first caught sight of the fillet knife, but something else struck her. An idea—a savage idea—burst into her twisted mind. Her fingers went past the blade and grabbed a bore brush.

The brush wasn't meant for your hair. That was easy to see. It was about an inch long and round, like a cylinder. She'd seen them used many of the times for their intended purpose, cleaning out the barrel of a shotgun. The bristles were thick wire and the handle on the brush was just about two feet long. Perfect for getting those hard-to-reach places in a gun or fucking a woman with.

Raylynn smiled, knowing exactly what her friend was up to. They'd talked about using the brush before, but female victims weren't that easy to come by. And neither of them wanted to stick it up a hairy ass of the many guys that had died there. Raylynn picked up the fillet knife again. She bent down and whispered in Sadie's ear.

"I'm gonna take those nice tits right off." She scraped the edge of the blade over Sadie's puckered nipple. The tip of the knife brushed against the leather string from which the pendant hung. "Oh, and I think I'll take a nice souvenir first." She sliced the leather, releasing the pendant.

"Fuck oo," Sadie spat. Her face was a mess, mixed with blood and tears.

Raylynn tied the leather around her neck, resting the pendant right between her breasts. "There, it looks better on me anyway, don'cha think?"

Tammi Jean grabbed Duke by the cock and pulled him to the base of the table, near Sadie's mangled feet. She dropped onto her knees, but Duke was already one step ahead of her. His fingers worked his snap and zipper in one motion as he yanked his pants down. Tammi Jean was nearly smacked in the face with Big Jake as it came towards her drooling a line of pre-cum.

Hungrily, she took Duke's cock into her mouth. The bulbous glans filled her throat like she'd swallowed a plum. There was no reason for her to blow him—he was already plenty hard, and she was dripping wet—but she knew it was good for the camera.

THE CHATTER OF NIGHT BUGS

Duke groaned and whimpered as she sucked him and paused. Tammi Jean stood up and turned around, pulling her pants down. She stood nude, with the bore brush in her hand. Sadie's pussy stared at her as she bent over the table, giving Duke and the camera a perfect view of her sex and ass.

Tammi Jean reached back and grabbed Big Jake, pulling Duke forward. She guided his massive cock into her as she lined the bore brush with Sadie's vagina.

Sadie jammed her legs shut as the bristles touched her thighs. The wires slipped into her flesh as easily as Duke had slid into Tammi Jean.

"Fuck!" Sadie shouted. Her reflexes kicked in and she yanked her thighs apart. Dozens of little pinholes dotted her flesh, weeping drops of blood.

Tammi Jean felt herself stretching with pleasure and pain as Duke unceremoniously rammed himself into her. As badly as she wanted to enjoy his rough fucking, they had a movie to make. She composed herself and used her free hand to open Sadie's lips. Without hesitation, she drove the bore brush into the woman's vagina.

Sadie screamed. Blood poured from her sex as the brush drove deeper.

Tammi Jean held it firm, and every time Duke railed her, the brush went deeper.

In and out.

Blood and meat.

Flesh ripped, and soon Sadie's vagina was a gory mess of meat and pubic hair. It didn't stop Tammi Jean. It made her fucking even better. Watching the brush tear Sadie apart as Duke ravaged her. It was all too much.

Raylynn felt just a twinge of jealousy but knew she shouldn't—they were a couple anyway. The sound of wet sex and torture filled the room. A smell of blood and shit—she assumed Sadie had lost control of her bowels—permeated the air. Raylynn knew the woman couldn't take much more, and she'd made a promise she would keep. She was going to take her tits.

Raylynn grabbed Sadie's nipple and lifted her breast. She put the fillet knife to the base of it and sliced, like she was cutting up a fish.

Sadie grunted and her eyes rolled into the back of her head. Her body seized and foam began running from her mouth. She bit her tongue, severing it with a drool of gore.

"Oh fuck," Raylynn muttered. She tossed the breast, which oozed yellow fat and blood, across the room.

"I'm gonnn cum," Duke grunted.

Raylynn knew that was her cue. Quickly, she sliced off the other breast from the quaking woman and dropped the knife. She rushed over and fell to her knees next to Duke, her mouth open, waiting.

"No, fill me up," Tammi Jean said. The bore brush lay in a puddle of mushy shit, piss, and blood at the base of Sadie's desecrated sex. "Eat it from me," she said, looking at Raylynn.

Duke grunted one last time, as he drove Big Jake so far into Tammi Jean, Raylynn thought she could see it in the woman's stomach. Then he was still. His cock throbbed as it deposited spunk into Tammi Jean. He pulled out, bringing with him an ooze of slimy jizz and pussy juice.

Raylynn slid over, pushing him out of the way. He stumbled—his pants still around his ankles. She spread Tammi Jean open, giving all the pervs a look at her dripping pussy. Raylynn ate her and the camera watched, unblinking.

Sadie's dead eyes saw nothing. They gazed at the ceiling, still wet with tears of agony. Her eyes saw nothing, but another eye—the one resting on Raylynn's chest—saw all.

CHAPTER 5

IT HAD BEEN two days since anyone had heard from Sadie. Renee knew her granddaughter had a wild side, but it was unordinary to not at least check in. Maybe when Sadie was in her teens, but not now that she was growing up.

Renee sat in her old recliner, a smoldering cigarette in the ashtray on the end table next to her. A game show flashed colorfully on the old tube TV, but she hadn't been paying attention. Renee sat lost and staring at nothing, her mind racing—her fingers itching to use the magic.

When she'd given Sadie the pendant—the identical one rested on her chest— she promised she wouldn't use it to spy on her. Sadie was a bit of a skeptic, dismissing the old ways of their ancestors, but to Renee, it was as natural as the sunrise. She promised her granddaughter that she would only use the pendant for an emergency—something that was a fail-safe for modern technology. Renee picked up the phone sitting next to the ashtray. The cigarette had gone out, leaving only the filter behind. She punched in Sadie's number slowly, ensuring she had it right. She did that, she knew.

The phone rang only once before it was picked up.

Renee thought her heart would explode. She sat forward on the chair, the receiver clenched to her ear. "Sad—" she began.

"Hey, this is Sadie. I'm probably doing something cooler than talking to you, so if you leave a message, I might call you back. Or just text me, weirdo." The phone beeped.

Renee's lip quivered. The sound of her granddaughter's voice echoed in her brain. The last member of her family, missing. She wanted to leave a message, to tell her how much she loved her and wanted her to return home but didn't. She knew Sadie would make fun of her for it, returning home safe and sound, joking with her old Gran about how scared she was. Renee would give anything to hear Sadie pick on her now. To scold her and make jokes at her expense. Gently, she lowered the receiver onto the cradle. Renee grabbed her cigarette, but it was out. Her fingers shook as she plucked another from the pack and put it against her dry lips. The lighter wavered.

No, no, something is wrong. This isn't a little jaunt that she took with a few friends. No, she's missing, I know it. And Renee did. She felt it in her old bones. Call it second sight, or just intuition, but ever since she'd been a little girl, Renee could *feel* things. She knew when someone was going to get pregnant or hurt. Or when her dog, Bingo, was going to get hit by a car on her dusty street as a girl. She even saw the image of her daddy—long since dead—shoot the crippled dog with a shotgun as it came, dragging its mangled legs back into the yard. Renee knew things, but she also had a way to be certain.

The cigarette crackled as she pulled deep, standing up. She smashed it into the ashtray alongside the others. Her chair creaked and rocked as her weight left it.

Her kitchen was small but was plenty big for her and Sadie. They didn't do much complicated cooking, so some cabinets were sparse. Except for one. That was Renee's cabinet. She opened it, and gazed upon the array of jars, vials, and pouches. Random pottery was scattered, along with feathers, animal hides, bits of stone and a few crystals. Renee knew what she needed, and her fingers snatched everything. She went to work right there, mixing liquid and powder into a mortar. Renee chanted as she worked, combining it all. Her hands were steady, but her heart raced. She felt something bad, something evil. Whatever had happened to Sadie wasn't good. She knew it the first night the girl hadn't returned, but she had to see, to know for sure. Part of her couldn't *feel* her granddaughter anymore. Like she'd been a candle that went out. Poof. Gone in a flash and puff of smoke. Renee hoped she was wrong, even prayed to whatever god would listen. This, this was how she'd find out for sure. Then she'd figure out what to do next.

The concoction was nearly done. Renee dumped the slurry into a small, fine screen, separating the liquid from the chunks. A few drops of blood-colored fluid landed in a small bowl. Renee reached into the cabinet and removed one last jar: Sadie's tears. It had been a struggle to convince her to give them to Renee, but eventually,

THE CHATTER OF NIGHT BUGS

she won. The jar only had a few drops, but Renee only needed one to make this work. Gently, she used an eyedropper to gather a tear. She put it into the mixture and stirred. Renee filled the eyedropper with the completed mixture, whispered another incantation and put two drops into each eye.

Renee blinked, allowing her eyeballs to be coated with it. Her hand wrapped around the pendant, and she closed her eyes. And opened her mind . . .

. . . *the car wouldn't start. Dead on the side of the road. Another car with young folks, seem nice, but stink of evil. No choice, have to go or be stranded. The car, a Buick, smelled of cheap perfume, smoke and badness. The tire. Have to help, it's my fault. The hit, the pain. Can't breathe, can't see. Cold, naked. Their faces clear, staring at my nudity. Animals—a fox, a mouse, a deer. Scared, so fucking scared. Pain. My body, the sander. My toes . . . gone. Never do ballet again, even if I wanted to. The knife, the brush, the invasion of my body. My world growing dark. I'm so fucking scared right now. Gran, help me!*

Renee opened her eyes and collapsed on the floor. "No. No. No," she moaned. Fresh tears mixed with the concoction, making look like she was weeping blood. "My baby, they took my baby." Snot flowed freely, wetting her lips. Her mouth hung agape, and drool fell onto her lap. "What did they do to you? Fucking monsters!" she shrieked. The images were burned into her mind. The pain, the fear, the blood.

The faces of the killers. Oh yes, they were there too, and they were oh so clear.

Renee let it hurt. She let it burrow into her mind. An insidious worm of grief, morphing into pure hatred. Their time would come, of that she was certain, but she needed to mourn.

Renee laid on the kitchen floor and wept.

Renee didn't check the time, nor did she care. It was night; that's all that mattered. The woods were dark, but the cold moon shone bright above. Renee didn't shiver, even though she was nude. Her body was warm with rage. Even her feet, which rested on stone, felt made of fire. The only thing she wore was the pendant around her neck.

DANIEL J. VOLPE

The blaze she'd created was out and growing cold. Her incantation was complete, but she didn't know if it had been heard. She would wait, though. She'd wait forever for vengeance.

The night was still and only a few of the normal bugs made any chatter. The cool air kept them at bay, but some of them skittered and crawled. Renee closed her eyes, her lips moved in silence. A sound, just barely audible, caught her ear. The sound of wings flapping. She opened her eyes and looked.

A moth the size of her hand fluttered. Gently, she put her hand out, allowing it to land. It was delicate, but Renee knew its true power. The insect faced away from her and spread its wings. A skull—a death's head—stared back at her.

Renee watched the insect open and close its wings. Without warning, the moth flew away into the darkness.

Renee gazed up at the moon, her faithful companion. The moonbeams bathed her in silver as the woods came alive. The night bugs sang and cried, multiplying with every second. A dead branch cracked, followed by another.

Renee looked into the inky dark of the woods. Something was coming towards her. Something big.

She clenched the pendant around her neck and smiled.

CHAPTER 6

"We're gonna get fucking paid on this one, I know it," Duke said. He parked the Buick behind the clubhouse and killed the engine.

After killing Sadie and dumping her body, they'd watched the movie. It was perfect, every part. The lighting was just what they needed and really set it off. Sadie's pain and fear was captured perfectly, and the gore was top-notch. He thought Tammi Jean was sick with the bore brush, but it was perfect, especially paired up with him railing her. Raylynn cutting Sadie's tits off was another brutal scene, really adding to the film. And of course, him pumping a hot load into Tammi Jean and watching Raylynn eat it out of her was the icing on the cake.

Duke was getting hard thinking about that and the wild fuck session they had afterwards. He knew he'd probably be hard watching the movie again in the Shiner's clubhouse in the next few minutes. Those two girls were in for a pounding when they got home—got home with the cash they were about to make.

"You have something good this time?" R.J. asked. He stood by the door of the clubhouse.

Duke pulled the SD card from his jacket pocket. "My friend, your boss and the clients who buy this are gonna shit. This is our best yet, by far."

R.J. unlocked the door but didn't open it. "I hope so. Grady wasn't too thrilled with you last time." He stepped closer. "And when people piss him off, they have a habit of disappearing." He nodded a little, raising his eyebrows. "Understand?" the young man said.

Duke didn't know if it was a friendly warning or a threat. Possibly a combination of both. R.J. was practically a kid, so it was a little hard to take him seriously. Although the gun he carried seemed legit enough.

"Got it," Duke said.

"Hey, what's the hold up?" Tammi Jean asked. She had her arms across her chest. "This fucking weather is all over the place and I'm freezing my tits off."

Raylynn stood next to her, a cigarette in her mouth. She inhaled and dropped it on the ground, extinguishing it with her shoe. "Well, at least you have plenty to spare." She looked at R.J. "But seriously, let us in."

R.J. smiled and pulled the door open.

Grady and Roger sat at a table, their heads close, whispering.

They stopped and looked up at the newcomers. Grady said something to Roger and patted him on the shoulder. "Well, I hope you three have something better for me this time," Grady said. He leaned back in his chair and lit up a cigarette.

Roger stood and walked over to them, holding out his hand.

"Here it is, my man," Duke said. He handed the SD card to Roger, who took it without a word. "And yes, this is our best yet," Duke said, looking at Grady. "We found this nice skank way out of town. Her car was broken down, so we gave her a lift," he chuckled. "Let's just say the ride didn't end the way she'd expected."

Grady looked at him through a veil of rising smoke. "For your sake, I hope you're right. The last one," he held out his hand and shook it side-to-side, "was so-so. The buyers could brighten it enough, but still took time and money."

Duke and the girls walked over to the couches, and Roger to the TV. Raylynn and Tammi Jean sat, but Duke stood waiting for Grady to join them. He knew the moonshiner was going to want a front-row seat.

"Trust me, we went all out on lighting for this one. There wasn't a shadow in the entire cabin, that's for sure," Duke said.

Grady stood and joined them. He plopped down on a couch, unleashing an army of dust motes. "I hope so, Duke," he pointed with his cigarette between his fingers. "There are other sick fucks like you three out there, so don't think you're the only show in town." Grady took a drag and let the smoke drift out of his nose. "Your only saving grace is those two," he gestured to Tammi Jean and Raylynn. "The buyer loves to watch them fuck. You could probably just sell him a few dyke-out videos with them, and he'd pay."

"Ready, boss?" Roger asked. He had the video loaded onto the computer, which was displaying on the big screen.

THE CHATTER OF NIGHT BUGS

"Let's see what we have," Grady said. He crushed his cigarette out in an ashtray and leaned forward.

Duke had cold sweat coating his crotch and armpits. It was that nervous sweat when you know you're in trouble. When something is wrong, but you don't quite know what it is.

The video started and Grady was already nodding. "Hey, she's quite the looker." He gestured to his face. "Even with the busted jaw. Wouldn't take the drugs, I assume?"

"Yeah, we had to improvise this time, but it worked," Raylynn said. "She was scrappy, but Duke laid her right out."

Grady smirked and nodded. "And the lighting looks much better. Let's hope your performance is up to par. You three might look at a good payday."

R.J. stood next to the couch, watching. His mouth was agape, and he licked his lips.

Roger sat close to the TV, still near the laptop. He watched and seemed impressed, but suddenly his face changed. Worry and fear flashed over his eyes like a bolt of lightning. He paused the video.

"What gives?" Grady asked.

"Yeah, man, that was getting good," R.J. said, trying to hide the fact he had an erection.

Roger stood and pointed to the naked woman on the table. "What is that?" his shaking finger hovered over Sadie's necklace.

Tammi Jean leaned forward. "Her necklace?"

"Yes, her fucking necklace. But what is it? What did it look like exactly?"

Tammi Jean shrugged. "I don't know. Some stupid amber looking thing, with a black, eyeball looking chunk in it. It looked like some gift shop bullshit, if you ask me."

Roger was sweating and looking at Grady. "No, no, this is no bullshit. That's bad fucking magic right there."

"Hey, relax," Raylynn said. "It's just a necklace. Nothing magical about it." She reached into her shirt and pulled the pendant out. It shone in the light, dangling from the leather strap.

Roger's tanned skin went white. He raised his pointer finger and pinkie and spat between them. He muttered something and turned off the movie.

Grady was looking at them. His pallor had changed, and his hands clenched and unclenched, like he was looking for a gun.

"Get this the fuck out of here!" Roger shrieked. He ripped the

SD card from the computer and threw it at Duke, who put it back into his pocket. "These fuckers are cursed, and they brought it upon us." He was pacing. "Sage, we need sage. Now! This entire building has to be cleansed of this evil."

Duke and the girls were standing. "Whoa, whoa, take it easy, Roger. It's literally just a necklace. There's no fucking magic in it."

"Ah, you stupid fucks. You're from around here. You've heard the stories of pow wow, of the old magic in the hills from the early people. Don't fucking play dumb with me!"

"Come on, those are fucking legends." Duke looked at Grady, who was shooting daggers at him. "Wives tales that our parents would tell us to make us go to bed on time so they could get wasted." He laughed, but it was clearly forced. "Look, we're the actual monsters out here, not some bullshit magic necklace."

Grady looked at Roger. Roger's head was shaking like a wet dog.

"Get out. All of you, and don't fucking come back," Grady said. "You bring a curse to my house, to my fucking people!" he spat, walking towards them.

Tammi Jean and Raylynn were taking refuge behind Duke.

"Grady, we didn't mean any harm," Tammi Jean squeaked. "Honest, we didn't think anything of the necklace, and we're not trying to cause you any trouble."

Grady looked at R.J. as he continued his march towards them. "Well, guess what? You fucking did. Get them the fuck off of this property," he said to R.J. "Our business is done, forever. If I catch you back here, I'll fucking kill you myself. We'll make our own movie out of the three of you."

Raylynn's back hit the door. She groped behind her for the doorknob, opening it into the cool night air.

"Do you fucking understand?"

Duke wanted to argue, to fight for their livelihood and movie, but he had a feeling getting out alive was the best they could do. And he wasn't sure that was going to happen. His eyes kept close watch on Grady's hands, expecting him to pull a gun any second and start shooting. No, if that were going to happen, it would be outside.

"Okay, okay, we're out of here." Duke had his hands up in surrender. "You won't hear from us ever again." He could feel the

THE CHATTER OF NIGHT BUGS

coolness of the night air on his back. He didn't dare turn around, but he knew the girls were out already. R.J. stood next to him, ushering him the rest of the way out.

"Get them out of here and if they give you any trouble, kill them," Grady said to R.J. He looked back at Roger. "We have to cleanse this immediately."

"Got it, boss," the young man replied. He picked up a rifle by the door and checked the chamber just for show. All the guns on Grady's property were loaded.

Duke started the car and Tammi Jean and Raylynn both huddled together in the backseat. It was mainly for warmth, but they were all scared of a bullet in the back.

Headlights of R.J.'s truck lit up the Buick as Duke drove out. He wanted to floor it in the worst way, but he kept his resolve. They'd done nothing wrong, but still, he felt like they'd signed death warrants.

The car groaned as it made its way off of the property. A closed gate came into view and Duke slowed down.

"Fuck, fuck, fuck," he muttered. His foot was on the brake, but he left the car in drive. If R.J. came out shooting, he'd hit the gas and pray. The gate looked flimsy enough, but the Buick wasn't exactly a tank. Duke jumped when he heard the door on R.J.'s truck slam shut. "Fuck, fuck," he said.

Tammi Jean and Raylynn looked back, trying to keep their heads low.

"He doesn't have the big gun," Tammi Jean said in a whisper.

"That don't mean shit. You know they all carry pistols too," Duke replied. He rolled the window down.

R.J. stood next to the driver's door like a cop, looking into the car. He sighed and reached down.

Duke's foot was just releasing the brake, ready to push the gas pedal to the floor. Instead of a gun in his hand, R.J. pulled out a wad of cash.

"I want it," he said, unrolling bills.

Duke sat dumbfounded. His heart felt covered in acid and lodged in his throat. "Want what?"

R.J. looked back at Tammi Jean and Raylynn.

"He wants the movie, Duke," Tammi Jean said. She leaned forward, pushing her chest out. It was dark in the car, but more than enough light for R.J. to stare at her tits.

"Oh, fuck," Duke dug into his pocket. "Of course," he took out the SD card.

R.J. handed him a stack of money. Far less than what the going rate was, but it was better than nothing and certainly better than a bullet in the head.

R.J. pocketed the card without another word. He walked in front of the car and opened the gate.

Duke gave him a wave as he slowly drove out, leaving R.J. in the red glow of his taillights.

CHAPTER 7

Tammi Jean locked the door just as the first peal of thunder boomed in the night sky.

Duke threw his jacket on the couch and began turning on lights around the house.

Raylynn left her jacket on, still cold, and sat down. "Well, that was certainly interesting," she said.

Tammi Jean looked outside as the rain was falling. "Yeah, I'd say so. But at least we got something out of it, right?"

Duke pulled the money from his pocket and held it up, showing them. "It isn't our going rate, but at least we're not fucking dead." He shook his head in disbelief. "Who would've known a stupid fucking necklace would cause so much trouble?"

Raylynn pulled it from her shirt, letting it rest in the open. The amber danced in the light and the black smudge looked more and more like a dark eye. "That pow wow stuff is bullshit. My family bought into it for years and what did it get them? Huh, poverty and violence." She looked at the pendant but didn't remove it.

"I'll drink to that," Duke said, walking towards the kitchen.

Tammi Jean plopped down next to Raylynn and sat close to her. Absently, she began rubbing the other woman's leg. They locked eyes and Tammi Jean blew her a kiss.

Duke came walking back in with three beers and a small bottle of bourbon in his pocket.

"Is that a bottle in your pocket or are you just happy to see me?" Raylynn asked, taking the offered beer.

"Oh, I'm always happy to see you." He looked at Tammi Jean, who was moving over to allow him in between them. "And you."

Tammi Jean took her beer as Duke sat. He rested his unopened beer on the coffee table and took out the bottle of bourbon. The cap cracked as he broke the seal. He threw it over his shoulder, clearly not caring where it landed.

"A toast," he said, holding it aloft, "to killing, fucking and making money." He upended the bottle and gulped. "Ah," he grimaced. Tammi Jean took it next.

She held it up, looking at them. "And to new beginnings," she said. "Fuck the Shiners, we don't need those backwoods cunts, anyway." She drank.

Raylynn took it next. "I'm not even thinking about them." Her dusky eyes were locked on Tammi Jean and Duke. "I'm just thinking about getting drunk and fucking and sucking the both of you until we're numb." She took a gulp.

Duke smiled and wrapped his arms around both of them. "Well, now that sounds like a hell of a night to me." He took his arm off of Raylynn and leaned forward to grab his beer.

A fly—a single fat garbage fly—shimmering green, fluttered through the air. It landed on the ceiling fan and rubbed its legs together. In the thousands of eyes on its little face, it watched.

Duke put the beer bottle down and stifled a belch.

Tammi Jean finished hers and grabbed his empty as well, standing up. "Anyone want another?" she asked with a slur.

Raylynn took a swig from the near-empty bourbon bottle and set it down. Her eyelids were droopy, but she had a mischievous gleam in her eyes. "Ah, I could have one more, if you're getting up," she said.

Tammi Jean looked at Duke. "Sure, why not," he said.

Tammi Jean shot them both a sloppy salute, heading into the kitchen. "Well, I think we're shit out of luck," she said. "Nothing left in here."

Duke yelled from the living room, which wasn't far enough away to warrant his shout. "There's more in the garage."

Tammi Jean stood on the threshold with her arms across her chest. "Can you go get them? You know I hate going out there?"

Duke smiled at her. "Oh, come on, babe. It's just a few spiders and cobwebs." He adjusted on the couch, looking at her. Her tits looked immaculate, pushed up even further thanks to her crossed arms. He didn't even really want the beer just to get them both naked.

THE CHATTER OF NIGHT BUGS

Raylynn stood. "I'll tell you what, why don't we shoot for it? The loser grabs the beer and the winner heads upstairs with Duke and gets the *real* party started." She looked at Tammi Jean and licked her lips.

"What do you think, babe?" Tammi Jean asked.

Duke looked at both of them. Big Jake was already swelling with desire, as he thought of the filthy things that were about to happen. "It sounds like a win-win for me, so I'm in."

Raylynn made a fist with her right hand, holding it above the palm of her left hand. "Ready?" she asked Tammi Jean, whose hands were prepared in the same fashion.

"Rock, paper, scissors, shoot," they both said.

Raylynn showed paper and Tammi Jean a rock. She covered Tammi Jean's hand in victory.

Tammi Jean grabbed her and pulled her close. She kissed Raylynn hard and deep, plunging her tongue into the other woman's mouth. They broke the kiss and looked into each other's eyes. "I'll be up soon; don't finish without me," Tammi Jean breathed.

"You wanna head upstairs, stud?" Raylynn asked Duke, but he was already standing.

"I think I can be persuaded," he said, stretching.

They headed towards the stairs, as Tammi Jean prepared herself for her journey into the garage.

The fridge in the garage—which was older than Tammi Jean—hummed quietly. It was a sickly shade of sea foam green and screamed 1950s, but the relic still worked, keeping everything cold. Old shelves were full of trash, stuff that her Gran had accumulated over a long life. Nothing that Tammi Jean wanted or even had the desire to go through. She had hated the garage since she was a kid and had seen a rat huddling in the corner. Now, she used it mainly for the fridge.

The bulb shone brightly as Tammi Jean yanked the door of the refrigerator open. A handful of beers was left on the top shelf, but that was it. She grabbed a few, banging the necks together as she tried to manage them. She was sure the fuck session they were about to have would leave them all dehydrated, even though beer wasn't the best thirst quencher.

A flash of lightning, followed by a crash of thunder, made her jump, almost causing her to drop one bottle. "Fuck," she said, pressing the bottle against her chest before it could hit the ground. Tammi Jean wrestled it back into her grasp, when another loud bang crashed. This time it wasn't thunder—it was the side door ripping open.

The wind whipped, causing the ancient sensor light to activate. She wasn't sure the last time that bulb had been replaced—years, if not decades—but it still shone. Weakly but still worked.

"Fuck me," she grumbled, looking for a place to set the beers down. Tammi Jean put them on an old piece of wood that had once acted as a crude bench.

Her feet were cold and in the house's warmth, she'd forgotten to put on shoes before walking out into the dusty garage.

Tammi Jean shuffled towards the door, which slammed against the building with each gust of wind. The rain started picking up, dropping fat blobs to the earth.

"Ow, fuck!" Tammi Jean yelled. A sharp pain tore through her big toe. She must've stepped on a nail, or other piece of debris from a time long ago. She looked down in shock and revulsion as the burning intensified.

A bug—one she'd never seen before—pinched her toe. Black pincers sunk into her pale flesh, squeezing it into an angry nub of red.

Tammi Jean shook her foot, but the little fucker was sunk in good. Another jolt of electric pain rocked her as the other pincer slid under the nail of her next toe.

"Fucking cocksucker!" she cried. Tammi Jean fell to her behind and reached down, plucking the offending insect from her. The pincers remained, as if they had a mind of their own. Tammi Jean quivered as she ripped them free, tossing them after the skittering body.

"Fuck, that hurt," she said, trying to get a better look at the blisters and cuts on her toes. Quickly, she rose, not knowing if more of the little bastards were around. She went to grab the beers and head upstairs, but realized the door was still blowing in the wind. Tammi Jean—moving with a limp—rushed towards the door and grabbed the knob. She pulled . . . but it was stuck.

"You've gotta be kidding me," she said. The rain was falling harder, and wind pulled every dead leaf from the branches

THE CHATTER OF NIGHT BUGS

overhead. Tammi Jean yanked, but the door was stuck, like it was set in cement.

Harder and harder she tugged but stopped. Over the din of the storm, something else was standing out to her—the night bugs. The sound was grating, whining, chirping and screaming. It was as if every bug for miles had made its way to her yard just to watch her fight with the door.

"Dammit," she said. Three wasps, soaked and barely able to fly, had their stingers buried in the back of her hand.

Tammi Jean brushed them away, feeling their little bodies crunch as they continued to sting with abandon.

There was something moving in the darkness. Something large. Something loud.

Tammi Jean froze as the sound of bugs grew to near-deafening proportions. A shadow rose in front of her. Lightning flashed and Tammi Jean screamed.

It was an abomination. Something that had no business in this world, yet in that flash of lightning, it was real.

Tammi Jean's scream was drowned out by the crash of thunder. A hand—a massive paw made of squirming, writhing bodies—snatched Tammi Jean from the garage.

The creature seethed, like a churning river, as water sluiced over the millions of bugs. Four fat beetles sat in the center of the face, moving like hard-shelled eyes.

Tammi Jean pulled the hand wrapped around her throat. The grasp was iron-like and each time it rewarded her with a series of stings and bites. Her eyes were bulging as the pressure increased. An urgent thumping echoed in her ears as blood and air became a commodity she no longer had access to.

Fat, lumbering scorpions crawled from the abomination's hand, skittering onto Tammi Jean's face. Their tapered legs dimpled her flesh as they climbed her wet skin. The pressure around her neck abated slightly, allowing her a precious sip of wet air. Blood flowed back to her brain and her vision became clearer. Just clear enough for her to see the scorpions in front of her eyes.

They struck in tandem.

Tammi Jean closed her eyes, as if the thin flesh could stop the stingers from entering her eyeballs. It didn't.

Twin barbs of venom-dripping fury pierced Tammi Jean's eyes, pumping them full. The stingers pulled free, only to strike again and again.

Tammi Jean, now blinded, opened her mouth to scream. It was the invitation the beast was waiting for.

A stream of centipedes—black as night—seemed to appear, seeking her gaping maw. They rushed into Tammi Jean's mouth, biting and tearing bits of flesh. Her uvula was severed in a pulse of gore and consumed as the centipedes made their way down her throat. More of them piled in, as Tammi Jean tried to spit them out, to bite them. They bit back.

She was blinded, but if her venom-filled eyes still had sight, she would've seen a smile made of night bugs on the monster's face.

The beast continued to squeeze, harder this time. Tammi Jean's eyes leaked pus and ichor, running down her swollen and bitten face. Her body shook with convulsions as she soiled herself in its grasp. Still, the monster squeezed. Tammi Jean's head lolled as her neck finally broke. Yet, it squeezed and squeezed. Fingers made of nightmares buried into her flesh. Deeper and deeper, they sank until they were almost touching. The monster made a fist wet with gore and wriggling bodies, as Tammi Jean's head fell off, landing on the wet earth. It let her fall heavy to the ground. A steam of blood and black bodies poured from the torn flesh of her neck. They rejoined their master. Legs rubbed and jaws clicked in glee. They all knew the night was far from over.

"Fuck, you need to slow down," Duke said. He put a hand on the back of Raylynn's head, pulling her hair.

She reluctantly let Duke's cock flop out of her warm mouth. Her hand reached out, stroking him.

"Oh, what's the matter? Poor baby can't hold his load?" she cooed. Raylynn stuck her tongue out, moving forward to lick the banjo string under his glans. The stolen necklace bobbed and bounced against her chest as she jerked him.

"Ah, ah ah," Duke said, keeping a firm grip on her head. "Give me a minute."

Raylynn gave him sad eyes like a lost puppy. "Why don't you give me that cum down my throat and I'll suck you hard again?

THE CHATTER OF NIGHT BUGS

Then you can give us a good fuck. Whenever Tammi Jean gets up here." She looked to the door as if expecting Tammi Jean to burst in.

Duke was on his back and looked down at her. A flash of lightning lit up the window across from him. It went back to darkness, allowing him to see Raylynn's ass and pussy in the reflection.

"What do you say?" Raylynn asked. She pulled, inching closer to his swollen member.

Duke's grasp wavered and released. He shuddered as her mouth closed over him again. This time there would be no stopping her, and Raylynn knew that.

Raylynn did what she did best. Her right hand was almost an extension of her mouth, as her left kneaded his balls. She felt him tensing up and wriggling, knowing it was almost time. She looked up at him, knowing he loved to make eye contact when he came.

Duke's eyes found hers and snapped to the window.

Raylynn sucked faster, pushing her tongue against the taut strip of flesh. She looked at his face, but his eyes were no longer watching the performance. What was once a look of pleasure was now fear and confusion.

"Oh fuck," he said, wriggling back. His cock ripped from Raylynn's mouth as he nearly fell off the bed.

"Hey, what the fuck?" Raylynn asked. She sat up and wiped her mouth with the back of her hand. A slew of questions sat ready on her lips, but the fear in Duke's eyes killed them before they could come to life. Slowly, she turned her head.

Tammi Jean looked at them from the window. Her face was pushed against the glass, leaving a streak of slime and blood. Her eyes oozed, nearly bulging from her skull. A fat, swollen tongue lolled from her mouth, but something moved inside: a black centipede crawled out, bits of flesh stuck in its maw. The stump of Tammi Jean's neck was pinched and raw, weeping gore. But something held her severed head aloft. Bugs crawled through her hair, raining down her face, fighting to bite her cooling flesh.

Bugs . . . in the shape of a hand.

Raylynn moved as Tammi Jean's head smashed against the glass. The old pane rattled and cracked but didn't shatter. The bug-hand pulled the head back again, this time much farther. A crack of lightning made Tammi Jean's ruined face seem to smile as it came hurtling towards the glass. Raylynn rolled off the bed and skittered away as the head smashed the window, rocketing into the room.

Rain, thunder and bugs, poured into the small bedroom.

Raylynn bounced up to her feet, watching the torrent of legs, wings and segmented bodies, rush in.

"Duke, get the fuck up," she said. Raylynn bent down to help lift him, but he was frozen. His eyes locked on the severed head of Tammi Jean. "We need to get the fuck out of here, now!" she shouted. The necklace against her chest felt warm, like it was alive. Raylynn pulled at it, trying to get it over her head, but the leather strip had shrunk. What easily came off and on, was now almost as short as a choker. "Fuck," she said, winding her fingers into the necklace. Raylynn pulled, hoping to break it, but it might as well have been braided steel.

"Ah, fuck!" Duke shouted. He was ripped from his trance as a host of fat, red worms covered his legs. His eyes were no longer on Tammi Jean's head, but on the writhing mass stripping the flesh from his lower extremities. Duke swatted at them in vain. Each swipe killed more and more of them, but others took their places, consuming.

Raylynn backed away from Duke. The necklace felt like a hot stone resting on her nude flesh, but her mind was pulled from the pain as more and more bugs poured in—and took shape.

It wasn't quite humanoid, but it was something like a person. The beast was a wriggling, writhing mass of filth and bugs. Its body hissed with the sound of armored and soft insects crawling over each other. There was no speech, but a dull chatter of sharp mandibles as they clicked in joy. A hand formed—the same one that had thrown Tammi Jean's head through the window—and grabbed Duke.

"No!" Duke screamed. A stream of piss splattered on the carpet—his erection long gone.

Raylynn pushed herself away, thankful the ire of the beast wasn't focused on her. She searched for the doorknob but didn't dare pull her eyes away. She wished she had.

The hand of bugs morphed and wrapped around Duke's left arm. With a wet snap, it pulled, yanking flesh and bone free in a cascade of gore. Jagged white and shredded muscle were all that remained of his shoulder. The monster shoved the limb into its

THE CHATTER OF NIGHT BUGS

torso. Glistening bodies of every color of hell crawled over the arm, sucking it deeper, eating the ruined meat. Duke screamed as his Achilles tendons gave way under the feasting worms. One—a fat one—latched onto the tip of his penis. Its bulbous head, ripe with snapping jaws, pushed into his urethra, biting its way in. Duke, in a last desperate attempt, tried to swat at the invading beast, but his arm was immobile. A fist of insects held his arm firm. The giant beast let out a low rumble, almost like laughter, and twisted. Duke's arm snapped like a rotten chicken wing, breaking at the elbow. White bone peeked out of his flesh as his hand faced the wrong way. Despite that, the monster twisted, snapping tendons, breaking bone and ripping flesh. Duke was fading, no longer concerned about the worm that was burrowed into his cock. His urethra bulged and wriggled, allowing drops of blood to run down his leg.

Raylynn felt her gorge rise as she looked helplessly at Duke's eyes. The eyes she'd been looking at moments earlier in the throes of passion, were now devoid of life. A blanket of bugs rushed over him, covering him in a writhing, wet mass. Raylynn found the doorknob and ripped it open. The door slammed into the wall with a crash, like the sound of a starter pistol. She ran nude, taking the stairs three at a time.

A wet, grinding sound followed her down, but she didn't dare look back. She knew what hell followed her.

Her bare feet slapped on the floor, but she didn't know where the fuck she was headed. Out of the house, that was for certain. She'd face a storm butt ass naked as opposed to sitting in there.

The gun, the thought flashed into her mind. She didn't know if the monster could be killed or even hurt, but she knew she had to try. Raylynn wouldn't die without a fight.

The back door was calling to her, welcoming her out of the house, but she needed the gun first. She stopped at the closet and nearly took the door from its hinges. The rifle—a wood stock, scoped hunting rifle—leaned against the wall.

"Fuck," she yelled as the necklace singed her skin. Raylynn pulled at it, burning her hand. The wet grinding was growing, and she was out of time. Raylynn grabbed the gun, praying there were a few bullets in it.

The storm raged outside. She was pelted with fat drops of rain, and she nearly lost her footing in the wet grass, but still she ran.

Raylynn's nudity was an afterthought as she raced towards the only other house nearby. She didn't know if it would save her, or doom the young couple to a horrible death, but she didn't fucking care.

Laughter and chatter followed her, closer. Her arms pumped in front of her, the rifle held tight. Closer the beast came. Raylynn could feel the beat of the insect wings, like a lover's breath on her neck. She had to look. She needed to look.

Raylynn turned her head and slipped.

The rifle stock met her jaw as she smashed into the wet earth. Blood and bits of teeth flooded her ruined mouth as she rolled onto her back. The rain fell hard, numbing her body, but her fingers still worked. Red drool ran down her chin, but she could shoulder the gun.

A flash of lightning gave her a snapshot of Hell.

It was well over twenty feet tall. Bugs dripped from it like water from a dog, only to be reunited again. Arms shifted and morphed, becoming many and then none. Its head was wide, and mouth made of bristling spiders smiled at her. The beetles that made up its eyes shifted with glee, knowing her end was near.

The rifle barked, creating its own flash. Raylynn cried as the bullet passed through the beast, doing nothing. Still, she cycled the bolt, loading another round. Again, the rifle erupted.

Bugs flowed from the monster's feet and headed towards Raylynn. She pushed her heels into the mud, trying to move away from the onslaught.

"No, fuck you!" she screamed, kicking at the torrent of biting bodies. She wasn't fast enough.

The first bite.

She didn't see what bit her, but whatever it was, hurt like a motherfucker. "Fucker!" Raylynn screamed. Her fingers—chilled by the rain and wet earth—fumbled with the bolt of the rifle, ejecting the spent casing. Without aiming, she fired. And again, nothing. The bullet passed through the monstrosity like a pebble into a churning river.

Tiny legs sunk into her muddy legs, climbing higher and higher. Raylynn knew the rifle was obsolete, but she still couldn't let it go. She cycled it again and pulled the trigger.

Click!

"Fuck," she said, using the now empty gun to push the biting creatures off her legs.

THE CHATTER OF NIGHT BUGS

More of them swarmed her as the hulking mass lumbered above. Her feet were black-booted with squirming, biting little monsters, digging into her meat. Raylynn screamed and kicked, but still they came.

She felt a tickle of antennae on the opening of her vagina. "No, no, no," she shrieked. Raylynn reached towards her sex, pulling offending insects from her folds. They were endless, biting and stinging her. Her hands became a mass of black. Dead bugs, mud and blood fell from her burning fingers. Yet, they still came.

They had found their way inside of her warmth—her anus, too. She was spread and violated—being eaten from the inside.

"Ah! Fuck!" Raylynn screamed to the storm as rain pelted her open mouth. A flash of lightning ripped across the open sky, but her vision swam. The pain, the pain, was like nothing she'd ever felt before.

Thousands of legs, mouths, jaws, and stingers violated her body. She no longer had a vagina or anus, but a gaping opening gushing blood, bugs and shit. Yet still, they ate.

Raylynn's breathing was ragged and wet. Her body quivered and shook with untold agony as more skittering bodies made their way into the chasm of her ruined orifices.

She could feel them in her stomach, eating through her guts. But, in her last moments of clarity, something else stood out to her in the night's coldness.

The pendant was burning like a drop of molten metal. Raylynn couldn't even scream as her flesh sizzled and burned. Wisps of smoke rose from her chest where the pendant lay.

Raylynn's vision went dark. The pain was in the back of her mind, but in the forefront was the feeling of tiredness. Her lungs were deflated—chewed to pulp by an army of little jaws. Her eyes closed for the last time, but her ears worked.

Before the sweet embrace of death took her, her brain echoed with two sounds: the chatter of night bugs and chewing.

CHAPTER 8

The clubhouse was dark except for the glow of the TV. R.J. had the remote in one hand and his cock in the other. On the screen was the snuff film in all of its glory. The girl was fucking hot, too hot for snuff, but it was already done.

When they'd played that brief clip—before Roger and Grady lost their shit—R.J. knew he had to have the video. His cock got hard at just that clip, let alone seeing the entire thing.

Grady and Roger had a meeting with some of their associates, but R.J. wasn't high enough on the food chain for that kind of shit yet. One day he'd be up there but for the time being he just held down the fort. It worked for him, especially that night. With them gone, he had the clubhouse to himself. R.J. had already cum once, unable to contain his excitement, but this was round two. He'd make this one last for a little while.

The sound of crunching gravel and doors slamming stopped him mid-stroke.

"Oh, fuck," he said as the doorknob turned.

". . . fucking roads suck," Grady said, as he flipped on the light switch against the wall.

"It's always been that way. Especially when it's rai—," Roger stopped. His eyes widened when he saw the brutal film on the screen. "What the fuck?" he muttered.

R.J. scrambled, stuffing his greasy cock into his pants. "I—ah—I can explain," he stammered.

Grady saw the movie playing and his subordinate jerking off on his couch. His eyes narrowed and turned black as he picked the laptop up and slammed it on the ground. The computer shattered, cutting off the movie mid-murder.

R.J. hustled to zip his pants as Grady rushed him.

"You piece of shit!" Grady sneered. He slapped the young man

THE CHATTER OF NIGHT BUGS

in the face and followed through with a knee to the balls and still-erect penis.

R.J. saw stars as he fell back onto the couch, clutching his genitals.

"You disobeyed me! A fucking direct order," Grady pulled out a pistol from his hip and put it to R.J.'s head. The muzzle was cold, but R.J. knew it spewed hot lead.

"I'm sorry, Grady. I'm fucking sorry," R.J. blubbered.

Roger stood by the open door. The rain had stopped, and, in the distance, thunder rolled. "A curse, a fucking curse brought on us," Roger muttered.

"I should fucking kill you, you little shit!" Grady's finger kissed the trigger but didn't put any pressure on it.

"Kill him," Roger said. "Kill him and save us. That's bad magic, Grady. Bad fucking magic those three—and now this cunt—played with."

"Please, I'm sorry. I couldn't help myself. I—"

"Shut the fuck up," Roger said, putting his hand up for silence.

Grady took his finger off the trigger, for which R.J. was grateful.

Roger looked outside into the darkness. His head was turned like a dog who'd heard a whistle in the distance.

"What is it?" Grady asked. He lowered the gun from R.J.'s head but aimed it at his crotch.

"Listen," Roger said. He waved his hand for his boss to join him. "The bugs. It sounds like there's a whole fucking mess of them."

Grady looked at R.J. and re-holstered the gun. "We're not fucking done yet." He nodded towards Roger.

They joined him by the door and listened.

It wasn't uncommon for the night bugs to come alive after a storm. A cheer for making it through the deluge, letting their friends know they'd survived another one. But this was different.

"Get a flashlight," Grady said.

R.J. ran into the clubhouse coming back with a spotlight they'd used to shoot deer at night. "Here'ya go, boss," he said.

Grady looked at him like he was a dipshit. "I don't fucking want it." He pointed to the sound of the mass of insects, which seemed to get closer. "Go find out what the fuck is going on."

R.J. licked his lips. He couldn't stand bugs, but the thought of a bullet to the skull was a great motivator.

"Sure thing," he said, stepping out into the darkness. R.J. walked but could hear the other two men creeping along behind him. He turned on the powerful beam, dispelling shadows with each swipe of the light.

Something black moved in the tree line. Something large.

"What the fuck was that?" Roger asked. He was next to R.J. pointing towards the quivering branches.

R.J. spun the beam slowly into the woods and saw a face.

A face nearly twenty feet tall. A face with beetles for eyes and spiders for a mouth. A mouth that was smiling.

The men screamed and ran, dropping the light into the mud. But it was faster, much faster.

Thunder rolled in the distance. But outside of the clubhouse was the chatter of night bugs and wet screams.

THE END?

Not if you want to dive into more of the Dark Tide series.

Check out our amazing website and online store
or download our latest catalog here.
https://geni.us/CLPCatalog

Looking for award-winning Dark Fiction?

Download our latest catalog.

Includes our anthologies, novels, novellas, collections,
poetry, non-fiction, and specialty projects.

WHERE STORIES COME ALIVE!

We always have great new projects and content on the website to dive into, as well as a newsletter, behind the scenes options, social media platforms, our own dark fiction shared-world series and our very own webstore. Our webstore even has categories specifically for KU books, non-fiction, anthologies, and of course more novels and novellas.

ABOUT THE AUTHORS

Multiple award winning author, **Jasper Bark** is infectious—and there's no known cure. If you're reading this you're already contaminated. The symptoms will manifest any time soon. There's nothing you can do about it. There's no itching or unfortunate rashes, but you'll become obsessed with his mind-bending books. Then you'll want to tell everyone else about his visionary horror fiction. About its originality, its wild imagination and how it takes you to the edge of your sanity. We're afraid there's no way to avoid this. These words contain a power you're hopeless to resist. You're already in their thrall, you know you are. You're itching to read all of Jasper's bloodstained books. Don't fight this urge, embrace it. You've been bitten by the Bark bug and you love it!

Candace Nola is a multiple award-winning author, editor, and publisher. She writes poetry, horror, dark fantasy, and extreme horror content. She is the creator of Uncomfortably Dark Horror, an indie press, which focuses primarily on promoting indie horror authors and small presses with weekly book reviews, interviews, and special features.

Daniel J. Volpe is the Splatterpunk Award-winning author of *Plastic Monsters, Talia, Left to You*, and many others. His love for horror started at a young age when his grandfather unwittingly rented him, "A Nightmare on Elm Street". He can be found on Facebook @ Daniel Volpe, Instagram @ dj_volpe_horror , X @DJVolpeHorror , TikTok @danieljvolpehorror1

Readers . . .

Thank you for reading *F.U.B.B.* We hope you enjoyed this 14th book in our Dark Tide series.

If you have a moment, please review *F.U.B.B.* at the store where you bought it.

Help other readers by telling them why you enjoyed this book. No need to write an in-depth discussion. Even a single sentence will be greatly appreciated. Reviews go a long way to helping a book sell, and is great for an author's career. It'll also help us to continue publishing quality books. You can also share a photo of yourself holding this book with the hashtag #IGotMyCLPBook!

Thank you again for taking the time to journey with Crystal Lake Publishing.

Visit our Linktree page for a list of our social media platforms.
https://linktr.ee/CrystalLakePublishing

Follow us on Amazon:

Our Mission Statement:

Since its founding in August 2012, Crystal Lake Publishing has quickly become one of the world's leading publishers of Dark Fiction and Horror books. In 2023, Crystal Lake Publishing formed a part of Crystal Lake Entertainment, joining several other divisions, including Torrid Waters, Crystal Lake Comics, Crystal Lake Kids, and many more.

While we strive to present only the highest quality fiction and entertainment, we also endeavour to support authors along their writing journey. We offer our time and experience in non-fiction projects, as well as author mentoring and services, at competitive prices.

With several Bram Stoker Award wins and many other wins and nominations (including the HWA's Specialty Press Award), Crystal Lake Publishing puts integrity, honor, and respect at the forefront of our publishing operations.

We strive for each book and outreach program we spearhead to not only entertain and touch or comment on issues that affect our readers, but also to strengthen and support the Dark Fiction field and its authors.

Not only do we find and publish authors we believe are destined for greatness, but we strive to work with men and women who endeavour to be decent human beings who care more for others than themselves, while still being hard working, driven, and passionate artists and storytellers.

Crystal Lake Publishing is and will always be a beacon of what passion and dedication, combined with overwhelming teamwork and respect, can accomplish. We endeavour to know each and every one of our readers, while building personal relationships with our authors, reviewers, bloggers, podcasters, bookstores, and libraries.

We will be as trustworthy, forthright, and transparent as any business can be, while also keeping most of the headaches away from our authors, since it's our job to solve the problems so they can stay in a creative mind. Which of course also means paying our authors.

We do not just publish books, we present to you worlds within your world, doors within your mind, from talented authors who sacrifice so much for a moment of your time.

There are some amazing small presses out there, and through collaboration and open forums we will continue to support other presses in the goal of helping authors and showing the world what quality small presses are capable of accomplishing. No one wins when a small press goes down, so we will always be there to support hardworking, legitimate presses and their authors. We don't see Crystal Lake as the best press out there, but we will always strive to be the best, strive to be the most interactive and grateful, and even blessed press around. No matter what happens over time, we will also take our mission very seriously while appreciating where we are and enjoying the journey.

What do we offer our authors that they can't do for themselves through self-publishing?

We are big supporters of self-publishing (especially hybrid publishing), if done with care, patience, and planning. However, not every author has the time or inclination to do market research, advertise, and set up book launch strategies. Although a lot of authors are successful in doing it all, strong small presses will always be there for the authors who just want to do what they do best: write.

What we offer is experience, industry knowledge, contacts and trust built up over years. And due to our strong brand and trusting fanbase, every Crystal Lake Publishing book comes with weight of respect. In time our fans begin to trust our judgment and will try a new author purely based on our support of said author.

With each launch we strive to fine-tune our approach, learn from our mistakes, and increase our reach. We continue to assure our authors that we're here for them and that we'll carry the weight of the launch and dealing with third parties while they focus on their strengths—be it writing, interviews, blogs, signings, etc.

We also offer several mentoring packages to authors that include knowledge and skills they can use in both traditional and self-publishing endeavours.

We look forward to launching many new careers.

This is what we believe in. What we stand for. This will be our legacy.

Welcome to Crystal Lake Publishing— Tales from the Darkest Depths.

Made in the USA
Middletown, DE
16 March 2024

51018299R00116